YOU DANCED ON MY DREAMS

BEYOND THE BALLROOM

THERESA E. LIGGINS

Chapter
One

Tyana grew hot under the collar while sitting in her air-conditioned car, glaring at her watch, waiting for her fiancé to meet her in front of their wedding planner's office. She snatched her phone from her purse, but then hesitated, looking around once more and hoping that he would show up before she had to call. Chewing on her thumbnail, her impatience, as well as the heat, got the best of her. She punched in his number and waited.

"Hello," Antonio answered.

"Antonio, I swear..."

"I'm on my way!"

"But, you've kept me waiting! You were supposed meet me here over thirty minutes ago! What is detaining you *this time?*"

"I'm leaving right now. I'm sorry; I'm sorry. A situation came up that needed resolving."

"Oh, really. I can only imagine." Tyana had heard every excuse in the book when it came to Antonio's tardiness — tardiness that, coincidentally, only occurred in their personal lives. She continued. "This is our wedding we're planning! We've been planning it for *five* years! And now we're late meeting the wedding planner — again! She's booked solid and it's hard to get appointments around your schedule. She has another couple scheduled in twenty minutes. I've already been to two appointments without you. I really need you to be part of this. It's always been something with you and the business for the last five years that's prevented us from moving forward with these plans."

"You make it sound like I'm avoiding our wedding, which isn't true."

"Aren't you?"

"No. Absolutely not! I'm sorry I'm running late. I really tried leaving on time, but I was unavoidably detained. It couldn't be helped. I'm on my way. I'll be right there."

"As usual, you let your work get in the way of us. It's been this way ever since I agreed to marry you. We should be married by now! Why is this so hard? When I sold my business to go into a partnership with you and the dance studio after you proposed, you promised me that I wouldn't regret it."

"Are you saying you regret it now?"

"No. I don't know."

"Which is it Tatyana?"

"Look, I know things got a little crazy with all of the personal adjustments and legal ramifications with both of our businesses, but I didn't expect that it would mean our wedding plans would be put on hold *this* long. And, I know we decided not to rush into getting married because of your daughter, but she lives with her mother and she's turning eighteen soon, so she should know by now I'm not trying to become her mother or come between you and her mother."

"Where's all this coming from?"

"What do you mean where is all this coming from? I'm sitting here in a hundred degree temperature waiting on you to help plan the rest of our lives with me. I'm feeling stood up, unimportant, neglected…"

"I love you. You know that. I love you…I love *you*! We're getting married, I promise. I'm sorry I'm late— again," he glanced at his watch, "but I'll be there. I'll be there in ten minutes." Antonio knew that was stretching it, but he truly didn't want to disappoint Tyana again. He didn't want her to lose faith in him. She meant everything to him.

"By the way, what was so important that kept you from being on time *this* time?"

Antonio let out a long sigh as he sprinted to his car, knowing that whatever comes out of his mouth next will not go over well with his very upset fiancée.

"Babe, I'm sorry I let you down, but what happened was Dottie stopped by with a payment; then she insisted on opening up about a problem, which made her emotional talking about it." Antonio cringed, and then heard nothing on the other end. "Tatyana? Tatyana?" he called out to her, but felt the silence on the other end. He looked at his phone to confirm that she had in fact hung up.

When Antonio realized Tyana had actually hung up on him, it didn't surprise him. He shook his head and sighed heavily. He tried to call her back, but she didn't answer. His honesty didn't pay off; not when it came to a select few of his students' narcissistic behavior. She has witnessed all of their dramas, including his methods of pacifying them, and has reached her own conclusion about the intrusions.

♥♥♥

Antonio Lorenzo had built his dance studio from the ground up through twenty-five years of hard work, dedication, determination, and mostly charm, which easily encouraged most of his female clients to remain long-term fixtures of his dance studio. His talent and natural good looks lured them in, but it was his scrupulous and personal attention to their dancing needs that kept them interested. That's how he attracted his young, beautiful, and talented prized student, Tatyana Dominique—not to mention the fact that he, surprisingly, fell head over heels in love with *her*, side-lining his philandering and flirtatious ways. Well, at least modifying them to a degree.

He, more recently, turned the dance studio into a profitable business for both Tyana and himself as they planned for their future together. However, his loyalty to his domain and to his demanding students, who need him like a bad drug, has hindered him from having any semblance of a social life through the years with anyone special, but he fell in love with Tyana despite that.

Tyana learned early on where his priorities lay, which she expected, from seeing firsthand how women idolized him. But finding out that he also had a high-maintenance teenage daughter, had thrown her for a loop since she had no previous knowledge of this information when she was taking lessons as a student and prior to his proposal. Since becoming his fiancée, the road to Tyana's highly anticipated wedding day had been bumpy and oftentimes littered with obstacles such as a high-energy business, fussy clients, and a coddled daughter.

As a man who wasn't born in the States and still spoke with a very distinct Latin accent, Antonio felt extremely proud of his accomplishments and never rested on his laurels—not for a minute and not even for Tyana. As a matter of fact, he had never successfully maintained long-term relationships before meeting Tyana, particularly because he found them to be more of a liability to his business than an asset. He thought it best that his female clients know as little as possible about his personal life; marketing himself as a suave and talented Latin dancer who could transform their lives in order to keep *them* happy and dancing, and this kept his business fruitful. One of those liabilities surfaced eighteen years ago when he learned, unexpectedly, that he was becoming a father at thirty-two, when his business was still young and struggling. His Lothario demeanor and actions on the dance floor— mesmerizing every woman whom he seduced into his hypnotic grasp—led him to be overly confident with women—women who were hopelessly attracted by his magnetism and good looks. That created a firestorm of opportunities for him to sleep with any woman of his choice. And one young woman, Shana, got her hooks in him. As a new dance instructor, Shana trained with Antonio and fell for his charisma, his good looks, and his dance skills. Not long after they had been working daily as dance partners and canoodling nightly as lovers, she announced her pregnancy. She also expressed her desire to keep the baby, which certainly did not fit into his plans. Respecting her wishes, yet not wanting to marry her, he convinced her to transfer to another associated dance studio managed by a close business associate, which crushed her. But when he wanted something done his way, he could be quite persuasive. She had fallen in love with him almost instantly once their very heated and private affair, on and off of the dance floor, commenced. He, on the other hand, didn't exactly feel the same way. After the baby was born, she returned to the dance business, but her dreams as his dance partner and lover were doused. He agreed to provide financial support for his daughter, but ended their romantic relationship almost immediately at the point in which he learned of her pregnancy. He had never given any thought to raising children, and he didn't want her existence in his personal life to become public knowledge. It wasn't until his daughter, Alyssa, turned nine and made regular appearances at his studio, did the rumor mill explode and confirm his personal relationship with a much younger instructor.

Since fatherhood, Antonio became more cautious about getting romantically involved with women, particularly women connected to his business. His practice of maintaining aggressive business goals over his own personal goals had made him successful. His business became a priority over everything. That priority meant that everything else, including a social life, suffered or became non-existent. This formula had become a way of life for him—a habitual work schedule. Gone were his carefree, Lothario ways. His job gave him all of the social amenities and interactions that he needed. He met new people every day; he traveled frequently with large or intimate groups within the dance world for work and pleasure, and he partied with the studio family and friends on a regular basis—all surrounding his world of ballroom dancing.

Falling in love with Tyana and surrendering to a committed relationship proved challenging for Antonio since he had avoided becoming serious with anyone, especially a student. But driven by his immense desire for her, he wanted to try hard to accommodate a relationship with her and make her part of his life, without compromising his work life. He also felt that Tyana could be a business asset to him. Tatyana, he called her by her birth name, seemed different than all of the others who basically threw themselves at him. Unlike the others, she didn't put him on a pedestal or gawk at him with star-struck eyes. She was different. The only man in her life that she would ever idolize was her father, who often put *her* on a pedestal.

Tyana's love for Antonio came from an honest and unpretentious place. He couldn't ignore his feelings for her even if he wanted to; and for the sake of his business, he tried in the beginning, when she initially trained under him as a student. But as an engaged couple, they struggled. He often found himself constantly disappointing her; reminding him that he was failing in his efforts to love her and support her as he subsequently promised to do.

♥♥♥

Tyana phoned the wedding planner from her car and apologetically cancelled the appointment again, with no imminent plans to reschedule. When she hung up, she gazed down at the multi-carat, brilliantly faceted diamond and platinum engagement ring that embellished her left hand, and began to fondle it while wondering if she'd ever have a complimentary wedding band placed next to it. With that thought, she flashed back to the night Antonio proposed to her—in Miami, Florida. That starry, moon-drenched night held such romantic memories for her after hearing Antonio confess his love to her, and after rescuing her from that painful face-to-face encounter with Ellis and Charlotte—a pregnant Charlotte. In her mind, he saved her from the unimaginable pain of losing a long-time lover and first love. She had never really gotten over that loss or had time to grieve it when her "Knight in Shining Armor" galloped in and protected her by stepping in front of Ellis, blocking him from going after her. He went after her instead. She quickly skipped over that unforgettable scene of seeing Ellis with Charlotte and fast-forwarded to Antonio gallantly carrying her back to his hotel room where they, for the first time, gazed deep into each other's eyes—farther than they've ever gone—feeling their souls converge, before passionately making love in a haze of fantasy. That regal moment had all of the fiery affections of a first-time love affair. She felt a flutter in her stomach just thinking back on that night, but eventually shook off the sensation, and drove away.

As Tyana drove home, she reflected on many things, such as her life growing up as an only child; her interior design business which she gave up for her partnership with Antonio; her first love and ex-boyfriend, Ellis; her love of ballroom dancing, and her promising future as Antonio's wife.

As business partners, Tyana shared the responsibility of ownership with Antonio—a partnership that accompanied his unexpected proposal of marriage. They were not only partners in running the business, but she willingly and eagerly trained to become one of the advanced instructors at Antonio's desire and encouragement. Like always, whatever he wanted, he generally always got. She didn't need much encouragement though. She genuinely loved everything about dancing and enjoyed teaching others to dance and move in a way they never thought possible. She felt especially giddy about working side-by-side with her new fiancé. Once she immersed herself into a teaching and ownership role, she quickly found out how consuming that business could be. She also saw, firsthand, how demanding and intrusive twenty percent of the students were eighty percent of the time, and without regard to their instructors' own personal lives or space. She immediately incorporated boundaries with her students when at work. But, she soon noticed that wasn't always the case with Antonio—something she didn't see as a student of his. Although she expected him to set similar boundaries, he had a different philosophy of handling and interacting with his students. It had never occurred to him to modify *his* way of dealing with his clients. He consistently, through hard work and dedication, held a prestigious ranking of Top Studio Owner and Top Instructor year after year among his peers, proving to all and to himself that he didn't need to change a thing; as change didn't come easily to him. He figured if his business was thriving, why rock the boat? "Don't fix what isn't broke," he would often say.

But as romantic partners, they connected on all levels, more so than her emotional connection with Ellis. When she and Antonio spent rare private moments away from the business and the rest of the world, all of his attention was on her. He was putty in her hands and he enjoyed the closeness and bond they had created between themselves in their private world and sanctuary. It was only then had she gotten to know the real Antonio Lorenzo—to see his vulnerabilities and sensibilities. She remembered how they would lose themselves within themselves for hours and days on end. Their sexual chemistry consumed their entire space and being, when they let it. They were addicted to each other sexually and maintained insatiable appetites, drinking in their essence at every conceivable opportunity. She became his confidante and he would confide in her almost everything. He trusted her explicitly and eagerly welcomed her into his world with absolutely no reservations and no doubts.

Inside their private walls, they created the perfect, envious relationship. However, once outside of their safe haven, Tyana became acutely aware that Antonio rarely thought of anything other than the dance studio. Most of the time, his appointment calendar didn't allow them any personal time on the job to interact. To most of the staff and clients, they seemed ordinary — like two professionals working together. They weren't seen together that much, so few knew they were engaged to each other. Of course, the long-term staff members were aware, but often wondered what could be keeping them from getting married. And, of course, some of the students who had become regulars of the studio were privy to their relationship status; not through Tyana or Antonio, but through idle gossip and the occasional personal inquiries. Antonio never went out of his way to inform anyone associated with the dance studio of his relationship with Tyana, even though she was now part owner of the business, which was also something that wasn't ceremoniously announced. She often wondered if he even thought of the business as theirs; but instead only his, especially with matters that concerned the highfalutin students who trained exclusively under him, at their insistence.

As Tyana approached closer to home, her increasingly frustrated state of mind focused on the times she and Antonio traveled together to every organized competition that the dance studio participated in, which at one point amounted to about five national competitions a year, and countless local and regional competitions. That kind of schedule often kept them off track of their personal lives — particularly the portion of time a couple needed to plan a proper wedding. He made her aware of his reasoning that since his career began in the dance business, he has never maintained close friendships outside of the ballroom dance world, so he didn't have the same needs as Tyana for balance—more specifically, for "work/life balance." He rarely spent time with his own family before his engagement to Tyana. Because of her, they scheduled time to enjoy family events and incorporated those events into their lives—with both families—when they could. She suspected that things probably would have been different had they dated a few years, prior to getting engaged. The engagement, indeed, fast-tracked their relationship, perhaps too quickly. One minute she is Antonio's star student with a promising dance life, and then with one swoop into his arms, she became his fiancée, his business partner and custodian of all of the problems and headaches that come with ownership of a business that is viewed as more of a luxury than a necessity, and not to mention she became a threat, in some ways, to his daughter. His mother showed hot and cold behavior toward her, knowing the intentions of most of the women from the studio with her son. And his prime students resented her for simply being the chosen one. They all had hopes that he would, in fact, pick them as his mate. Once she said yes to his marriage proposal, unbeknownst to her, Tyana gained a number of passive-aggressive enemies through association.

♥ ♥ ♥

When Tyana ended up on her street, she wiped away tears that had leaked from her eyes. She loved Antonio with all of her heart. She did. And, she wanted nothing more than to spend the rest of her life with him as his wife, not a fiancée. He became the most important person in her life from the moment that they committed themselves to each other. No one else took precedence over him at that point—no one and nothing. She made it a point to protect their private relationship with her heart and her love. She would support him one hundred percent.

When her phone rang, she knew it was Antonio.

"Yes!"

"Hi Tyana, it's me, Ellis."

"Ellis!" She nearly missed her turn. "Why are you calling me? I thought I asked you not to!"

"I know, but I've been thinking about you since the last time we talked. I want to see you."

"You can't! Please don't call me again. Please!" She ended the call and her whole body tensed up. She could barely catch her breath. Hearing from Ellis conjured up their past together, which included her nemesis, his wife, Charlotte. Tyana tried for months and even years, after Charlotte single-handedly destroyed their relationship, to put the past behind her and get over Ellis, but his occasional phone calls would stir up those horrific times and her recurring nightmare where Charlotte stalks her, terrorizes her, and threatens to kill her with a gun.

In an attempt to calm her nerves, Tyana made a phone call to the one person who kept her grounded.

"Hi, Trevor, it's me."

"Hey, what's going on?"

"Is this a bad time?"

"No, where are you? What time is it? I thought you'd still be tied up with all the wedding planning stuff. Isn't that today?"

"No. I mean, yes; I cancelled. I'm on my way home."

"Why did you cancel? What happened now?"

"I'd rather not talk about it right now. What time do you get off work? Is Cleo waiting for you at home?"

"Well, I told her I'd be straight home, which I should be finished in about half an hour or so. What's going on? Where are you now?"

"Close to home. I will be in about thirty seconds."

"I'll be in Scottsdale in about an hour and a half—depending on traffic. Do you want me to call you when I get there? I can let Cleo know I'm meeting you and will be a little late, or you can come over and have dinner with us.

How serious is it? You sound serious," Trevor asked, detecting a hint of stress in her voice.

"No, no, it's nothing—not important. I don't want to interfere with your plans—it's no big deal."

"Tyana..." Trevor and Tyana had been friends much too long for him not to be able to read her moods. Not to mention that they usually got right to the point during their calls and typically scheduled time to visit in person.

"Hey, I'm pulling into my garage now. I was going to take the evening off and catch up on some paperwork, but I think I should call Kellie. She's left several messages that I haven't returned yet. It's not that I don't want to spend the evening with you and Cleo, but I really do owe Kellie a phone call. It'll take you a while before you can even get up here anyway. You and I will catch up real soon, I promise."

"Sure, if you say so. I'll hold you to it, though." He hesitated for a moment; not convinced by her assurance. "Are you sure you're all right? The truth."

"Yes, I'm positive! Trust me." She glanced in her rear view mirror. "Uh...hey look, I gotta go. I'll call you later, okay?" She hung up abruptly after seeing Antonio pull up behind her. She got out of her car. He got out of his car.

"Tatyana, what are you doing here?" Antonio sounded slightly agitated, but more confused, as he approached her in the garage, eager to escape the mid-afternoon desert sun.

She closed her car door and stood facing him. "I left. You were late, again, and involved, so I cancelled and left."

"I told you I was on my way. I called to apologize and they said you cancelled. Why did you hang up on me? I apologized to you for being detained—it couldn't be helped. I left as quickly as I could."

"Antonio, it's the same story and I didn't want to hear more excuses; not at that particular time. It's embarrassing to constantly arrive late and to such an important meeting. It looks bad. Besides, what's done is done. You did what you needed to do and it's over." Antonio started to say something, but Tyana interrupted. "You make me feel that this wedding isn't as important to you as I initially thought; otherwise, we would have been married by now. It's also very clear to me that the dance studio and your clients will always come first."

"Tatyana..."

"No, I admired that of you when I met you, so I don't hold it against you. It's your life and you need to give of yourself the way you do. It makes you happy. But, I gave up *my* world when you asked me to marry you and to share your life. I did it because I not only love you, but I love the dance world, too. I do. Then we transformed this beautiful house together — to make it our home — because you proposed to me to get *married*; not to be engaged forever! You have to make time for us, too!" She swiftly turned away and reached for the doorknob. "Excuse me."

Tyana walked into the house and closed the door behind her, leaving Antonio standing in the garage alone with the echoes of her rant. She walked directly to the couple's bedroom, and once inside, she closed and locked the door. She stood right on the other side of the door for a moment listening to her heart pound and feeling it shatter. Antonio followed her and attempted to open the door, but couldn't.

"Tatyana. Please open the door. Let's talk about this. I'm sorry."

"Not now. I'm resting. I want to be alone for a little bit. I'm not mad, but I am frustrated. I just need a few minutes. Please."

She never liked to argue with him because she knew his intentions were to be loyal — to his business. She also knew he adored and loved her, so she didn't want to come off as the jealous type. On several occasions she tried to convey to him that she never felt jealous at all of his attention to any of his students, especially the privileged ones; privileged to his catering ways; but she felt hurt and neglected at times, by his lack of attention to their relationship when important situations or issues arose between them. She had to share him with all of that, and his daughter, who learned early on to run to him for everything because he gave her everything—mostly a reason for her to choose him over her mother because he could be easily manipulated and her mother could not. To make up for his lack of time spent with her, he granted her every wish. It didn't take Alyssa long before she knew she had her daddy wrapped around her little finger. He was always too busy to notice how spoiled she had become.

"Hey, I'm going to head back to the studio then," he announced through the door. He waited for a response. None came. "Té quiéro." Still nothing. "Tatyana, please open the door so I can see you; to kiss you good-bye. Are you going to be all right?"

"I'm fine. Yes, I'm going to be all right. We'll talk tonight when you get home."

"You're not coming back in tonight?"

"I don't think so. I have something else I need to do."

Feeling a twinge of jealousy, Antonio's curiosity piqued, but he refrained from prying. Instead he surrendered to her wishes to be left alone.

"All right. I understand. Té quiéro."

"I love you, too," she responded.

Antonio left Tyana to her thoughts and returned to work to finish out his schedule. He almost wished he didn't have any more lessons on the books so he could stay to see how bad the punishment would be. But as usual, duty called and he, as predicted, answered. Actually, he had a full schedule, which meant he wouldn't get home until almost ten. He had no choice but to wait to talk to her then. He foremost hoped that she would forgive him. He hated himself for letting her down. He cherished her and knew he messed up. He processed over and over in his head his decision to tend to a needy student instead of being where he needed to be, for his relationship. He wondered if he had become too available to his clients; too much of a pushover; too easily influenced by their trumped up tears and emotions. And then he wondered if perhaps Tyana was too insensitive to the students' needs.

As soon as Antonio pulled away, Tyana called Kellie and made plans to meet her for dinner.

♥ ♥ ♥

"I can't believe you took the night off! What did *I* do to deserve this treat of your company in the middle of the week?" Kellie inquired sarcastically. "And why *aren't* you at work?"

"Can't I visit with a dear friend without a reason? I felt bad that I've been working so much and not spending any time with you."

"Yeah, right, like I believe that. I *don't,* you know, but I'll take it if it means I get to spend a few hours with you. So, what's new? How's the Salsa King?"

"Good," Tyana replied nonchalantly while studying her menu. But then she sprung her face from out behind the menu as if a light bulb went on in her head. "Kel! I'm thinking about taking this weekend off and going up to Sedona. I know it's short notice, but would you like to go with me? I've been feeling badly about not spending much time with you, *seriously,* and pretty soon Antonio and I will be getting married and going on our honeymoon, so I thought…"

"Wait, what's this *really* all about?"

"Nothing! Nothing more than that. I thought you and I could spend some time at a spa resort in Sedona. Kinda like a girls' bachelorette weekend. But, if you don't think it's a good idea…"

"No, don't be silly! I think it's a great idea! I'm just shocked to hear you suggest something like that. I can barely get you out to dinner and now you're talking a spa weekend in Sedona. Sure! I'd love to go! Let me check with Paul and see what he's got going on and I'll let you know. I'm sure he'll be okay with it, though. Wow! I'm thrilled and looking forward to it. But don't you have to check with Antonio? I mean, does he know about this and he's cool with you being away from the dance studio for a whole entire weekend?"

"No, he doesn't know yet, but it doesn't matter, he'll be fine with it. I'm a grown woman, you know, and I can make a decision to spend some much overdue time with my best friend; can't I?"

"Of course you can. I didn't mean to imply…"

"I know. I just think we should do this before the wedding and all. Things will get busy after the wedding and we have a calendar full of competitions coming up in a few months."

"I've never seen you take time off before a competition, especially."

"Kelly, do you want to go with me or not? It's just a weekend and I'm going whether you do or not."

"No, I'm in! I'm definitely in! But I do need to check with Paul, since this is the first I'm hearing of it. But, I'm sure he'll be okay. It doesn't give me much time to plan or shop."

"What are you talking about? We'll shop when we get there! So, just grab some essentials and an empty suitcase. It'll be fun! I can't wait! Well, then I guess it's all set. So, let's order! My treat!"

The two friends talked over dinner for several hours. Tyana caught herself checking the time on her phone every so often, wondering about Antonio and who might be twisting him around her little finger tonight. She consciously decided to keep her earlier conversation between Antonio and herself out of her dinner conversation with Kellie. She didn't want to involve her or Trevor with something so personal, prematurely. It would probably work itself out anyway, she hoped. She wasn't sure how to resolve her recurring issue with Antonio's inattentiveness to their wedding plans, so she certainly didn't want to alarm her overly protective friends or encourage them to resolve it for her. She figured a cooling down period in Sedona would do the trick to put things into perspective and then everything would eventually get back on track. She and Antonio had been working around the clock lately and she had convinced herself that they were both a little stressed from the hours and the demands of the job. Her time away could do them both some good, or so she thought.

Tyana and Kellie wrapped up their evening and their plans of the upcoming weekend in Sedona and said good night. Tyana took a deep breath before turning on her car and heading home. She crossed her fingers that Antonio won't give her any grief over her plans to skip town for a few days. She wanted to take a break—to gain a new perspective and perhaps put some much-needed adventure back into her life. On her drive home, she thought of her phone call from Ellis.

Chapter

To Antonio, the dance studio meant everything and he ran it like a well-oiled machine. He took it personally when the instructors bailed on him by taking unscheduled time off because the studio was finally running at full schedule—practically every hour booked with either private and semi-private lessons or group lessons. Tyana knew Antonio had become even more driven to succeed, especially since he had committed himself to her. He had not been personally responsible for anyone in his whole life, until now. He didn't even have primary custody of his daughter—she lived with her mother since Shana and Antonio never married.

Antonio grew up the third of six siblings—all of whom were married, and both of his parents were still alive, so he was never put in a position where he had to step up and help out. Having never married, at forty-nine, he was about to embark upon one of the biggest events in his life with a beautiful, young thirty-four year-old woman, who went from being his prized student to his lovely fiancée practically overnight, and it made him nervous. He wanted the best for her; he felt personally responsible for her happiness, and to him that meant he had to work even harder to see to it that he could support her and take care of her in the manner he thought she deserved.

When Tyana pulled into her garage, she took another deep breath. Antonio would be home in about an hour. She proceeded into the house and tidied up some to expend her nervous energy. She abandoned her work schedule not only that evening, but she was about to abandon it for the weekend, too. After an hour of cleaning, she took a hot bath and retired to bed where Antonio found her half asleep when he eventually came home—later than he expected.

"Hi," Antonio whispered upon opening the bedroom door. He slowly approached the bed, fully waking her in the process. She glanced over at the bedside clock after opening her eyes and saw that it said eleven-twenty. Then she looked up at him, unsure of what to say. It was much later than he would normally arrive home.

"Hi," she replied in a soft voice. She continued to stare at him, waiting for an explanation.

"Té quiéro," he whispered, as he leaned in closer to her. He sat down next to her on the bed, nervously stroking her hair, and then he lightly kissed her forehead.

"I love you, too," she replied, being soothed by his touch on one hand, but on the other hand, she nearly gagged from the obnoxious, old lady perfume on his clothes. But that was normal. It was one of the unpleasant side effects that came with the territory. He had gotten used to it over the years, but for Tyana, it tested her trust and faith in her fiancé every day. Working side-by-side with Antonio daily gave her comfort in knowing that he loved only her. But she had seen other instructors sell out their integrity and engage in illicit affairs with students. After all, she, herself fell in love with her instructor and found herself in his hotel room after one emotional, willpower-tested night together. They both lost that battle of the wills, but in the process, found something worth gaining in the end after a year of denying the sexual tension that held them captive to one another. Tyana eventually came to realize that no one in that business was exempt from faltering and backsliding into a point of no return. No one.

Without another word or gesture, Antonio left her side and retreated to the bathroom to take a hot shower—a ritual for him after an exhausting day of dancing. When he returned to bed, he slid his warm, naked body into bed next to her, until their bodies touched — skin on skin. Touching her body always aroused him and this time was no different, in spite of their earlier episode. She, herself, could not resist the sexiness of his physique next to her. Even the slightest touch of his lips against her neck sent chills down her spine. He lay facing her, brushing back the hair from her face with his left hand and then lifting her chin to meet his face and his lips. He kissed her tentatively at first, testing her mood temperature. When he continued and increased his intensity, she kissed him back, but not matching that intensity. Her mind had communicated to her body that all wasn't yet forgotten and that she hadn't completely forgiven him for his error in judgment earlier that day. She, however, was receptive to him making love to her — a very passionate act that they indulged in often and regularly. To that point in their relationship, she has never denied her desires of him or the act of making love to him, and no minor spat could deter either of them from a moment of genuine loving passion.

When Antonio finally lay quiet catching his breath, he noticed Tyana relatively calm and unfazed, staring off into some corner of the room. Once the dust had settled and his head cleared, he refocused on her disposition.

"Hey, what's going on up there?" he asked as he gently tapped her forehead.

"What do you mean?"

"Well, you didn't seem…exactly in the moment with me just then and now you're so quiet. Are you okay?" He dove in and kissed her neck, hoping to arouse her.

"I'm fine. I guess I was tired. I was asleep when you came in at nearly eleven-thirty. Plus, I've been working a lot of hours lately."

"Are you sure that's it? Can I help you…you know?" Antonio began caressing her in an intimate way. He leaned in and began kissing her again in an attempt to arouse her.

"No, Antonio, don't. I'm okay. I'm just tired." She squirmed from underneath him, uncharacteristically refusing his encore gestures.

Antonio surmised that she might still be angry with him about what happened earlier.

"What did you do tonight after I left? You said you had some things to do. Did you go out?" He became suddenly aware of his insecurities. Since Tyana started working at the dance studio with him, he had around-the-clock access to her. She rarely kept him in the dark about her comings and goings.

"I've been thinking..." Ignoring his inquires about her evening, she sat up to address him. While twisting her hair she confronted him. "I'm going to reschedule my students this weekend and take the weekend off. I feel like I need some time away for awhile—a breather, so to speak." She paused for a reaction. Being the workaholic that he was, he would ordinarily object to such an impromptu decision by any instructor.

"What do you mean—time away? Away where? We have competitions coming up in a month. We can't afford to act irresponsibly by not being prepared."

"I'm not irresponsible. I just need a few days to...decompress. Yes, decompress and relax. I was thinking of going to Sedona with Kellie for a spa weekend. Just a weekend."

"Decompress...from what, the studio or me?"

"From everything. I've been working non-stop and trying to plan a wedding by myself and I've gotten, well, out of balance, you can say."

"So, you're still mad about today."

"No, I'm not still mad about today. I wasn't ever 'mad,' I was frustrated. And instead of becoming mad over something that's in the past, I want to take some time to unwind and breathe...and gain some perspective you could say."

"So, why can't you do that here, with me? We can set up a massage appointment with what's-her-name, Karen, Kathy…"

"Caitlin? The twenty-three year-old massage therapist who's taking dance lessons at the studio? No! Have you had massages from her?"

"One time when she brought her chair in to give massages to the staff and some of the students."

"What? And you let her massage you?"

"What are you getting so worked up about? It was nothing. Everyone signed up and I thought it was a good idea."

"Of course, you did, as if you don't have enough students touching you and pressing themselves up against you all day long."

"Tatyana, you're talking crazy."

"Don't call me crazy!"

"I didn't; I said you're talking crazy."

"Same thing."

"Well, you're not crazy. I didn't mean to insinuate that you were. And, I won't have her massage me again if it bothers you."

"Antonio, I'm going to Sedona — with Kellie."

"Fine, go. What about your…?"

"I'll re-book the students that I have this weekend with either someone else or I'll take them when I get back. It's not the end of the world."

"Okay. And, I'm sorry I haven't been there for you like you want me to be. I've been up to my nose with scheduling the regionals, and some staff issues. Crystal and Shaun don't want to go."

"Yeah, I know; remember, I work there, too."

"I'm sorry. I'm tired; you're tired. Let's go to sleep."

"So, you're alright with me going this weekend?"

"Sure. Of course. You do what you need to do. I'll be here when you get back."

"Thank you. I love you."

"Good night," he sulked. He kissed her before turning over.

"Good night."

Tyana drifted off to sleep with imminent concerns about her relationship. She wondered if marrying Antonio would be a mistake of gargantuan portions or would it be the best decision she had ever made?

♥ ♥ ♥

Early Saturday morning, Tyana and Kellie headed north on I-17, to begin their two-hour trek to the Red Rock Country of Sedona where they would indulge in a leisurely weekend involving a revitalizing full-service spa treatment, some hiking, horseback riding, and if time permitted, squeezing in a tour. But the primary purpose of the trip, which remained at the top of Tyana's list, was to hang out by the poolside at the resort, relaxing and drinking in the sun and silence—in terms of no ballroom tunes. She desperately welcomed the tranquil sounds of nature in the desert. She also looked forward to some girl-time with her long-time and closest friend in an attempt to clear her head over the whole wedding plans versus dance studio fiasco. Ironically, though, that was all she thought of during the entire ride into Sedona.

Tyana began isolating herself from the rest of the world once they started traveling north of 101, which unintentionally included tuning Kellie out for most of the trip. Her distraction with Antonio's lack of enthusiasm toward their wedding plans consumed her. She felt that not yet being married after five years of engagement meant something other than they were too busy to schedule it in. Something else bothered her more.

"Finally, we're here!" shouted Kellie, as they arrived at the front entrance of the magnificent club resort. Tyana's trance took a backseat to the drop-dead gorgeous scenery of central Arizona.

"Wow, it's beautiful! I can't wait to stretch my legs." Tyana suddenly felt restless. And right on cue, the attendant approached the door of her Lexus SUV to open it and welcome the attractive ladies to the Four-Diamond rated resort.

"Since it's only a little after ten and we scheduled an early check in, let's get settled, get something to eat, and then relax a bit by the pool. You look like you need to get your bearings first before we take this weekend by the balls!" Kellie suggested, reading her friend's disposition. She sensed her distraction throughout the ride.

Kellie had known the moment she saw Tyana at dinner the other night that something seriously bothered her, but she would wait for Tyana's cue to talk about whatever troubled her. Kellie's job became quite clear to her — to just be there for her dear friend. And wait she did.

When they reached the suite, Kellie unpacked while Tyana called Antonio to let him know that she arrived safely. She had to leave a message because he was conducting a lesson with a student at the time. She wondered when he would retire from teaching and focus on just managing the business like he had always talked about. She knew how much he loved teaching though, so she didn't hold her breath for that day to come very quickly.

They both changed into something more appropriate for the ambiance of the resort before returning to the lobby to take a quick tour of the resort. They headed straight to the pool after that, unable to resist the pull of the inviting water. The temperature reached ninety-eight degrees on an early June afternoon, which didn't faze those who were acclimated to the region at that time of the year. The mountainous breeze kept the air temperature in perspective most of the time. Shade was crucial.

Kellie and Tyana talked casually by the poolside about Kellie's work and latest family news before moving on to Tyana and her numerous accomplishments at the dance studio. As much as the dance studio has been a distraction to her personal life, she still loved her job as an instructor and owner.

"Do you ever miss your interior design business?" questioned Kellie, wondering if some of Tyana's quiet mood had to do with the absence of the career to which she once committed her life.

"Where did that come from?"

"It wasn't that long ago that you had a very successful business that you, yourself, built from the ground up. That's huge, you know. Not an easy thing to do, and yet you did it. Who can forget that?"

"I guess sometimes I do, but I love what I'm doing now. I *love* dancing! At first, I didn't think I would like teaching that much, but I do! It's very rewarding and I get a sense of purpose from it. My students' accomplishments are my rewards as well. Plus, that business is mine, too. I'm in a partnership with Antonio, remember?"

"I know. But, you know what I mean."

"No, I guess I don't know. If you think because it's not mine alone, it's okay that it's not. I love him and I love the fact that we're doing this together. It's nice to share an exciting venture with someone—especially with someone you love. With the interior design business, Ellis barely recognized my business or gave me credit for having a business. He kept himself too involved with his own thing." Her mind drifted off to his infidelity issues. "But with the dance studio, I'm doing it with someone who cares about what I think! God, that feels so, so amazing! Plus, we're actual partners. I *love* that." But her mind, once again, took her off course to Antonio's disassociation toward their plans of becoming the ultimate partners—husband and wife.

"That makes sense." Kellie took a sip of her drink. "But what about all the baggage that comes with him?"

"Like what?"

"Oh, like the obsessive students who cut you out of the picture every chance they get, his dubious mother who's hot and cold with you; his drama queen daughter who's jealous of your relationship with her daddy, and what about the ex?"

"Whose ex?"

"His, of course!"

"She's not a factor. I've only seen her a few times and she's always been cool with me."

"Maybe she's not a factor yet. Remember, she'll always have leverage with him—their daughter. She will be forever involved with him."

"Kellie, you're being ridiculous."

"Am I? Think about what he, all by himself, means to all those attention-starved people. And, they're all women! And, he's always under the watchful eye of his mother. She practically lives at the dance studio, always there to tend to his every need."

"She takes lessons about four days a week from the staff, what's wrong with that?"

"You told me yourself how his groupies have befriended her and she barely talks to you."

"I'm usually working when she's there. We talk sometimes."

"And in what language does his bilingual mother speak to Antonio in your presence?"

"Spanish."

"Exactly. And you don't find that a bit disrespectful; like she's deliberately excluding you from their conversation? And it's even more rude that he lets her do it, and he, too, talks in his native tongue to her in your presence. How would he feel if you conversed with your parents in your native language when he's around? Oh, wait! When have you two even visited your parents?"

"You made your point."

"Have I? Let me ask you this. Does he have any pictures of just the two of you in his office where he entertains his groupies?"

"No."

"Do you have a picture of him in your office?"

"Yes."

"Tyana, I'm happy for you. I really, really am. I know how much you love him and how much he loves you in spite of the weird way he shows it. I'm just saying that your love for each other comes with baggage, and it's all on his side. And that baggage isn't something that he's ever going to discard, in spite of your relationship. I think maybe he knows some of that, which is why he's not been eager to move forward with the wedding plans—he knows he's putting a lot on you and maybe, subconsciously, he's trying to spare you. Otherwise, he should show how proud he is to have you by his side and as his fiancée! He shouldn't be hiding the fact that you two are engaged. Maybe he's purposely dragging his feet and doesn't want to get married!"

"I'll be right back." Tyana began feeling an emotional surge coming on. Her throat tightened. She quickly got up and rushed inside of the hotel so Kellie wouldn't see her fall apart.

What the hell is wrong with me? She asked herself under her breath when she reached the lobby. She kept her head down and desperately tried to ward off the awkward and ill-timed flare-up of emotions. She wanted to think that maybe she had too much to drink and too little sleep. But she admitted to herself that she knew Kellie was perhaps right with some of her theory. But now wasn't the time to have that conversation. She wanted to spend a relaxing weekend not thinking about anything too serious or upsetting. Kellie would only keep at it until she got Tyana to agree with her and see things from her perspective—outside looking in—and Tyana didn't want to be interrogated—not there. She wished she had gotten to talk to Antonio first, thinking that their conversation would have given her clues to what he was thinking. She hoped he would come around and say something encouraging about their wedding plans. She didn't think she could wait much longer, and yet she didn't want to give him an ultimatum. She would just as well end the relationship before doing that. Controlling or manipulating a man had never been her style. That made her think about Ellis and Charlotte. Charlotte had manipulated Ellis right out from under her. She wouldn't have put it past her to have purposely gotten pregnant in order to trap him. Then she wondered if Ellis was happy. She reflected back on that night at the hotel in Miami when he slipped a note under her door apologizing for hurting her and then his random phone calls that he still insisted on making to her. But none of that mattered anymore. He is now married to Charlotte, and they have a child together, at least she assumed so since the last time she saw Charlotte her belly was quite swollen. But she tortured herself further with the reality that at least Charlotte was married and had a family.

Tyana vigorously shook her hands to fend off the tingling feeling, and took a deep breath before turning around to head back out to the pool where she abandoned Kellie.

"Tyana?"

"Huh?" She turned toward the voice, catching a whiff of expensive, yet familiar cologne.

Chapter
Three

Losing all momentum from her escape from Kellie's interrogation, Tyana was stopped dead in her tracks. She couldn't feel her legs. The six foot tall, dark, handsome and very familiar man now standing in front of her literally took her breath away. She gasped. He smiled and spoke first.

"Hi. I thought that was you. God, you look...how are you? How have you been?"

"Ellis! I, I...What are you doing here?"

Words were suddenly foreign to her. Her confused heart pounded rapidly and yet it seemed to have stopped beating at the same time. The noise in her head was deafening, as if the earth just split open. Her knees shook uncontrollably behind her sarong, but she played it off and held her composure and her balance with every bit of strength she had in her. She looked for something to hold her up. Then sensing something even more disturbing, she looked down and caught a glimpse of the two darling little girls patiently standing behind each of his legs. Ellis' eyes followed hers.

"Tyana, these are my daughters, Hailee and Hannah. Time flies, huh?" He directed the girls to come out from behind his legs. They appeared shy and well behaved; definitely feeling protected by their daddy's stature and presence.

"Hi; pleased to meet you," Tyana replied, introducing herself to the timid little four-year-old identical twins. She couldn't believe her eyes or her luck.

"Hi," Hailee responded. Hannah shyly hid behind her daddy's leg again and smiled.

Tyana smiled back at the girls, and then looked up at Ellis, lost for words—uncharacteristic of her natural unerring response in any situation. She shuddered at her luck of standing face-to-face with her ex-lover and boyfriend of ten predictable years—until his betrayal, that is—and his two children from his affair with his co-worker and now wife, Charlotte St. Jean-Montgomery. Seeing him like that only brought back the painful aspect of her life, which was like taking a bullet between the eyes. Oddly, she was experiencing the same fluttering feeling inside as she did during one unforgettable event in her life—when she was pregnant with their child for a brief time. Recovering quickly, she was reminded by how his good looks still managed to fluster her. His drop-dead attractiveness still turned heads even more so in his mid forties, than when he caught Tyana's attention fifteen years ago, as a college student—unfazed by how accomplished he already had become at thirty. As for Ellis, he found himself tongue-tied on occasion around her. He realized she was too young for him, but he became defenseless against her beauty, maturity, and intelligence.

Once again, the raw emotions were rushing back, but she couldn't just run away from Ellis this time, like she did in Miami. Nor could she hang up on him as she had done numerous times before. No, this time, she had to check her emotions, stand up straight, and deal directly with him and the situation. *Why now?* She could hear herself screaming inside of her head.

"Are you all right?" he asked with concern since she wasn't talking.

Ellis watched Tyana's facial expression gradually change before his eyes. Her face took on a more serious and sad countenance. He lived through the worst part of her life with her because he was responsible for it, so he had seen that look on her face before and he understood its meaning. They both remained staring at each other with so much anguish in their hearts and pain in their eyes. Her sorrow represented the loss of something significantly precious to her, and she didn't need the reminder now. His sorrow represented the most significant loss of *his* life—her. Various thoughts were scrambling through both of their minds. He wanted to say so many things to her, but he didn't know where or how to begin or if he even had the right. After all, it had been nearly five years since they had last seen each other and since he betrayed their love, crushed her heart, and married someone else.

"Tyana..."

"Daddy, I wanna go! I wanna see Momma!" whined Hannah, tugging at his leg.

"Okay, Hannah, we're leaving. Momma should be back soon." He looked back at Tyana not wanting to bring up Charlotte, seeing that she was still holding on to too much of their painful past. "I better take them back. I think it's time for their nap. Hannah is starting to sound cranky." He tried to divert their minds from their shared thoughts.

"Uh...how's Charlotte?" Tyana asked nervously, not knowing what else to say. She didn't want to utter her name nor did she care how she was, but nothing else came to mind. She thought that if she didn't ask, it would seem like she still held a grudge, which she did. Actually, she wasn't sure how she still felt about herself and Ellis until she saw him. But there was one thing she felt certain about now, and that was, she wanted a baby. It became an absolute, clairvoyant conclusion. She suddenly felt sadness for the baby she lost.

"She's good. She's somewhere getting a facial or a manicure, or something." Ellis became just as nervous as Tyana. "How's your business?"

"I'm not doing that anymore."

"Really? Why? You loved interior design and you were so good at what you did. I'd always admired your talent."

She looked surprised to hear him say that. He had never talked about her business in that way during her four years of ownership.

"I'm partners with Antonio — of his dance studio, I mean, our dance studio. I teach full-time now."

"Really. That's…"

"Ellis, why are you here?" she asked suddenly realizing where they were. The last she knew he still lived in San Diego with Charlotte.

"I'm actually here on business. This is one of my properties. Then we thought we would make a little vacation out of the trip for the girls and head on up to the Grand Canyon…and, I'm saying all the wrong things, I know."

"No-no. Yes. I'm sorry, I'm just stunned to be standing here talking to you. And, your girls…they're adorable." She placed her hand to her heart.

"Thank you." Ellis gave Tyana a longing look, and then looked at his daughters to see them busy talking to each other being distracted by another toddler passing by. "Tyana," he whispered, "I never meant to hurt you."

"Ellis, don't."

"I never stopped loving you," he confessed.

"Daddy, let's go!" shouted Hannah, louder this time. Hailee inquisitively looked on.

"You better get them back. I'm here with Kellie and I better get back out there before she sends out a search party. Bye Ellis."

Tyana awkwardly waved good-bye to the little ones and abruptly left Ellis standing, longing after her as she walked swiftly away from them. Her heart lodged somewhere in her throat and she could barely take in air. With the girls in his care and at his side, he could do nothing, but watch her go. He still concealed so much regret for his actions against her. To him she looked more beautiful than she did when he last saw her that night in her elegant ball gown and in the arms of another man. He knew he was a fool to have ever cheated on her and destroyed what they had together. She didn't deserve it and he felt painful regret because of that truth. He sadly turned around and carried his tired little girls back to their suite, looking back only once.

Tyana darted around the nearest corner and stopped to catch her breath before returning outside. She couldn't control her nervous shaking. Seeing Ellis had completely unraveled her. His daughters were cute and precious. It never occurred to her that she would ever meet them; and they only reminded her of what took place between Charlotte and him, not to mention the baby she lost—their baby. She had lovingly devoted herself to Ellis once and welcomed the chance at conceiving a baby with him.

She vigorously shook her hands again to try and thwart the uneasy feeling shrouding her entire body, but it didn't work. She blew out several short puffs of air to help as well. She tried everything short of putting her head between her knees. She thought she was about to lose consciousness when she heard a woman's voice speaking to her.

"Hey, there you are!" Kellie startled Tyana.

"What? Oh, hey. I was coming back out. I need to get a drink first. Do you need anything? What time is it? I need to get some more sunscreen from the room. Are you hungry? I think I need something to eat, or to lie down. It's really hot. Are you hot, or is it just me?" Tyana's rambling raised concern.

"Time out! Slow down. What's the matter with you? What gives? You've been acting weird ever since we got here. First you're all quiet, now you seem freaked about something. Girl, what's going on with you? And, don't say it's nothing; I know you. Here, sit down over here." Kellie attempted to guide Tyana over to a seat in the lobby.

"No! We have to get out of here! Let's go!"

Tyana looked around and dashed over to the elevator. Kellie spun around to catch up with her.

"Hey, wait up!" She eventually caught up with her. "What are you doing? Why are you acting so freaked out and...upset? You're starting to freak me out, Tyana!"

"I'm really sorry. I just need a minute. I need to go back to the room for a moment. Can you give me a minute? I want some time alone—just for a little while. I promise."

"Are you sure you're all right? Is it the heat?"

"I'm fine. Come up if you need to in about twenty minutes. If not, I promise to come back down to the pool in half an hour, and then we can go from there with our plans. Just please give me this time."

"Sure. I'll be down here at the pool if you need me. But, can you tell me a little of what's got you like this?"

"Not right now." The elevator doors opened. "I'll be back in a little while. I need to lie down for a few minutes. I'll be fine after that. I got a little dizzy."

"Okay, take your time."

Kellie stood puzzled as the doors closed and Tyana disappeared. Nothing came to mind about what she could do or say for Tyana at the moment and that made *her* feel useless as a friend.

Meanwhile, Tyana entered the suite, crawled across the bed, and lay back against the pillows with her eyes closed. She dissected over and over in her head her unexpected run-in with Ellis. She couldn't get his face, and those girls of his, out of her mind. She tried shutting her eyes tightly, but nothing she did would remove the images from her mind. And then the phone rang.

"Hello," she answered on the first ring.

"Tatyana, it's me," replied Antonio. He finally broke away from his duties long enough to call her back.

"Sounds like you're really busy today."

"Yeah, Elizabeth didn't come in today, so we had to juggle her students around and we had some new walk-in business. Hey, I forgot to ask you… how many students do you have going to the competition next month?"

"Antonio, I thought I gave that information to you already. It's on my desk—on the calendar. If you can't find it there, look in the folder marked September Competitions. It's filed in the right-hand drawer. Can it wait until I get back?"

"Rita was asking for it, that's all."

"Aren't you going to even ask me how I am?"

"What's wrong? Is something wrong? Are you sick?" Antonio grew concerned, thinking only of her ability to dance.

"No! I'm just saying you jumped right into a conversation about work before asking about me or us! What about *us*? Don't you even care about *us* anymore? Or *me*? I want us to get married. I'm tired of waiting. What are we waiting for? Do you remember when you asked me to marry you?"

"Of course I do. And, I do want us to get married. We will. Things have been kind of crazy with the business and we've been busier than ever…"

"Antonio, I want to have a baby. I can't wait any longer."

♥ ♥ ♥

"Momma!" exclaimed Hailee, as she happily greeted her mother coming through the door of the suite.

"Hi! How's my Baby Girl?" Charlotte asked, giving her daughter a big hug.

"And me!" shouted Hannah, running out from the bedroom with Ellis following behind her.

"Yes! And you, too, Baby Doll! I missed you both! Did you have a good time with Daddy while I got my toenails and fingernails painted pretty?" She kissed the girls, and then her husband. He politely kissed her back for the sake of the girls.

"We were good, Momma!" they chanted in unison.

"Can you watch them for a minute while I make a call to the office?" asked Ellis.

"Of course." Charlotte took the girls into the living room to show them the new bathing suits she bought for each of them.

"So, what all did you do today while I was gone?" she asked the twins.

Hannah spoke first. "We watched Daddy exercise first, then we walked, we ate, and Daddy talked on the phone, then Daddy talked to a pretty lady."

"Oh?" Charlotte's interest was piqued. She thought at first her daughter meant someone from the hotel staff, but it was the way Hannah said it that made her think otherwise. "Who, Hannah?"

"Her name was Tina," interjected Hailee.

"Daddy told her he loves her—like a secret—but I heard him," added Hannah.

♥ ♥ ♥

Antonio swallowed hard. "A baby?"

"Yeah, a baby. Why do you sound so shocked? Wouldn't you want to have a baby? I thought that would be the next logical step after we got married. I'm sort of running out of time here—biologically speaking."

"You're not that old."

"No, but I don't want to have a baby when I'm forty! I'm already in my mid-thirties. I thought I'd be farther along in that department—by now." She thought once again of Ellis' children. They should be hers.

"What about your dancing?"

"Antonio, what are you saying? This is my life we're talking about. I'm not giving up having a baby and becoming a mother just to dance. I thought..." tears welled up in her eyes.

"Look, can we talk about this when you get back? I have students waiting and the phone's ringing off the hook—everyone's teaching—it's chaos around here. I sure could use you here today. Well, have fun and I'll call you later tonight, okay?"

"But..."

"Tatyana, té quiéro. I'll call you later."

"I love you, too. Bye."

Tyana didn't think Antonio had any reservations about having a family; but his avoidance of the topic gave her the impression that he did—at least from that conversation. She needed to find out how seriously he regarded the subject—and soon! She continued to lie, staring up at the ceiling, deep in thought about her future as Mrs. Antonio Lorenzo.

♥ ♥ ♥

Charlotte put the girls down for their afternoon nap and headed straight to the master bedroom to look for Ellis who appeared to be buried in his work. She thought about what the girls told her and came to only one conclusion. They were in Tyana's territory and Charlotte has always known in the back of her mind how Ellis felt about Tyana, even after five years of marriage with her. She knew that he only married her because she threatened him with her pregnancy, and she also knew that if he had his druthers, he would be with Tyana instead of her. Now, she needed to find out if he did run into Tyana that afternoon, and what transpired between them. However, she was determined not to let him make a fool out of her or leave her and the girls at that point—or at any point in their marriage—without putting up a fight. What it was like getting him to marry her in the first place would resemble a cakewalk compared to what divorcing her would turn into.

"Ellis! I need to speak with you!"

"In a minute; I need to run this package downstairs to the front desk. It has to get out today. I'll be right back."

Ellis dashed past Charlotte and out of the suite before she had a chance to start her rant.

♥ ♥ ♥

Kellie glanced at her watch and saw that she needed to send out a search party for Tyana. She got up and headed for their suite. She doubled back to pick up some brochures at the Concierge's desk to entice Tyana with some tours in the area. With her nose into the brochure, she turned right into another guest who was approaching the Concierge's desk; both were lost in their own thoughts until they nearly collided.

"Oh! Excuse me," Kellie apologized and then did a double take.

"No, my mistake, excuse *me*," Ellis politely insisted.

"Oh, my God! Ellis?" Kellie removed her shades to get a better look at the man who nearly destroyed Tyana.

"Kellie…" He deduced by the degree of shock in her voice that Tyana hadn't told her that she ran into him earlier, or maybe she had.

"What are you *doing* here?" she asked in a threatening manner, as if he staged it. She darted her eyes around the lobby to see if Tyana might be anywhere nearby.

"It's okay, she knows."

"Shit! Are you kidding me? It's not okay. You *bastard*! You have no idea. You have a lot of nerve!"

Kellie left Ellis standing in the lobby looking dazed and confused by her words. She instantly theorized Tyana's earlier behavior by Ellis' comment of her knowing he was there. She thought if they had run into each other, then that would explain her strange request for wanting some space; and her gibberish conversation earlier. She became obviously unnerved by Ellis' presence. Kellie pushed the elevator button repeatedly in a panic to get to Tyana.

"*C'mon, c'mon, c'mon!*"

"Kellie, wait!" urged Ellis as he approached her.

"Not now, Ellis!" Then she turned around to face him. "Did you speak to her?"

"Yes, we spoke, why?"

The elevator doors opened and Kellie got in. Ellis followed her.

"What are you doing?" She pushed the button for her floor.

"I'm going back to my suite," he replied, as he pushed the button for his floor.

"Leave her alone, Ellis."

"Why are you so paranoid? We're all adults here."

"Just do it!"

"Why are you so protective of her? She's a grown woman who..."

"Who you screwed over! You destroyed her and stomped all over her heart with that...that slut!"

With that insult, the elevator doors opened on Kellie's floor first. She sneered back at Ellis and got off. Ellis stood alone in the aftermath of her attack on him. She walked briskly toward the room, but couldn't seem to get there fast enough. She inserted the keycard and let herself in without warning.

♥ ♥ ♥

Antonio returned to work, but could barely concentrate, given his last conversation with Tyana. She brought up a sensitive subject that he hadn't much wanted to give any thought to since the birth of his daughter. He never envisioned himself as being a father—again—let alone, as being married. He had his business that required a great deal of his time and attention, which more than fulfilled his needs. He knew that when he asked Tyana to marry him, his life would change somewhat, however, the change that he had envisioned involved the studio—like a partnership, opening of more studios, and even perhaps, with the help of Tyana, coaching. It hadn't occurred to him that he would take on domestic changes, such as babies and parenthood! It was not exactly what he had in mind as he inched toward his fiftieth birthday.

As Antonio continued mindlessly dancing with his student, he remembered the conversation that brought Tyana and him together five years ago, that night in Miami. She confessed the scandalous details of her ex-boyfriend's affair that resulted in their breakup and the loss of the baby she so urgently wanted. He remembered himself hurting inside from the pain she had endured, and his concern was genuine. He couldn't bear to see her like that again, and because of him. What was he thinking by denying her the opportunity of a second chance at being a mother, he thought, and with someone who loved her the way he did? But could he be a good father to their child and an attentive husband to her, he wondered? Could he be devoted enough to a family and not let her down? He knew of no other life than that of his world—his dance business and his clients. They have all come to depend on him for everything. He wasn't even a full-time father to his daughter. Could he give everyone everything they needed, and at the same time, keep everyone happy? He didn't know the answer.

♥ ♥ ♥

When Ellis returned to the suite, Charlotte stood posed like a model in a bikini bathing suit with her hands on her hips ready to fire off questions. Even after giving birth to twins, she managed to maintain a sculptured body—toned and tight—that didn't go unnoticed.

♥ ♥ ♥

"Tyana, why didn't you tell me Ellis was here and that you saw him? Are you okay? We can leave if you want to. We can leave right now!"

"Kel, Kellie! It's okay! No, I mean it's weird. I'm a mess. I'm freaking out!"

"Of course you are! What did he say to you? Tell me every detail!"

"It's not so much what he said to me, it's what Antonio didn't say."

"Antonio? What are you talking about? What does Antonio have to do with *this*?"

"I talked to him a little while ago—after I saw Ellis."

"And...you didn't tell him that you saw Ellis, did you?"

"No! But seeing Ellis and his girls got me thinking. And, after talking to Antonio, he doesn't sound like he's on the same page as I—with this whole wedding/baby thing."

"Baby? What baby?"

♥ ♥ ♥

"So, Ellis, did anything out of the ordinary happen this afternoon? Where did you go and what did you do? And, I want the truth!" Charlotte glared at her husband of five antagonistic years. She didn't give Ellis a chance to close the door once he stepped foot inside of the suite before she started drilling him verbally.

"What? Why the tone? I took the girls out, we walked around the property; that's about it; and then we came back. Why are you looking at me like that, with daggers in your eyes? Knock it off."

"You're not leaving me, so don't get any ideas. For one thing, you can't afford to leave *me*. I'll see to that when I lawyer up."

"Charlotte, what are you talking about? Who said anything about leaving?"

"I'm just saying..." With those last words, Charlotte exited the suite. She decided to go for a swim—a long swim. She poked her head back in, "Keep an eye on *your* girls!" She was gone again.

♥ ♥ ♥

"Kellie, I plan to have a baby once Antonio and I are married. What did you think I was talking about? What's with everyone? I want a baby! *Is that such a crime?*"

"No, calm down. I just didn't know how we got from Ellis to you having a baby, that's all."

"I'm sorry. I'm all frazzled. The Ellis sighting really threw me. Ellis said he still loves me and I saw his twin girls. They're adorable."

"He said what?! He's a damn fool! Don't listen to him. I hope you told him off!"

"Kellie, he had his girls with him."

"He told you this in front of *them*? How stupid *is* that man?"

"He whispered. They didn't hear."

"I don't believe this is happening. For your information, I ran into the son of a bitch downstairs and I *did* tell him off! And, if he even *thinks* about coming near you *or* this suite while we're here, he's going to have to come through *me* first!"

"What? Why did you do that?"

"Because he's *stupid*! Do you not remember what he did to you and for God knows how long? Did you take a long look at those two little girls? Tyana, he slept with that slut over and over and over, while living with you, in case you forgot, then got her pregnant, while you were pregnant with his child, too! And because of his sorry ass, you lost the baby!"

"Yeah, I remember! *I remember*!" Tyana, horribly confused, got up and ran into the bathroom and shut the door.

"Damn!" yelled a frustrated Kellie after Tyana shut her out.

♥ ♥ ♥

"Damn." muttered a miserable Ellis after Charlotte left and slammed the door.

♥ ♥ ♥

"Damn-it!" shouted a desperate Charlotte when she left the suite.

♥ ♥ ♥

Antonio, worried about his future, continued dancing with his students.

Chapter

Tyana remained locked in the bathroom for nearly fifteen minutes before she exited without a word and began changing her clothes.

"Tyana, are you going to speak to me? I said I'm sorry. I just don't want to see you devastated again. He put you through so *much* back then and I had never seen you so messed up before. We were all worried about you. Your life was turned upside down! He did that, with *her*! I just don't want to see you go through anything remotely close to that again."

"I appreciate your concern for me, really I do. But, we both have moved on from that. He's married; I'm with Antonio and will be married soon." She paused. "It's over. I don't need you to run interference for me like I'm not capable of handling myself. Granted, I came a little unglued because of the unexpected sighting of Ellis *and* his twins, but that's because of what Antonio and I are going through at the moment. And, I didn't tell you about *that* because I didn't want to focus on it this weekend. I knew you wouldn't let that go if I had told you."

"So what is going on between you two? And you should have said something sooner. I want to help."

"It's not your problem and I was hoping things would have worked themselves out by now. He's so committed to the studio and everything tied to it—more than he is to me, I'm afraid. I know he loves me, but I'm scared he really doesn't want to marry me."

"That's crazy! Of course, he wants to marry you; I'm positive of that. I was just talking. What do I know? But I'm sorry you're going through that other stuff with him and I did wonder why you guys were waiting so long to tie the knot."

"Like you said, he has baggage that comes with the territory."

"What are you going to do?"

"I'm going to change my clothes and go out and enjoy this weekend and this fabulous resort. What do you want to do first, a spa treatment before dinner? I could definitely use a foot massage and a full body massage. I think I'll indulge in a full-service. What about you?"

"Sure, whatever you want to do is fine with me. I'll change, too. But if you want to take it easy..."

"Kellie, don't! This is why I didn't want to talk about it."

"Okay, I got it. We're here for a girls' getaway weekend, so let's go out there and get our groove back...or something not quite like that."

When they left the suite, Kellie took a deep breath. She worried about Tyana and her future.

♥ ♥ ♥

When Charlotte returned to the couple's suite, the girls had awakened early from their nap and were occupying Ellis' time with children's games, books, puzzles, dolls, learning videos and the occasional spilled juice. Ellis hated to travel without their nanny, especially when they traveled for business, but Charlotte promised him that she would take care of the girls since they didn't intend to stay away for very long. Charlotte also didn't expect Ellis to run into Tyana. Plans had changed.

"Where the hell have you been? I've been trying to make my business calls and the girls are running all over the place. They didn't sleep long at all. I fed them a snack already, by the way. You didn't take your cell phone—I couldn't reach you. You left it here!"

"Don't you raise your voice at me!" Charlotte cut Ellis a stern look.

"Momma! Momma! Can we go swimming? Can we wear our new bathing suits?"

"Yes, Baby Doll. Daddy will take you both swimming. How about that?"

"Yay!" shrilled the girls.

"What?" questioned Ellis. "Charlotte, I need to get this work done—I have deadlines!"

"You also have a wife and children. Just remember that. Now take your daughters swimming." Charlotte stormed into the bathroom.

Ellis let out a long sigh and then looked at his girls' big blue eyes, which always melted his heart. They had Charlotte's blue eyes and soft blonde hair, but they looked more like him. He assisted them with their bathing suits and within ten minutes the three of them headed for the hotel pool. Slightly annoyed by the interruption of his work, Ellis grabbed his documents and his phone.

Charlotte still held her executive position with the hotel, and didn't cut back her hours as significantly as Ellis had hoped she would after having the girls. They hired a nanny to help out with most of the chores around the house, where the girls were concerned, as well as with the occasional travel. But, they usually granted their nanny time off when they traveled to visit family or when their business travel didn't require the involvement of both of them. However, Ellis now regretted not having the nanny on this trip, and also regretted not taking the trip alone.

Charlotte came out of the bathroom after Ellis and the girls left. She sat down on the sofa to enjoy a glass of wine and the peace and quiet of the suite. However, she suddenly became acutely aware of the quiet. Her mind traveled back to the day she found out that she was having twins. From that moment forward in her pregnancy, her feelings for Ellis grew stronger, even though she knew he still resented her for setting up Tyana to discover his affair with her. She gambled on his heart thawing toward her after the birth of the twins, but with no such luck. He began to exhibit more compassion and respect for her once they found out about the twins, but it wasn't the same kind of love that she felt toward him. After she gave birth, his daughters were the only ones who could tug at his heartstrings. Charlotte turned up the glass and finished off the wine.

♥ ♥ ♥

Antonio sat in his office alone, lost in thought over Tyana being away for the weekend and their conversation before she left. It was Saturday, so the studio hours were abbreviated—at least they were scheduled that way. He intended to get caught up on some paperwork after his calendar cleared. The thought of going home, knowing Tyana wouldn't be there, didn't interest him, so he continued to work a little longer. He noticed some discrepancies in the financial reports and, although he had an accountant who took care of his books, he wanted to review them himself. But his concentration became compromised. He wondered what she and Kellie were doing. He made a move to pick up the phone to call Tyana, but a soft knock on his office door interrupted him.

"Excuse me, Antonio?"

"Yes, oh, hi. What are you doing back? Did you forget something?" Antonio wondered why Dottie returned after hours. He put his phone away when she barged into his office uninvited.

"Uh, no, I wanted to talk to you about the competition next month. I have some concerns."

"Concerns about what? Sit down." The call to Tyana fled his mind. "You sound upset. What's wrong?"

"I just don't think I'll be ready. I'm not sure I can do this anymore."

"Why? You'll be fine. You've been dancing and competing for years. Why all of a sudden the cold feet and change of heart?"

"I just don't feel confident and talented enough." Her voice quivered and tears blurred her eyes.

"Here." He handed her a tissue. "You're a great dancer. I don't know where all this is coming from. What do you want to do?"

"I should quit. I don't think I'm progressing and I'm probably just wasting my time and yours."

"Nonsense! That's absurd, Dottie. You're doing a fantastic job! Now, I want you to get those crazy thoughts out of your head and get ready for the competition. We're going to do great!"

"But…never mind." She got up and turned toward the door to leave.

"What is it? Wait, come back!" Antonio jumped up and went after her. He grabbed her shoulder and turned her around. She put her hands on him and cried in his chest. He awkwardly comforted her.

♥ ♥ ♥

After the spa service, Tyana and Kellie dressed for dinner at the five-star restaurant at the resort. They were initially going to venture out, but they felt so relaxed and Tyana felt exhausted after the trip and the eventful day so they decided not to go too far on their first day. Kellie had reservations about staying around the resort and being a target for Ellis to run into Tyana again. Tyana had the same concerns, but thought it highly unlikely that it would happen again. After all, it was a big hotel with three restaurants.

♥ ♥ ♥

Charlotte insisted that they order from room service because the twins fell asleep early and she didn't want to hassle with getting them up and prepared for dinner. Ellis didn't argue. He had a chaotic day. They sat and ate in silence while Ellis looked over his work documents and intermittently thought about Tyana. He had to prepare for a meeting with a client first thing on Monday morning, then after that, they were off to the Grand Canyon. Charlotte couldn't wait—two more days. Tyana and Kellie were also scheduled to leave early Monday morning.

♥ ♥ ♥

"That was a great meal—I'm stuffed," raved Kellie.

"Too good. I'm stuffed, too." Tyana agreed while dabbing at her mouth with her napkin.

"Do you want another cocktail?" Kellie finished off her drink.

"No, I'm actually very tired and ready to leave whenever you are." Tyana motioned for the check.

"Okay, sure. I am ready. I need to call Paul soon, too."

"What's he doing this weekend without you?"

"He's probably up to his eyeballs in research and documents. He's got a big high-profile case in court coming up and he's not exactly thrilled with the judge who's assigned. That's adding to his stress."

"So, then this is a perfect weekend for you to be gone."

"Oh, he gave me the guilt trip anyway. I think I spoiled him by always being right where he can find me at all times."

"Kel, can I ask something personal?"

"Sure."

"Why haven't you and Paul had any children? Is that something you both decided early on in your marriage?"

"You know, for the most part, we haven't thought about it too much. Neither one of us were too keen on the idea of raising children, or at least we didn't think we would be good at it."

"Really. And that's it?"

"No, that isn't exactly it. One night when we were on a romantic getaway in Paris—remember that trip? Well, one night, in bed, I felt particularly 'romantic' and maternal and had the wild idea to start a family and I felt sure that Paul would go along with that idea. He had been quite amorous since the moment we landed in Paris and catering to me like crazy. And, I'd been watching him interact with his little nephew prior to that, and he's been amazing with him. Little Brian loves his uncle and Paul loves little Brian. When we're visiting his sister, those two are inseparable! So, I'm thinking to myself, maybe he *does* want kids."

"What happened?"

"Well, when I brought it up, he nearly exploded. He became angry that I had changed my mind. He said I left him out of the thought process, which made him feel like the bad guy for not wanting kids now that I did."

"Oh, wow. I'm sorry to hear that."

"I tried to explain that I hadn't been thinking about it very long; it was more of an impromptu suggestion to, like, open it up for discussion. But he didn't see it that way. He felt ambushed and thought that I picked a bad time to bring it up. I apologized and told him that I didn't mean to toss out the idea at that particular time in any attempt to manipulate him or to catch him off guard, but it did ruin the moment. We haven't talked about it since."

"Why? Why not? You can't just drop it after you brought it up. Do you still want children or has that now changed?"

"I don't know. Once we got back home and back into our crazy, chaotic routine, there really hasn't been a good time to bring it up. I haven't thought about it much."

"Much? But you have thought about it, right?"

"Really, no, I haven't thought about it. We love our lives and I don't think either one of us misses not having children, plus I'm inching toward forty and it may be too late."

"Nonsense! It's not too late for you to have a baby."

"Maybe not for me and my body, but for us, perhaps."

"I think you should bring it up again, so you'll know for sure before it *is* too late."

"We'll see. But first things first…you and Antonio need to get your situation figured out and set a date."

"We'll figure it out, but our situation has nothing to do with yours. Let's get out of here. I'm really tired."

"I'm with you."

They paid their dinner tab and returned to their suite. Tyana hadn't heard from Antonio yet and wondered why he hadn't called, knowing he should have finished up at the dance studio hours ago. She tried calling him when she returned to the room, but didn't get any answer at home either. She couldn't imagine him still working, but it wouldn't be the first time he stayed late on a Saturday. So, she tried him there, but only got the voicemail. She bolted out of the bedroom.

"What's the matter?" asked Kellie. "Did you get a hold of Antonio?"

"I'm going to get some ice. I need some ice."

"Okay." Before Kellie could say another word, Tyana disappeared into the hall.

Tyana fabricated the ice story. She had become distracted over Antonio's whereabouts and she didn't want Kellie to know. She began thinking about his lack of concern about their personal lives, particularly, the wedding plans. And now not being able to reach him escalated her worries. She stormed down the hall—ice bucket in hand.

♥ ♥ ♥

After Ellis had put the twins down for the evening, he tiptoed out of the suite when Charlotte dozed off after consuming three glasses of wine. Ellis needed a breather.

He decided to walk the halls to clear his head and strategize his upcoming meeting. After he started feeling mesmerized by the carpet design, he found himself in the elevator occupied by two couples. He gave a courtesy nod to the other guests also heading to the lobby. He thought he would visit the bar. But before he settled in for the ride to the lobby, at the last second, he pushed the button to Tyana and Kellie's floor and then got off. Once he stepped out, he almost turned back toward the elevator to escape, but he didn't. He told himself he would walk the halls just once, and then leave.

♥ ♥ ♥

Tyana entered the ice room and began to fill her ice bucket, while still disoriented over her issues with Antonio. She put the ice bucket down and retrieved her phone expecting to see a message. Nothing. Suspicion shrouded her when she recounted to herself the amount of time that had passed since she had first tried to reach Antonio. It was late, really late, and he should be home by now, or at least reachable. Still staring at her phone contemplating her next move, she exited the ice room and stood idle on the other side of the door.

"Tyana!" Ellis' voice jolted her out of her trance causing her to juggle the bucket and spill the top layer of ice cubes onto the carpet.

"Shoot!" She stooped down to pick up the ice.

Ellis immediately stooped to help her. "I'm sorry, I didn't mean to startle you."

"You scared me! Are you following me?" she asked as she quickly reached for each ice cube scattered all around them. While scooping up the ice, she noticed he still wore impeccable shoes—always shined and well taken care of. Nothing about his appearance and how well dressed he had always been, had changed. If anything, his clothes were more expensive today. Her eyes traveled up from his Armani Suit and Perry Ellis tie to his hypnotic hazel eyes. His face looked smooth and meticulously shaven. From head to toe he looked the epitome of a corporate executive, which seemed out of place for him. But his face and his body actually looked more like a male fashion model, with piercing eyes, a strong jaw line, full narrow lips and perfect eyebrows. His dark brown semi-wavy hair never seemed out of place.

"No, I was, uh, taking a walk, but I'm glad I ran into you — alone."

"Yeah, I heard you had an interesting encounter with Kellie."

"Yeah, when did she become your bodyguard? Is she around, by the way? I don't want to get my ass kicked?" he chuckled.

Tyana chuckled. "She's in the suite. And, I believe she will do it. She, uh, well, she doesn't like you much." They picked up the last of the ice and stood up together. "So, what about your wife?"

"Uh, about her. I think, somehow, she figured out that you're here and now I'm on lock-down. Speaking of which..." Ellis pulled Tyana toward a door marked "Laundry Room." He yanked her inside causing her to spill more ice onto the floor in the process. Once inside, he locked the door. Tyana looked confused and almost frightened.

"What are you *doing*?"

"I meant what I said."

"What are you talking about? Why did you pull me in here? Let me out of here!"

"I still love you."

"Ellis, you're married. You made your bed..."

"Yes, I know, but that doesn't mean I don't feel what I feel. I told you what happened back then. I got in over my head and wanted to be successful, and she did that for me; for us."

"For us my ass!"

"It's true! But her mentoring came with a price — a hefty price and before I knew it, I was screwed."

"Yeah, literally!"

"I know, Tyana, she got to me and I sacrificed so much for my executive position with the hotel."

"You sacrificed our relationship, our future, and our baby!"

"I know it! Don't you think I know it? I screwed up everything and I've been paying for it ever since, and I hurt you and I destroyed *us*. But I'm still in love with you. I need you to know that."

"Ellis, you're smart! I don't understand why you needed her help at all. And why, why do I need to know all this—*now*?"

"Because I've been wanting to tell you everything for the last five years. And, when I ran into you here, I took that as a sign that this was my chance—my only chance. I didn't want another day to go by without you knowing how I feel about you. If you just say the word, I swear I'll leave her. I'll give you whatever you want—anything. You're not married, so…"

"How do you know I'm not married?"

Ellis gave her a confident stare. "C'mon, Tyana. First of all, you're not wearing a wedding band, and second, you're here with Kellie and why would she be so protective if you were happily married? Wouldn't that be your husband's job?"

"That doesn't mean anything."

"Well, then are you?"

Embarrassed, she replied, "No, but…"

"I'm serious, Tyana, I love you." Ellis moved in closer and took the ice bucket out of her hands and placed it on a shelf.

"Ellis! You don't love me. That's ridiculous!" She backed away, but he pulled her in closer to him. She caught a whiff of his intoxicating aroma. He always smelled fresh and rich, she recalled.

"It may be ridiculous to you, but not to me. I've missed you so much. I miss what we had. It was perfect."

"It wasn't perfect, apparently! You slept with someone else, for months, and right under my nose!! Oooooh, I hate you for that!"

"I know you do. I humiliated you and embarrassed you. I'm so, so sorry for my lack of judgment and sensitivity. I lost my head!"

"Yeah, between her legs!"

Ellis lowered his head in shame. He agreed with everything she said, which made fighting for her that much more difficult. But he wasn't about to give up.

"You had a baby, I mean, babies, with *her*, and you married *her*!"

"I'm sorry. None of that was planned. Nothing was! Not by me anyway. You don't understand."

"Oh yeah? Then enlighten me!"

"She trapped me. She literally had me by the balls. She would have ruined my career!"

"And that's all you could think about, was *your* career. What about me? What about us and what we had? I loved… "

"I know, you loved me and I'm so *incredibly* sorry for hurting and betraying you. I was weak and I did a dumb and regrettable thing. You didn't deserve it. Will you please forgive me? Please."

"Let me out of here! You're delusional!"

"Tell me that you're over me and that you don't still love me."

"I'm not in love with you. I'm in love with Antonio!"

"Then why hasn't he married you?"

"Why weren't *we* married? You and I were together for *ten* years!"

"I was an idiot. And like the cliché, I took you for granted and I didn't know what I had until it was gone."

"Why are you doing this to me?" She suddenly got emotional, thinking about the day she found out about Ellis' affair, finding out how Antonio felt about her, and reading

Ellis' apology letter at the hotel only minutes before committing her heart and her body to Antonio for the first time. She turned away intensely confused about how she got there again with Ellis. Ellis touched her face with his forefinger and guided it back to face him.

"I know I hurt you so damn badly. And maybe I caused irreversible damage…"

"*You broke my heart!*"

"I know, Baby, I know. I'm so sorry," he stressed, as he gripped her upper arms. "I obviously cannot convey to you in words how sorry I am. I could say it over and over a million times, but I know you won't believe me. You will never understand how much I hated myself for what I did. I'm reminded of it every frickin' day."

She got fidgety and made a sudden move toward the door.

"Tyana wait! Please just think about what I'm telling you, please! Here, take my office number, too." He reached into his pocket, pulled out his business card and handed it to her. She looked at it for a quick second—long enough to see his new executive title, which of course was thanks to Charlotte. She got angrier. "Call me anytime if you need anything—*anything*—even if just to talk about everything or berate me some more. I totally deserve it. I want to help you."

"I don't need your…"

Without warning or premeditation, he leaned down, tightened his grip on her arms to hold her captive, and then spontaneously kissed her softly with his whole mouth and tongue for several long seconds. He moaned quietly as a reaction to tasting her lips once again after so long. He truly missed her and she felt it in his kiss. She couldn't stop it. It was unexpected and it paralyzed her. They both drank in the moment with unquenchable thirst. His kissing became more passionate and hungry for her. He hadn't kissed anyone like that since her, and his kiss captivated both of them, rendering them weak to the force of nature. It took him back in time to what seemed like only yesterday when she belonged with him and he belonged with her. Tyana stood devoid of all rational thought. She, too, was reminded of his taste and familiar sweetness, and soon the result of his passion traveled at lightning speed from her brain to her loins. He sensed it too, so he reached over and turned out the light. She tried to turn the light back on, but the light switch was out of reach from his grip on her. She dropped her hand and began to quietly sob. She couldn't sort out her erratic emotions or the reason why she gave in. She couldn't think; she couldn't reason, she couldn't speak. Most of all, she couldn't resist. His determined love for her made it impossible. And in the flash of two hearts colliding, she carelessly submitted to the impromptu liaison with her former lover.

♥ ♥ ♥

When Tyana hadn't returned to the suite after thirty minutes, Kellie launched an all out search for her. She first checked the obvious place, the ice room, and when she didn't find her in there, she went to the lobby to look around the pool area, the spa, the gym, the bar, everywhere. Fifteen minutes later, she returned to the suite and found Tyana inside, staring at nothing in particular.

"Well, there you are! Where the hell have you been? I've looked everywhere for you! Is everything all right? Did you talk to Antonio?" Kellie approached her. "Hey, where's the ice?"

"Huh? I'm fine. Nothing happened."

"What do you mean, nothing happened? With Antonio? What did he say?"

"I don't want to get into it right now. I'm really tired. I'm going to take a hot shower and turn in."

Kellie became extremely suspicious, but didn't have a chance to find out more before Tyana locked herself in the bathroom.

♥ ♥ ♥

"Now do you feel better?" asked Antonio, as he wiped the perspiration from his brow. He and Dottie collapsed winded in the nearby chairs.

"Yeah, I guess so. I appreciate your time and the special attention. I'll see you on Monday as scheduled, right? I feel so foolish for worrying. You must think I'm crazy."

"Not at all. It happens. As long as you feel better, I feel better. I'll walk you out."

Antonio collected his keys and left. When he glanced at the clock before he turned out the lights, he knew he would have some more explaining to do the next time he talked to Tyana, having missed several of her calls that evening. It was late and he hadn't called her back since that morning. He would have a difficult time justifying his delay, but he knew he could never lie to her. He hadn't expected to give Dottie the unscheduled private lesson, and after hours at that; but he felt she needed the reassurance if he was going to successfully persuade her to remain on as a competitor in the upcoming competition, and as a student. Dottie appeared genuinely distraught to him—more so this particular time than the other times. She barged in requesting a refund, but left two hours later after signing up for more lessons. Antonio eventually left the studio feeling drained and guilty. He knew Dottie used her sensual potential to get what she wanted and he permitted it. If his clients thought it would make them feel better by doing so, then so be it; as long as he made the sale and retained happy clients. He didn't see the harm. He and Tyana have been at odds with his clients' methods used to manipulate him. Trickery, as she would call it.

The minute he entered the house weary and spent, he phoned her.

"Antonio, it's eleven-thirty. I'm asleep. I've been trying to reach you all afternoon. Where have you been? I really needed you today. I have to tell you something. But first, what happened to you? It's been over ten hours since you said you'd call me back!"

Chapter

Tyana sat straight up in bed as she listened to Antonio's familiar reason for not calling her back.

"Are you kidding me? When are you going to realize that these are just devious tactics to manipulate you?"

"Why do you think everyone is trying to manipulate me, Babe? Why is it so hard for you to believe that someone could actually have a legitimate problem or concern? You weren't there."

"I don't have to be there. You don't know women like I do — these women! They're the same ones I spent more than enough time with when I was a student, *your* student. Remember Heather or did you forget about what she did to manipulate you? Why are you so naïve?"

"Tatyana, these are my clients and I am responsible for them. And, I'm not naïve. I've been dancing with women for almost thirty years. Give me credit. I think I know a little something about them. And what's the harm in giving these women some attention; attention that they otherwise don't get — to make them feel special, if only for a few hours? A lot of them are just lonely."

"That's why I love you. You're so caring and attentive and thoughtful. But, what about me? What about me, Antonio? I'm your fiancée. I needed you today. I needed you." Tyana's mind flashed back to her shameful make-out session with Ellis a few hours ago. She began to cry.

"What's the matter?"

"I can't talk about it right now," she sniffled. "Good night."

"Tatyana..." He heard nothing. Her abrupt disconnection confused him. He actually became worried that he had missed something. Her saying that she needed him today was all that he could ponder. Her words were cryptic to him.

Antonio started to call Tyana back for answers, but then he stopped himself. She was tired, he was exhausted, and so he put the phone down and headed to bed. Tomorrow he would make a point to get to the bottom of her comment.

Tyana lay awake for several minutes longer, upset and confused. Upset by Antonio's lack of attentiveness to her, in comparison to the attention he repeatedly gave to his clients; and confused by her unexplained moment with her ex. Her whole day, starting with the first sighting of Ellis, had been a blur. She pounded her pillow in a fit of anger over her lack of good judgment with Ellis. She felt like a hypocrite when she accused Antonio of being manipulated by Dottie and the others, when she found herself in a manipulated situation with the one man whom she had loved more than anyone in her life for ten years. She replayed over and over in her head the entire sequence of what occurred in the confines of that laundry room.

Tears continued to stain Tyana's pillow until she finally fell asleep an hour later with Ellis' kiss on her mind and the essence of his taste still present in her mouth.

♥ ♥ ♥

Charlotte got out of bed to check in on the girls one last time before turning in, to make sure they were sound asleep. And when everything looked peaceful with the twins snug in their beds, she freshened up for some adult time and returned to the master bedroom to seek out Ellis, who appeared engrossed in a television program. She quietly closed the bedroom door, slipped off her silky robe, exposing a very revealing nightgown, and slithered into bed next to him, positioning her body between his legs to distract him. She began tugging at his shorts in an attempt to remove them, with the intention to arouse him.

"Charlotte," he tried to push her off, "not now." He clearly wasn't in the mood — least of all for her.

As always, she ignored his aloof attitude and continued applying more of her mastery, using the tools available to her, once again manipulating him into getting what she wanted. It became the only way she could get sexual attention from her husband. Charlotte could do many things well and sex proved no exception. When necessary, she leveraged it often to her advantage. The men she used to attract, captivate, and covet were helpless to her sexual prowess and Ellis easily became one of them — her main target. He was tall, sexy, extremely handsome, physically strong and fit, charming, and successful — he had it all and she, matching his success and attributes from a womanly perspective, wanted to claim him and all of his assets. He knew it and once they were legally bound, again through her manipulations, there was little he could do to fight against it — with his career on the line and twins on the way. The office rumor mill exploded when their affair had been exposed. Without the marriage, his career would have been destroyed. She often reminded him of how much he owed her for saving his career — the career in which she single-handedly controlled — and how much she would sue him for if he tried to dissolve their marriage.

Within thirty seconds, he had forgotten all about his thoughts, and relaxed his body while she pleasured him. The ritual had become routine with them. He would resist, she would insist, he would give in, and in the end, everyone got what they wanted. She knew exactly how long to work on him before he would surrender and then she would take over. She had him right where he could no longer oppose her — and he didn't. Instead, he submitted to her tricks. After all, he was still a man and he had needs. But the only way he managed to feel in control of her, or rather, she allowed him to feel in control of her, was to become the dominant one in bed. But this time, he lay with his eyes closed and with thoughts of Tyana in his head. While he was lost in his fantasy, Charlotte worked a little bit harder to remind him of where he belonged. And just then, with a burst of excitement, she had jolted his mind blank. He lost his vision of Tyana and without much control, he submitted to her efforts. He tried his hardest, but he couldn't get the visions of Tyana back. His body continued to shudder as Charlotte continued to kiss him passionately. He lay breathless under her spell. Her sexuality could never be denied—by anyone. That's what got him in his situation in the first place.

Ellis slowly got up after Charlotte drifted off to sleep. He stared at her naked body lying atop the bed like a sleeping model posed in a painting. Her beautiful, long legs stretched across the bed; her perspiration still glistening on her silky, flawless skin. No doubt, she was one of the most beautiful women he had ever known. No doubt that between the two of them, they created two beautiful children, who turned heads everywhere they went. Ellis stared at her for a long time while thinking how no one could master the art of lovemaking like Charlotte. He wasn't sure how she did it. But what was more puzzling to him was how she could be so artfully insidious. She was the farthest thing from a ditzy blonde. He shook his head in wonderment of her well-executed schemes in her business life and in her personal life, and then turned and quietly headed to the bathroom to remove all evidence of their passionate union that took place moments ago.

When he emerged, he poured himself a drink of Maker's Mark and sat out on the balcony in the dark, hot, Arizona night, in only his shorts, for about an hour. He relaxed and dwelled on his earlier liaison with Tyana—now worried about possible ramifications that could follow from his spontaneous choice to act upon his desires of her. He poured himself another drink, and then another.

At forty-five years of age, he had achieved a lucrative career, married a super executive who currently out-ranked him in seniority and pay, had two awesome and gorgeous children, and homes in San Diego and Lake Tahoe. He and Charlotte drove a Porsche Panamera, Aston Martin Rapide, and a Range Rover; he wore designer suits, traveled extensively, and yet he was about as unhappy, guilt-ridden, and empty inside as he could ever imagine someone in his position could be. No amount of money, material possessions, or gratifying sex could remove the chasm of loneliness that consumed him every day that he lived knowing what he did to Tyana and wanting to make it up to her.

Chapter

Six

On day two of the girls' getaway weekend in picturesque Sedona, Tyana and Kellie got an early start to the day and signed up for a horseback riding adventure that would take them out for several hours, and then if they hadn't gotten enough of nature, they would go hiking. Kellie planned the outings with the intent of keeping them away from the resort and away from Ellis. Whatever happened to Tyana the day before when she disappeared while retrieving the ice had Kellie concerned. She still never got the whole story and she was dying to pry, but respected Tyana's space for now.

As the sun dipped lower in the late-afternoon sky, they returned to the resort exhausted, dusty, and completely worn out. They cleaned up and decided to venture out to dinner to further enhance their weekend experience. There, Tyana continued to avoid all conversations of either Ellis or Antonio. They spent a few hours dining and shopping for souvenirs.

After returning to the resort, they decided to change and claim a spot poolside for a relaxing end of the day and weekend. The pool area was sparsely inhabited since most of the weekend guests had left the resort. Tyana and Kellie were planning on leaving Monday morning, as were Ellis and Charlotte.

The nighttime breeze flowing off of the mountains felt heavenly.

"I could stay here, right here in this spot for at least a week," announced Kellie, stretched out on a chaise lounge with her eyes closed.

"I agree. This is so nice."

"When we were at Gucci, I saw you talking on the phone. Was that to Antonio? How's he holding up with you gone?"

"Yes, I was talking to him. He's all about the work. Apparently, this wasn't the best time for me to be gone from the studio. He had his hands full."

"So, he's been anxious?"

"Somewhat. He's looking forward to me coming home; that's for sure. His big birthday is this week and the staff and I are planning a surprise party for him at the studio. It doesn't sound like he's on to it. He would definitely say something if he knew because as much as he loves the attention, being a Leo and all, he hates surprises."

"That sounds nice. What's the plan?"

"Well, we'll surprise him in the morning when it's less busy and we'll all have some time in our schedules to eat cake. He's so hard to plan anything like this around because he would be suspicious if everyone had an opening in their schedule, so we all had to block out the time with fictitious clients. We even pretended to book him some new clients so he wouldn't book that slot for himself."

"Sounds so under-handedly fun! Wish I could see his face when he walks in on that!"

"Yeah, it should be something. I hope it goes well because the staff wanted to do this so badly. Me, I'd rather not make the fuss so public, but that is his life."

"What did you get him?"

"He's sort of hard to buy for, but I decided to get him a new tux. That's something he'll definitely use and he needs a new one. I got him a new garment bag, too, for traveling."

"Wow! How generous of you."

"Well, he is turning fifty; and I love him."

"Maybe he'll wear the tux at your wedding, too!"

Tyana didn't say anything.

"Tyana, is everything okay between you guys, I mean about that earlier thing with having a baby, getting married and all?"

"Uh, yeah. We're fine. It's just hard for him to think of much else when it gets chaotic at the studio."

"Why did it come up now, I mean, the baby talk and all, while you were here and not before now?"

"I dunno. I guess something triggered the conversation."

"Like seeing Ellis' girls, who would have been the same age as your child, had you not miscarried?"

"Maybe. I feel like I'm right where I was five years ago—like I haven't moved on." She did not want to dwell on Ellis or his children. Any conversation surrounding Ellis made her nervous.

"You *have* moved on. You're with Antonio and you're happy and you're planning a wedding."

"Yeah, in theory. Who plans a wedding for five years?!" Tyana's mind flashed again to her and Ellis in that room. Her heart started pounding wildly, and she began to perspire. She took a long gulp of her drink, but it didn't help. She was beginning to panic. She jumped up. "I'll be right back, I need some air."

"But you're..." Tyana scrambled out of her chair and left. "...outside," Kellie finished her sentence. But it was too late, Tyana had disappeared.

Tyana scurried back into the hotel, through the quiet lobby, to an awaiting elevator. When she stepped in, she inhaled deeply. When she caught her breath, she pushed the button to her floor and exhaled. The doors were almost closed when they suddenly stopped. Tyana stepped back to make room for more guests—a woman with two little girls.

"Charlotte!"

"Momma, that's the lady from before with Daddy!" pointed out Hannah. Then she hid behind her mother.

"Tyana. Hi. Uh, I see you've met my daughters."

"Yes. Yesterday. In the lobby. They're sweet."

"Are you enjoying your stay?"

"Yes. It's lovely."

"Staying all week?"

"No. Leaving in the morning."

"We're going to Gram Cannon!" shouted Hailee.

"She means, Grand Canyon," corrected Charlotte.

"Yeah, uh, thought so. Um, that's nice."

They both looked up to see when the elevator would stop and relieve them from their awkward meeting. Both women displayed a great deal of nervousness during the ride up. Tyana prayed that she could get off before someone said anything about Ellis.

"Momma, Daddy..."

"You know what girls? As soon as we get in the suite I want you to start packing your clothes so we'll be ready to go in the morning. Okay?"

"Yay! Okay!" they both sang in unison.

The elevator stopped on Tyana's floor first. She turned and nervously grinned and nodded as she stepped out.

"Bye!" shouted the girls.

Tyana waved goodbye as the door closed. Seconds later, she leaned against the wall with her left hand over her chest. She closed her eyes and took deep breaths to calm her heart.

Charlotte did the same thing once the elevator doors closed. The last time she saw Tyana, it was also in an elevator. She and Ellis were exiting the elevator in a Miami hotel when Tyana and Antonio were entering. She was pregnant with the twins. That was the first time they had face-to-face contact with each other and it was Tyana's introduction to Charlotte's pregnancy. As ruthless as Charlotte had been throughout the whole ordeal with her stealing Ellis from Tyana, she couldn't handle seeing her in so much pain during that unfortunate encounter. Her heart actually went out to Tyana and it wasn't until then did she realize the lives she had destroyed—mainly those of Tyana and her unborn baby.

Seeing Tyana again brought it all back for Charlotte. It made it real. Tyana was real—the woman with whom she had focused her nefarious plots against was real. The same woman who lost her baby because Charlotte lured her to the hotel suite at precisely the moment she was engaged in an explicit sexual act with Ellis, was real. Charlotte, the tough, superior, ball-breaking bitch who got everything she ever wanted at any cost stood feeling nervous and inferior to Tyana. But that only fueled her aggression toward Ellis because she knew deep down that he had never stopped loving Tyana; that he would rather be with Tyana than her and no amount of manipulation could change for whom his heart longed.

When Charlotte and the girls reached the suite and found Ellis relaxing on the sofa, after a long day with clients, the girls ran to him with excitement. They loved their daddy.

"Girls, remember what I said we would do when we got back?"

"Oh yeah. Pack!"

Ellis gave them both a kiss and off they went. He looked up at Charlotte. She slowly and stiffly sat down next to him on the sofa and whispered, "Don't get any ideas about leaving me for Tyana. If you do, I'll make sure you'll never see her again." With that, she stood up and went to check on the girls.

♥♥♥

Monday morning came quickly and everyone packed up and went their separate ways, leaving the scenic, breathtaking beauty of Sedona, Arizona and the club resort that assembled the current and past lovers. However, loyalty, desperation, betrayal and bewilderment lingered in the walls of the resort.

♥ ♥ ♥

Tyana pulled into her driveway around ten o'clock that morning. Antonio's car was parked in the garage. He felt it was important that he be home to welcome Tyana and had rescheduled his lessons. He couldn't wait to see her. When he heard her enter the garage, he sprung to his feet to meet her. Outside, Kellie transferred her things to her car while they chatted about the weekend. Antonio stood watching them from the door. Tyana saw him and smiled; he smiled back. The two women hugged good-bye. When Kellie drove out of sight, Tyana took a deep breath, exhaled, and proceeded into the house.

"Welcome home," greeted Antonio, as he held the door for her.

"Thanks. What are you doing here? I figured you would be working. I was going to change and head on in."

"I thought I'd wait for you here instead. I missed you. I'm glad you're back. Here, let me help you with that." He took her bag out of her hand.

"I missed you, too." They kissed each other before heading to the bedroom to deposit her luggage. She sat down on the bed to rest.

"Boy, am I tired." Tyana began to remove her clothes to change for work. Antonio sat down next to her and then gently pulled her into his body.

"Té quiéro mucho," he whispered in her ear before kissing her hard on the mouth.

"What are you doing?" She playfully squirmed free of his hold on her.

"What does it look like I'm doing?" He guided her down against the pillows, making his move to make love to her right then and there. She couldn't resist his touch or the magic passion they had always shared—the same fiery passion that their closeness and physical bond created and the same chemistry that attracted them to one another from the moment they shared their first dance.

Antonio removed the rest of Tyana's clothes, then his, but first he inhaled her natural aroma at her neck, untainted by any man-made perfumes or colognes. He craved her natural scent—it drove him wild—causing his body to quickly respond and want to take her instantaneously. He began to rub the smooth skin of her stomach, while taking in her natural beauty. He admired her body, like a priceless prized piece of art. He could sit for hours and stare at her nakedness.

Tyana admired Antonio's natural physical attractiveness as well. He maintained impeccable fitness, given his age, nearly fifty. He wasn't as tall as Ellis, but that only made them more of a perfect fit for one another—on the dance floor and wrapped in each other's arms. Once he had all of her clothes removed, and then his, he eased himself on top of her as their bodies connected together— perfectly. Neither had experienced symmetrical, physical chemistry with any other partner and it made what they shared—phenomenal.

Tyana's mind had prepared her body to receive Antonio at once. His strong arms, locked firmly on both sides of her, steadied himself above her, looking down at her eyes revealing the flame of desire in his eyes. She suddenly thought of Ellis and she shut her eyes tightly. She couldn't bear to look at Antonio in his face while daydreaming of another man, as he hungrily made love to her. He moaned louder when she received him. He had certainly missed her. She willfully dismissed the invasion of Ellis in her mind, refocused on her fiancé and joined him in their intimate reunion.

"I am yours, Babe, all yours," he spoke proudly and breathlessly.

"I love you," she responded and meant it.

During their passionate celebration, Tyana could only think about the magical way Antonio made love to her and how he was capable of making her feel adored with his sexy body, his confident hands, and his hungry mouth.

After about twenty vigorous minutes of reuniting with every inch of each other's body, they paused quietly in each other's arms for a brief moment, listening to their heartbeats and their shallow breathing.

"Tatyana, no one else matters to me the way you do. The business is my life, but so are you. And without my job and the business, I can't give you everything we've dreamt and talked about. We're already committed to the comps that are on our calendar this year. Let's get through these competitions first, and then I promise we'll get married after that."

"What about a baby?"

"You really *need* a baby?"

"I don't *need* one, I *want* one. Don't you?"

"First things first, we're going to miss our first lessons of the day if we don't leave real soon. Let's go to work." He kissed her lips then got up, leaving her behind still waiting for an answer to her question. He stopped and looked back at her. "Tatyana, let's get married first, then we'll talk about that."

She knew what that meant for her — another year down and another year older for Tyana before she could embark upon motherhood. She calculated at the earliest, she would be thirty-six before having her first child. She dreamt of motherhood since she could remember. Growing up in Seattle, she used to admire her parents raising her with so much enthusiasm and emphasis on love, affection, and a sense of family, and she had always imagined herself having a child whom she could spoil like her parents spoiled her. Her father, Oliver, an immigrant from Romania, didn't have a lot of money, but what he lacked in wealth, he made up for in love. He possessed an exuberant amount of love, which he freely dispensed from his heart. He fell head over heels in love with her mother, Celeste, an American, upon laying eyes on her. They met under unusual circumstances. He was a professional drapery maker and made custom draperies for top interior designers in America. Celeste met him through an interior designer friend of hers whom she befriended through one of her real estate dealings early in her career. It was instant love-at-first-sight for Celeste and Oliver and they married within six months of meeting, which from their fast-forward love affair brought forth the news of Celeste's honeymoon pregnancy. They were overjoyed with bringing a baby into the world — their first born. Tyana recalled when she was a little girl, how much her father talked about love, and told her the story over and over of how he met her mother and fell in love with her immediately. He openly displayed his love for his family every day and even more so today. Tyana called him Papa, which made his face light up at the sound of her voice. She was his world. She wanted to create that same atmosphere in her own home with Antonio — the new love of *her* life.

"Come on. Join me in the shower. If you hurry, we can go in together," suggested Antonio.

"Okay, I'm on my way." She got up. "Start the shower."

Tyana unpacked her toiletries from her overnight bag, and in doing so she came across Ellis' business card. She picked it up and looked at it feeling perplexed by so many emotions. She thought particularly of his offer to leave Charlotte and give *her* anything she desired. *What did he mean by that?* She wondered.

"Tatyana! Are you coming?"

Tyana flinched and dropped the card when she grabbed her toiletries. She rushed to join Antonio in the shower.

♥♥♥

Less than an hour later, Antonio and Tyana stepped into the impressive ballroom dance studio together where they immediately spotted Dottie eagerly waiting for Antonio's arrival. They both acknowledged Dottie, but Dottie strutted past Tyana without a word. Instead, she greeted Antonio with a warm smile and a hug that appeared to linger beyond a typical greeting. Tyana stood by and watched while rolling her eyes. When Dottie and Antonio stepped onto the dance floor, Dottie kept one cunning eye on Tyana. Tyana could do nothing but ignore the advances the women in the studio made toward her fiancé. As long as Antonio refused to confront the behavior and put an end to it, she had no recourse.

Every time Dottie could pull Antonio's strings like a puppet and get him to surrender to what *she* wanted, she felt victorious and it only gave her more confidence in her position with the man of her dreams—her dance instructor. In her fantasy, Antonio wanted her as much as she wanted him.

Tyana eventually retreated to her office where she could think and not be distracted by the exhibition on the dance floor between Antonio and Dottie. She shut the door to block out the music—some romantic song that Dottie requested. It played over and over. A sudden knock came at the door.

"Come in!"

"Hi Tyana; welcome back! How was your weekend?" inquired the studio's office manager.

"Hi Rita, thanks! My weekend was relaxing. How did things go around here over the weekend?"

"Oh boy…it was busier than I've ever seen it. We had some staff cancellations at the last minute, some new clients come in; some walk-ins, we were getting prepared for the coaching sessions this week. Some of the coaches arrived and wanted to drop off some of their stuff and we had to get them settled in the hotels. I thought Antonio was going to collapse. He had back-to-back lessons. One of his older students, Ms. Kremer, you know, who comes a good distance for her lessons, showed up and we didn't have her on the books for Saturday, but Antonio squeezed her in anyway. I don't know how he does it."

"Yeah, he's a wiz at it. Well, it sounds like I missed all the action. I had no idea it was so crazy. I'm sorry I wasn't here to help out."

"I think Antonio certainly missed you, but if anyone asked where you were, he said you were getting some well-deserved rest."

"That was nice of him."

"Yeah, you got a real winner there." Rita leaned in closer. "So, what's the deal with that out one there?"

"What?"

"That Dottie person hanging all over him trying to make out with him on the dance floor. That's so tacky."

"She is? Hmm… that's rather inappropriate and disrespectful to Antonio and to the business, if she is. But, in this business, you come to expect that behavior from time to time, I imagine. I think dancing with Antonio gives her the confidence that she otherwise doesn't have and when she's on the dance floor she expresses that confidence. I can see how certain privileges and attention didn't easily come her way in life, if at all. Antonio does that for women—like her—giving them the self-confidence and sense of friendship they lack."

"Wow, Tyana. That was nicely said. But we both know what you really wanted to say if you weren't Antonio's fiancée." Rita roared with laughter. Tyana quietly smiled. The phone interrupted them. Rita reached over to answer the line from Tyana's desk.

"It's a great day for dancing…" the caller interrupted Rita.

"Just a minute please; who may I say is calling?" asked Rita curious by the mystery man on the other end. "Sure, hold on." She pushed the hold button. "Some man named Montgomery is on line one. Is he a new client of yours?"

"Uh…thanks Rita. I'll take it. Would you excuse me please? And could you shut the door also. The music…"

"Sure, right away. And again, welcome back!"

Tyana smiled and waited for Rita to exit. She clicked over when the door closed.

"This is Tyana, how may I help you?"

"Hi. It's me."

"Ellis! What are you doing calling me here?" She panicked. "How did you know where to find me?" she asked in a hushed voice.

"You told me you were working with…him, so I've been calling all the dance studios in the Scottsdale area. I need to talk to you. You weren't answering your cell."

"You can't call me here! In fact, you can't call me at all! It's not right. I'm busy. You're married! You have children!"

"Did you give any more thought to what I said? I will leave her. I still love you."

"No, you don't. And, it doesn't matter anyway. I don't love *you*."

"Tatyana, your couple is here for their lesson— they're waiting for you," announced Antonio as he popped his head into Tyana's office. He overheard the tail end of her sentence.

"Okay, I'm on my way," she answered, nervously, as she covered the receiver. Antonio left, but didn't close the door completely. He left it ajar.

"Look, I gotta go," she insisted, returning her focus back to Ellis.

"Do you still have my card?"

"I threw it away!"

"Tyana, write down my number."

"Ellis!"

"Please, just write it down!" He repeated the number. Reluctant to legitimize his existence in her life, she wrote it down before hanging up. Her hands were shaking and her heart raced as she stood up to leave the room. She wondered how much of the conversation Antonio had heard. She stopped before exiting the office and stood behind the door to collect herself. She feared she couldn't hide the truth any longer. She had to tell Antonio what happened in Sedona. Her secret was torturing her.

Antonio watched Tyana's unusual behavior while on the dance floor with her students. She seemed antsy about something. He was interrupted by a phone call at the front desk. He took the call. During the call, he saw Birdie march into the front door with her head high and her nose in the air — her typical demeanor — and strut straight into his office where she routinely placed her personal belongings. Antonio instinctively glanced at Tyana, who caught the familiar scene. First Dottie, now Birdie. He and Tyana simultaneously redirected their thoughts and resumed their activities.

Tyana continued working with the middle-aged couple as she noticed Antonio escorting Birdie hand-in-hand into one of the smaller private ballrooms. As they disappeared out of sight, Tyana struggled to ignore the fifty-nine year-old, highfalutin client, who she thought looked a little like a stuck-up Eartha Kitt. She had been a permanent fixture in Antonio's dance life since even before he opened his first studio. When Tyana was finally able to divert her focus, it went directly to Ellis' phone call moments ago, still rattling around in her head.

♥♥♥

Ellis sat holding the phone, long after the call ended, thinking about the exchanges with Tyana in Sedona. She may still be resentful and unforgiving for what he did to her — understandably — however, the fact remained that she wasn't married and he felt he still had a chance with her. He remembered the way that guy ran after her on that night in Miami Beach, then carried her back through the hotel, so gallantly. And the way he kissed her... Ellis assumed, by the way Antonio looked at her, that they would be married by now—five years later. What did that mean that they weren't married? To him, it meant he had a shot at winning her back! It meant he still has a chance to prove to himself that he can be redeemed for his mistake and, hopefully, make it up to her and persuade her to change her mind about him. It also meant, if it wasn't too late, that he could persuade her to marry *him*. Of course, all of that remained contingent upon his divorce from Charlotte. That could take months; even years, depending on how much fight she had in her. And knowing Charlotte the way he did, Ellis was in for a long, long battle. Charlotte would undoubtedly hold Tyana as the reason for the divorce, which meant he would most likely not have a prayer at gaining anything from the marriage, but instead lose it all. He knew that, but he felt he would have at least a feeble leg to stand on as long as he had something to leverage over her, otherwise as much as he wanted another chance with Tyana, it could come at a very hefty price. He reamed himself for being a fool for not marrying her when he had his chance and for not being more in control of Charlotte. They proved to be two gigantic mistakes.

♥♥♥

When Antonio's back-to-back coaching sessions with Birdie had finally ended, he and Birdie returned to his office to chat. Throughout the years, as dance instructors had come and gone, Birdie had made it known to everyone in the business, not just to Antonio's studio, but also to those in the industry, that she would be held to a higher standard than most students. And in order to demand that privilege, she had befriended Antonio right out the gate, twenty-five years ago. She was an exceptional dancer, thanks to him, but was also a master manipulator. She had convinced almost everyone in the business that she was not only Antonio's star student, but that they had a special relationship beyond dancing. They had been seen together in a friendly way for years — participating in every competition. She certainly saw to that, and she had the means to finance such an endeavor. She had also spent hundreds of thousands of dollars, not only for the lessons, the competitions, the gowns, custom made dance shoes, costumes, and accessories, but for the featured dance excursions hosted by the studio that took them traveling to many parts of the world. She had him escort her on his arm to some of the most exotic and romantic places around the world. And people did talk — a lot.

At fifty-nine years of age, Birdie Pennington remained in great shape and projected strong presence, fluidity, and musicality on the dance floor — again, thanks to Antonio's training. In the last twenty-five years, she had never so much as taken a break from dancing. It had become her life's goal and obsession to become a competitive dancer and partner, along with the goal of becoming romantically accessible to Antonio. She was married, but that didn't seem to be an issue with her. She, like so many of the other female students, was enamored with him, and lived a delusional life once she entered his dance studio. He had never consciously made any advances toward her or any of them in that way, or at least in his mind, had never given them that kind of hope for a romantic tryst. But she, like some of the others, often misconstrued his physical touch on them on the dance floor while in character with the dance. After all, he danced the dances of love with them every day. For him, the difference between Tyana and the others was that they both felt the connection and chemistry before they stepped onto the dance floor. And Tyana, unlike the others, did not flaunt herself and her sexuality onto him. She respected him, and herself, and kept her emotions distant from him — giving off no signals or glaring gestures that she could be attracted to him. She was there to learn to dance and nothing else. And had her relationship with Ellis not disintegrated when it did, she probably wouldn't be with Antonio today. But even today, now that she was his fiancée, the other women still have not given up hope that he would come around to woo them and choose them.

When Tyana had wrapped up all of her lessons and updated her schedule for the week, she patiently waited for Antonio to conclude his business with Birdie. She became annoyed with herself for not choosing to drive separately. Birdie was never in a rush to leave when she had Antonio's undivided attention. And Antonio would entertain this lifetime client and benefactor for as long as it didn't interfere with his other clients.

After the last instructor left, Tyana impatiently drummed her fingers on the desk, growing increasingly angry. She had been gone all weekend and had a lot of things to get caught up on at home. She couldn't wait any longer so she sought him out in his office. She knocked while at the same time opening the door to peek her head in.

"Hi," said Antonio, simultaneously releasing Birdie's hand.

Tyana looked surprised by his sudden movement. He looked guilty of something. She stared at their hands.

"What's up, Babe?" he asked.

"Are you going to be much longer? I really need to get going."

"What time is it?"

"It's nine-thirty."

"Already?"

Birdie sat back to keenly observe the mounting tension between the couple because of her.

"We were just talking about the Bolero routine and the changes Jonathan incorporated for her during her coaching session. We were going to run through them again."

"Tonight?"

"It'll just take a few minutes. Can you wait?"

"Or I can give you a ride home when we're finished," Birdie suggestively interjected.

Tyana's eyes widened in complete and utter objection to Birdie's offer and to her interference in their personal matter.

"Do you want to take the car?" asked Antonio, oblivious to Tyana disapproving of the offer.

Tyana's blood pressure began to rise. She was torn between what she should say and what she wanted to say. How dare he ask her something like that in front of Birdie, giving her the upper hand? She stared him down, inviting him to read her mind and do the right thing. But he sat looking blankly at her, waiting for her to decide. Then as if all of her insecurities vanished, she spoke up.

"No, you keep it. I'll call a friend of mine. He wouldn't mind taking me home."

"Who, Trevor?"

"No, not Trevor. Look, I shouldn't have interrupted. Take your time and I'll see you…when I see you." Tyana popped back out and scurried to her office a few doors down and waited.

Antonio turned to Birdie and excused himself.

"Tatyana wait!" He rushed after her. He remembered the part of her phone conversation that he walked in on earlier in her office. He hadn't had a chance to quiz her about it. Trevor was the only male friend of hers that he knew about. He suddenly became insecure, because he knew she wasn't talking to Trevor.

When he caught up with her in her office, he entered and closed the door.

"Give me ten minutes; I'll take you home."

"I'll give you five."

"I'll be right back."

In walking back to his office where Birdie waited for him, Antonio's life suddenly flashed before him—a life without Tyana—and he tensed up from nervousness. He recognized that he was on the verge of losing her and it terrified him. He had gotten his way for five years and now realized that he had taken her for granted and it was a mistake. She seemed different to him since she returned from her weekend in Sedona and he didn't know why, but she did seem different. He knew she was already upset over their delayed plans and canceled dreams so he thought he would tread lightly until they could finalize the wedding plans. He didn't want to lose her. They drove home that night the same way they came in—together.

The next morning, while Antonio busied himself giving lessons, Tyana entered his office and placed a picture of her and him together on his desk. Two days later, Alyssa added a picture of her and her dad together next to it.

Chapter
Seven

Ellis and Charlotte entertained the girls at the Grand Canyon; however, the Grand Canyon was the furthest thing from Ellis' mind. Every time he thought about sneaking off to deal with his mind-boggling issues over his affections for Tyana, Charlotte appeared, right on cue, as if reading his thoughts. He couldn't turn his back on her for a second without catching glimpses of her keeping one suspicious eye on him at all times. He knew her very well, and didn't trust her to not have some private detective or spy guy watching his every move. He had to be very careful to not tip her off, but little did he know his four year-old daughters had, inadvertently, done that already.

♥♥♥

Throughout the three-day stay at the Grand Canyon, Ellis experienced bouts of sleeplessness trying to come up with a plan to abandon his marriage to Charlotte. The five-year marriage had been a farce from the beginning. It was the children who gave the union purpose and him the *only* reason for staying with her. He knew it and she knew it. He cared for her because of them and for no other conceivable reason. Because of Charlotte, Ellis lost Tyana—he could never forgive himself or Charlotte for that—ever. And now he was willing to do whatever it took to get Tyana back, if she would take him back. At least he wanted to do something to see if he had a chance in hell with her before she married the dancer guy, and then it would be too late. Conceivably, he couldn't begin that journey if he, himself, was still married.

Ellis breathed heavily, and then slowly closed his eyes, realizing the monumental task that lie before him—divorcing Charlotte. He could stand to lose his shorts in a divorce settlement with her. He would certainly lose his girls, his home and significant financial wealth—that was a given. But there's one thing he wouldn't put up with and that would be Charlotte tarnishing his reputation and integrity in the business. That meant war; a war in which he would be armed and prepared to fight because he didn't put anything past her. Aside from her anyone-who-is-anybody rolodex, he earned his positions in San Diego and Madrid, as well as the respect of his superiors and his clients, so it didn't seem likely that he would lose either, but he didn't trust her not to use whatever method she could come up with to sabotage him. The thought actually had him knotted and restless. She had a knack for expertly and expeditiously reducing anyone to a mere wretch—to a point that it sometimes appeared that she drew pleasure from it. Her reputation—stopping at nothing until she got what she wanted—preceded her in the hotel business.

"Do you mind? What's keeping you up, Ellis?" asked Charlotte, annoyed at noticing her husband tossing and turning night after night repeatedly for hours.

"Trouble sleeping," he uttered.

"Is that all? If you try to divorce me, I promise you'll have many nights worse than this. Now, stop fidgeting and make love to me like I like it."

"It's late; I'm tired."

"Fine." She paused. "Hmm, isn't Jack Benson on the fence about coming on board as a client? I hear he's got that multi-million dollar trade show booking. He would be a pretty big client to schmooze. I'd hate to see you lose that one to a competitor. That would really suck."

Ellis sat erect and glared at Charlotte. "If you even *think* about sabotaging *any* of my deals, I'll..."

"You'll *what?*" Charlotte never backed down to any threat.

"Is that all you have, are threats? You have to make threats to me in order to get sex?"

Ellis paused long as he glared at her undeniable beauty, wondering how he got himself in such a bad situation with such a beautiful woman. Sex.

"You're such a *bitch!*" He blurted.

No one uttered a sound after that insult. Even Charlotte became defenseless. It was as if all of the air had been sucked out of the room and they both quietly shriveled up. One of the girls could be heard crying from the other room.

"I'll go," insisted Ellis.

He broke the awkward silence and got up to investigate his daughter's crying.

Charlotte remained behind, still stunned by the word that echoed in her head—"*bitch.*" It shook her, coming from him. She loved Ellis, so his words stung her deeply. He had never called her a bitch before.

"Why are you crying, Baby Girl?" whispered Ellis to Hailee, trying not to awaken Hannah, who lay sound asleep in the bed next to her. The last thing he needed was two crying toddlers *and* a pissed off wife in the middle of the night, in a hotel in the Grand Canyon.

"Daddy—I'm scared," whined Hailee.

She appeared only half-awake.

"Wake up, Baby. Stop crying. Talk to me. What are you scared about?"

"Don't leave me, Daddy!"

"Hailee, I'm not leaving you. Look at me. C'mon, wake up. Why would you think that?"

Hailee finally opened her eyes.

"Why do you think I would leave you, Hailee?"

"Because they took me and Hannah away from you and I didn't see you when Santa Claus came. Daddy, I don't want to go with them. I want to stay with you."

"Go with who? You're not going anywhere without me. You know I love you, don't you?"

"Uh-huh." She rubbed her eyes through a long yawn.

"I also want you to know that no matter what happens between Momma and me, I will always love you and Hannah forever; you're my daughters—you two mean everything to me."

"We'll always be a family, right? That's what Momma said."

"Yes, of course." Ellis didn't know how to respond to his little one's question knowing what could lie ahead of them all. "Here, let me tuck you in. You need to get back to sleep. I love you, Baby Girl." Ellis kissed his daughter good night and hugged her tightly.

He certainly didn't want to lose the twins to Charlotte. He didn't think Charlotte had their best interests in mind. Sure, she made certain they had everything they needed—clothes, educational toys and games, a nanny, anything money could buy—but, whenever she could, she managed to pawn her daughters off on Annamarie, the nanny, or Ellis, as soon as he walked through the door. She usually spent more of her time pampering herself during her hours away from the office, than she did nurturing the girls. Her work always came first, and then time spent on herself. Her appearance meant everything to her. When she took one look at Ellis, she knew that they, together, would make the perfect, hot couple—the talk of everyone and the envy of many. He was just another asset to her. He had the looks, the physique, and the bank account. That was her formula. Her focus initiated on those attributes solely, until she later fell in love with Ellis, after expertly manipulating him into marrying her.

Ellis and Charlotte spent the rest of the trip barely speaking to one another and making rude comments under their breaths about sabotaging business deals and divorce threats.

♥ ♥ ♥

Antonio and Tyana spent the next few days being civil, but barely speaking to one another except for the occasional interaction at the dance studio—though they never let the staff or students become aware of their personal business. Also, their interactions on the dance floor, while practicing their own dance routines, were never compromised. They were professionals and role models. At home, they painted a whole different picture in shaky times. In the evenings, Tyana usually left the studio before Antonio, and managed to shower and fall asleep before he even walked through the door. She still hadn't forgiven him for wanting to stay late at the studio with Birdie instead of ending his day on time and insisting on taking her home.

"Tatyana, Tatyana..." Antonio tried to wake her.

"What is it? I was sleeping."

"I know. I'm sorry to wake you, but I wanted to let you know that I was home."

"You woke me for that?"

"No. I wanted to talk to you. We never have time to talk anymore."

"You never have any time for us anymore."

"That's not true."

Tyana sat up and looked at him with icy eyes.

"You embarrassed me in front of that woman!"

"I'm sorry. I didn't mean to. I was just thinking about..."

"You were just thinking of someone other than me—like always."

"That isn't true, but I know I didn't do what you wanted me to do."

"What I wanted you to do? What's the matter with you? You didn't do what *anyone* would have done in that situation. Antonio, I'm tired. I had a long day and I really need to get some sleep. Tomorrow is going to be busy. Good night."

Tyana lay back down on her back and closed her eyes. Antonio stared at her in silence for a few minutes, and then kissed her forehead. She opened her eyes to see him looking at her through the darkness. A single tear trickled down her cheek. He saw it and kissed it, and then he kissed her lips.

"I love you, Tatyana, I do." He kissed her again, this time with more passion and feeling.

It had been two nights of tension, but on that night they called it a truce and made love with a sense of purpose, both having missed the warmth of each other's body. Any night that they didn't make love was one night too many for the sexy and sex-driven couple. But since Sedona, Tyana had been preoccupied with more than her domestic issues. And Antonio had been preoccupied with a host of issues, including Tyana's happiness.

The next day began how the evening ended between Tyana and Antonio. They awoke to find themselves once again entwined and letting their love for one another dictate the mood.

"Happy Birthday, Babe," Tyana cheerfully greeted her fiancé on his birthday morning. They spent just enough extra time in bed to satisfy their insatiable craving for each other. They forgot all of their woes and worries and got his birthday off to a glorious start. They couldn't keep their hands off of each other's bodies.

Once they were up and moving about, Tyana showered him with gifts.

"Wow! What's all this?"

"This is for your birthday," she responded carrying a tray that consisted of his favorite breakfast foods: eggs over easy, hash browns, two strips of bacon, toast, a tall glass of juice, a bowl of fruit, and his vitamins.

"It's perfect." He kissed her. "You're perfect, thank you." He kissed her again.

"While you eat that, I'll get your presents."

"What? More?"

"It's your special birthday, of course, there's more!" She trotted off to the guest room to retrieve his gifts. When she returned, she presented them to him. He placed the tray aside so he could accept his presents so creatively wrapped with love.

"Tatyana, you shouldn't have gone through all this trouble. I don't need anything."

"Hush, and open them!"

Antonio felt like a kid at Christmas when he tore through the pile of gifts and uncovered a new black designer tuxedo, diamond cuff links, dress shirts, an expensive garment bag, and several designer ties. Not that he was ever a shabby dresser by any means, but with Tyana in his life, she saw to it that he was sophisticatedly dressed at all times. He didn't own the tailor-made suits that Ellis wore, but Antonio looked impeccable nonetheless. Tyana often told him that he would look good in jeans and a tee shirt, but that she preferred him naked.

"Tatyana, everything is beautiful. You shouldn't have done all this."

"I love you; I wanted to." She kissed him.

"*Your* birthday is in a few months; what do *you* want? How can I outdo all this?"

"I only want one thing for my birthday," she quietly remarked. "A wedding and a baby. Okay, those are two things."

"In two months?" He saw the melancholy look on her face. "Come here. I love you. Can we talk?"

"Of course."

"Sit down." He guided her down on the bed next to him. "Tatyana, I've been giving the baby thing some serious thought." She was getting a bad feeling based on his body language. "In all honesty, I don't think I can do it." With that she stiffened up.

"What?"

"I'm fifty."

"Yeah, so what? You're not dead!"

"I know you probably won't understand where I'm coming from, but I'm not sure that having children had ever been a priority or need for me."

"Why are you telling me this now?"

"We haven't really talked about it before and it never occurred to me. It's not something that I think about—ever."

"I see. You gave Shana a baby, but yet you can't give me one—for us?"

"I didn't get her pregnant on purpose. It was a situation that we found ourselves in and that's all there is to that. I didn't want that to happen."

"But it did!"

"Yes, it did and I'm dealing with it, but to consciously bring another child into my life, well, it's just not what I've wanted or am prepared to do."

"It's all about you! When is it ever about me, or us?!"

"Look, it's getting late. You planned this very special birthday morning for me and I don't want to ruin this. I love you, even now more than ever and I still want to marry you. We'll do that. Can we talk about this later? We're going to be late."

"Right. Umm...I better get dressed. We better get going. We've got a busy day today and we mustn't keep anyone waiting." Her emotions were surfacing and she felt herself starting to come unglued. She didn't want to create a scene, but she was in shock. Then she thought of the surprise party at the studio. She walked away from him.

♥♥♥

When Tyana and Antonio reached the dance studio nearly an hour later than normal, Tyana walked straight to her office, and Antonio was bombarded with questions, birthday wishes from the staff, and phone messages to return—no doubt more well wishers. The staff had time to decorate the ballroom area with balloons and streamers everywhere. The birthday song was playing when he walked in. No one noticed that Tyana had disappeared. No one except Antonio.

When Tyana sat down at her desk, her cell phone rang.

"Hello…" she knew who it was.

"Okay, I've waited a reasonable amount of time for you to call and tell me what's going on; I couldn't wait any longer. Now, I'm free tonight. I know it's Saturday and you and Antonio usually spend Saturday nights together…"

"Trevor, I'm sorry. It's been one thing after another since I've been back. Tonight is fine. Actually, I'll be finished up here around three, so if you want to get together earlier, that's fine with me. It's Antonio's fiftieth birthday today, but I've already given him his presents this morning and the staff is throwing him a party here at the studio today, so he's well-covered."

"The old man's fifty, eh? Are you sure you don't want to spend the evening with him? I will certainly understand. If I'd known I wouldn't have suggested tonight. Cleo is visiting her mother this weekend, so I'm free anytime that's convenient for you."

"Yeah, sure, tonight is fine. He'll probably be working anyway."

"Want to meet somewhere close to home or do you have another spot in mind?"

"Here is fine. I'm not in the mood to venture out too far or for too long. We can grab a bite to eat near the mall or in the mall. I have to go over that way anyway. Say, five-ish? I'm pretty sure I'm finished around three, but just in case."

"Five-ish is fine. You pick the place and text me later."

"Sounds good. Thanks for calling. I'll see you later."

Tyana hung up and returned to the main guest area to join in the celebration of Antonio's birthday.

"Where's Antonio," she asked Rita when she didn't see him in the area.

"He's in his office. You know who's got him holed up in there. She came in bearing gifts."

"Who?"

"Ms. Pennington."

"Oh." Tyana knew it was going to be a long day. She looked over toward Antonio's office to see his door shut. While she waited, she checked his calendar and saw Dottie booked, too, and was expected to arrive in a couple of hours. Actually, all of his fans had managed to book time with him on his birthday. How conveniently special, she thought. In the meantime, her first student had just arrived.

♥♥♥

Ellis and Charlotte returned to their home in San Diego to pick their lives back up where they left them, both trying to ignore the inevitable—discussions about divorce. It had been on both of their minds ever since Sedona where they had run-ins with Tyana. Charlotte didn't want to lose her man and Ellis didn't want to lose his children. He knew that the second he mentioned the word, "divorce," she would attack him with the word, "custody." He had to get his custody argument prepared from every possible angle. He needed to leave no stone unturned. And, from that point on, he had to watch his every move because he knew she would also be watching him. He didn't want her to have anything on him, so he played along with whatever she wanted to do in order to portray the illusion of a loyal husband, including making love to her on her command. If he showed his disinterest in her, she would try to prove that he might be having an affair or might be interested in another woman. He had to watch himself very carefully around her.

"I'm going for a dip in the hot tub," Charlotte said. "Would you like to join me?" She strutted past Ellis in her thong bikini.

"Charlotte, I'm busy. I finally got the girls to sleep and I'm exhausted, and I still have some work to finish. Why don't you go ahead; I'll stay in and listen out for them. I want to make sure they stay asleep. They were pretty restless tonight."

The girls were a handful, and Ellis spent most of his evening consoling them when they became cranky. He couldn't get them to settle down enough to finish their dinner and take their baths without resistance. Once he got them quieted and in bed, he didn't want to do anything, but relax and decompress. The girls turned into a bit of a challenge for him lately—perhaps sensing the stress between their parents and acting out in protest.

Whenever Annamarie had the day off and the girls remained in Charlotte's care, they were usually unmanageable by the end of the day. Charlotte didn't have a clue about how to raise her children—especially twins. She either gave them too much freedom and leniency or she applied too many restrictions on them. Ellis spent a lot of time on damage control, trying to restore balance in the little ones' lives. When he first recognized Charlotte's parental deficiencies, it became imperative to give the girls a chance at having balance in their development. Of course, they needed to know right from wrong, but he wanted them to have the room to have fun. Charlotte's idea of fun meant taking them on business trips and then leaving them cooped up in a hotel room with the nanny or hired staff. Ellis usually felt sorry for them and would end up forfeiting his meetings to take them out to do something entertaining for them.

For some reason, Ellis flashed back to the time Charlotte made sexual advances toward him in a hot tub five years earlier—the ruse that started it all. He would never forget that time in his life. He often wondered if he would have gotten the promotions without going through what he went through with her and ultimately becoming her sex slave. Once they got married and shortly afterward revealed Charlotte's pregnancy to the public, many assumed she had something to do with his untimely promotions. But soon those looks of disapproval turned into looks of pity, because of whom he tangled with and lost. Her arrogant reputation preceded her. Anyone who spent any amount of time working with her or for her, and wasn't trying to get into bed with her, usually didn't find her approachable or easy to get along with. Actually, she thrived on making others' lives miserable if they didn't meet her expectations.

Ellis never played up their marriage at the office. Fraternization had always been frowned upon in the business, but they couldn't be reprimanded once they were married. He also heard some of the rumors, mostly about Charlotte, and didn't think that she, or anyone, deserved such meanness. While she carried the twins, he protected her as much as he could from the rumors. But, after the girls were born and the real work began—for him—he couldn't keep up the semblance of a protective husband. He lost all energy for that kind of gallant protection. Raising his daughters became too exhausting and something had to give way—meaning Charlotte would have to fight her own battles. The girls suddenly reprioritized his home life. He not only gave them the things that they wanted to surround themselves with, but he also gave them plenty of love, as well as the occasional mild discipline, when necessary, but the girls hardly ever gave him trouble. He found it very difficult to scold them. He felt they were punished enough by their mother's parenting.

Ellis watched Charlotte sashay to the hot tub knowing she never once bothered to look in on the girls to say goodnight. He shook his head in disappointment over her lack of parental responsibility, but more in sadness over her emotional detachment to her own children. He got out of his chair once more to check in on the girls. He worried about them—especially if he divorced Charlotte and she would somehow end up with custody. He shuddered at the thought.

♥ ♥ ♥

Antonio enjoyed all of the attention and fuss he received from the staff and students over his birthday. The gifts, cakes, and hugs never seemed to stop. Everyone made a big deal out of his milestone birthday. After all, he was the boss and owner; so, many in the business respected him and genuinely liked him. He had spent his whole career transforming lives and making friends, and those friends wanted to show him their gratitude.

After about two hours, Tyana finally caught up with him in his office. She had not been able to think of much else all day other than the news Antonio slapped her with about not wanting a family. She loved him, but he broke her heart.

"Hi Babe!" Antonio greeted her with a hug.

"Hi. Having fun?"

"Thank you again for all of this. You're the best."

"The staff did the decorations and put the word out about your birthday."

"Yeah, everyone's been either stopping by or calling."

"Or booked lessons."

"I've been dancing non-stop. I have about ten minutes before my next student."

"Speak of the devil, your two o'clock is right on time." Tyana spotted Dottie entering the studio. "So, what all did you get?"

"I got a lot of wine, some liquor, some dancing paraphernalia…"

"What's this?" Tyana reached over and grabbed a gift box with gobs of tissue paper and a smaller box inside.

"Oh, Birdie gave me that," he answered nonchalantly.

Tyana peeked inside and began removing the tissue paper. She looked at the gift inside and then looked at Antonio.

"This is a very expensive shirt. Isn't that rather extravagant and personal?"

"You know her."

"Yeah, I do know her. But how did she know your shirt size? That's normally something only someone close to you should know."

"She's given me shirts before in the past. I guess she assumed the size would be the same."

"What do you mean she's bought you shirts in the past? How many shirts?"

"Tatyana… don't do that."

"Do what? I just asked how often does she buy you personal clothing. And what's in here?" She opened the little box in which she found a shiny Rolex watch. "Seriously?"

"Don't get upset, Babe." He knew the gift went too far and that Tyana wouldn't approve.

"Then why did she have to present the gifts in private? Why was the door closed when you were in here with her?"

"She didn't want me to open it in front of everyone. There was no other reason…" He touched her arm.

"Don't!" Tyana started to show her disapproval when suddenly Dottie swung the door open wider and pranced in.

"Hi, Happy Birthday Antonio!" Dottie announced as she hugged Antonio tightly around his neck before she saw Tyana. "Oh! Hi."

"Hi. I see you brought a birthday gift for Antonio. How nice. Excuse me." Tyana slid out behind her. Antonio wanted to go after her, but Dottie shoved her gift at him.

"Thank you! I'll open it later; we better get started with your lesson." Antonio grabbed Dottie's hand and pulled her to the dance floor.

Tyana marched to her office to collect her things. She sent a quick text to Trevor to let him know where to meet her. She locked up and left. She glanced toward the dance floor on her way out to see Dottie giggling and acting silly with Antonio while unashamedly draping herself all over him. She was drawing the attention of the other guests and teachers to her and Antonio. Tyana shook her head, smiled and then left.

Chapter

Tyana met up with Trevor for a late lunch/early dinner at Kona Grill in the Scottsdale Fashion Square mall.

"I can't believe you actually took the weekend off and went to Sedona. Good for you! Did it help? I mean, one minute you were going to have a casual dinner date with Kellie and the next thing I hear is you're taking an entire weekend off and heading for Sedona, without Antonio. Must be something serious. Are you going to clue me in?" asked Trevor.

"What makes you think that there's something to be clued in about?"

"C'mon, Tyana... Who do you think you're talking to?"

"Yeah, you're right. But first, how's Cleo? Why is she visiting her mother? Is her mother okay?"

"Oh, yeah. It's not her mother, it's Cleo."

"Cleo?!"

"Oh, no, she's fine. I didn't mean to alarm you. It's just that she's pregnant! We're going to have a little Trevor or Cleo, so she and her mother are spending the weekend together celebrating and shopping—spending all my money that is, getting ready for the baby."

Tyana suddenly had mixed emotions, which she tried extremely hard to disguise. But, she could never hide any of her facial expressions from her close friends, no matter how subtle.

"What is it?" Trevor asked, concerned about Tyana's sudden change in demeanor.

"Nothing! That's wonderful! Congratulations! When did you find out? When is she due? Do you guys know what she's having? How far along is she now? Is she going to continue to work up until her due date? Have you started picking out names for the baby? What about decorating the nursery? Do you need my professional help?"

"Stop, whoa....land your plane."

"What?"

"What do you mean what? Tyana, what's going on with *you*? We'll talk about the baby in a minute. Start talking. You can either sit here and stall all night, and delay your shopping trip, or you can cut to the chase and give me the straight scoop," urged Trevor.

"All right."

Their meal arrived and while they ate, Tyana began opening up to Trevor.

"I cancelled the wedding planner appointment the other day because Antonio was late — again. It's been five years, and we're not married. I hate it and it's getting to me. What's also getting to me is the fact that, because we're not married, I'm not pregnant."

"Oh, and I just..."

"No, see, I didn't want you to think that because you announced Cleo's pregnancy, I'm jealous or insecure. It's just the timing of it. It doesn't matter anyway because Antonio told me this *morning* that he doesn't want any more children."

"What? Is he serious?" Trevor asked.

"Yep."

"What about the wedding?"

"Oh, he still wants to marry me and he promised we'll do it sooner than later, but there will be no babies — for me."

"I'm so sorry. I know how much you want a baby."

"I'm not sure I've processed it yet. We went right into work after that and his students have swarmed him all day because of his birthday. Birdie gave him an expensive dress shirt and a Rolex watch."

"Get out of here! I don't mean to be insensitive, but are you sure there isn't something going on between those two?"

"I don't know anything anymore. I thought I would have been married and a mother by now."

"What are you going to do?"

"I don't know. I have a lot to think about." She paused. "Trevor, I ran into Ellis while Kellie and I were in Sedona.

"Okay, what? You're kidding, right."

"No. And, he told me he still loves me and wants me back."

"He what? Just like that. What did you say?"

"Say? I was in shock! It was kinda hard to have a conversation with him. He was standing there with his twins. I can't believe he had twins! Then on the second day, I run into Charlotte in the elevator. Just her, the twins, and me. I wanted to disappear into the floor. What was supposed to be a relaxing weekend was anything but."

"Wow! I'll say. So, then what happened?"

"If I wasn't so unprepared and stunned, I would have thought she was just as nervous as I was. We exchanged some small talk. I couldn't tell you what was said. I don't believe I took a breath the whole time."

"That's pretty remarkable. What are the odds of you running into both of them there? So, did you tell Ellis off? What was that exchange like?"

"It was upsetting. We sorta ran into each other at a different time — alone."

"How alone?"

"Very alone. Don't ask me what happened or why."

"Okay. But have you lost your mind?"

"Thank you for reminding me, and yes, I have."

"How does Antonio fit in all this?"

"I tried calling him that whole day and he claimed he couldn't call me until eleven-thirty that night when he woke me up. He's been all about the business and his gift-bearing students. Trevor, it's been five years and he's still not giving our impending wedding much attention. He doesn't care. He only cares about the dance studio."

"More on that in a minute, but back to Ellis...where did you guys leave things?"

"Nowhere. I've been walking around like a zombie ever since. Then he called me, *at the studio*, and is threatening to leave Charlotte and wants to give me anything I desire. *Great!* Antonio is not offering me what I want and Ellis is offering me the world."

"What are you thinking? You haven't forgotten what he did to you?"

"No, I haven't! Do you and Kellie think I suddenly acquired amnesia or something? Geez!"

"My bad, I'm sorry. I guess I should have asked, what is *he* thinking? What *is* he thinking? He's really going to divorce Charlotte?"

"That's what he says. He's very serious. He says he regrets what he did to me and he wants to do whatever he can in order to get me to forgive him and give him another chance—whatever that means. I guess that means he's willing to leave her. I don't know anything beyond that, except his children's names are Hailee and Hannah. They are *so* adorable." Tyana's mind wandered back to that point in time when the four of them stood together in the lobby of the resort.

"Hey, where did you go?" Trevor snapped his fingers in front of her face. "I've seen that look before. He's not good for you."

"You know what, Trevor? It's not like he was a womanizer or cheated on me with hundreds of women. He had sex with *one* woman, who manipulated him *and* set *me* up, as well. Remember the airport incident when he said good-bye to me at my gate, only for me to find them together at another gate where she 'accidentally' bumps into him there, after booking herself on the same flight to Spain? And the hotel incident in Madrid — the same trip — when she was there with him and when I called, she tricked me into finding her in his room — and I woke her? Well, if you don't, I do. My point is, she worked overtime to create the deception, and she did it remarkably well. She focused on one thing and stopped at nothing until she got it — Ellis. And, not that I'm defending his stupidity because it takes two, but he also fell victim to her schemes, mainly due to his greed, not because he wanted to leave me. Well, he's paying for his mistake now. So, everyone needs to stop making him out as some kind of sleazy, snake of a man who can't be trusted to genuinely be in love with me." She took a breath, and then continued, as Trevor listened.

"Antonio says he's in love with me, but what is he doing? Nothing, that's what! I'm still not married and I'm still not pregnant, and never will be pregnant with him. How does that make me feel after five good, reproductive years of my life gone knowing that my fiancé doesn't want to have a family with me? You're sitting over there about to become a father and telling me I should have a safe life with a man who'd rather *excessively* cater to desperate, delusional, and lonely women, than spend any time with his own fiancée, *and* who's been postponing our wedding indefinitely. No! I say no to that!"

"Are you saying you don't love him?" asked Trevor.

"I do love Antonio, more than anything and anyone. And, I love dancing more than anyone will ever know — including Antonio. But I can't accept having anyone suggest how I should live my life. Kellie ran interference in Sedona, out of concern, I'm sure, and literally threatened Ellis. She thought she was doing the right thing. But I'm a grown woman and I want the control of *my* life back. *I'll* make the decisions. If I make bad decisions, I have only myself to blame, but how will I know if I've made a good or bad decision if everyone wants to do it for me?"

"I don't think anyone is trying to make decisions for you. I'll speak for myself. I don't want to see you go through again what you already went through with Ellis. He chose her over you and that was a cowardly thing to do. If he really loved you then he should have chosen only you, regardless. He shouldn't have done what he did."

"He talked to me about that and it wasn't that black and white. And before you say anything, I do remember what I went through. I think about it all the time."

"Do you still love him?"

"I don't know how I feel about anything where he's concerned right now. I left my fiancé at the studio with a woman making a spectacle of herself draping herself all over him and he was quite comfortable with it. And, I left Ellis begging me to forgive him and promising me that he will leave his wife for me. I saw him with his daughters and I know how much he loves them. He stands to lose them if he divorces his wife and he knows it. Whatever I decide to do, I want to do what's best for me. Do you know that his mother still calls me from time to time? She was so disappointed in him when his affair came out and then the marriage and pregnancy as a result of the affair. Do you know that I have a closer relationship with her today than I ever did with Antonio's mother?" Tyana paused long enough to take a deep breath and another sip of water. "Trevor, I'm sorry. I didn't mean to go on and on like that. I think I've been holding in a lot of stuff and I'm stressed."

"No-no, it's cool. I totally understand. I get it. You have every right to feel what you feel and we have no right to question you."

"It's not that you shouldn't question me, but you guys have biased perspectives and it makes it hard on me when I want to talk about my true feelings and the whole picture."

"You can talk to me about your true feelings. I won't judge, I promise."

"Really?"

"Really."

"Thank you. I desperately needed to hear that right now. I need all the support I can get these days. I'm so confused and I feel isolated."

"Well, you're not isolated. I'm here for you—Cleo and I both will help you with anything you need."

"I appreciate that, thanks."

"Can I make an observation? And this is strictly me looking in from the outside."

"Of course."

"My gut tells me that there may be more going on with Antonio and his business—his financials to be more blunt—from what you're telling me. Maybe things aren't as profitable as he would like them to be and therefore, his focus is on his career and his ability to support you, more than it's on loving you. I don't mean to hurt you, but a man's pride is all about who he is and what he's become, first."

"That can't be it. The studio is thriving; we're making money."

"Okay, then maybe I'm wrong." Trevor was hoping, for her sake and peace of mind, that he was right. It would still be hurtful, but at least she would know why he was putting her and their wedding on the backburner.

"Look, I better get going. I need to talk to Antonio. He should be finished by now. Thanks for meeting me for a bite to eat. Oh! And, tell Cleo congratulations on the baby news. I'm so happy for you both. Keep me posted on her progress and condition. We'll catch up on all the details because I am extremely interested. And, don't forget, if you need me to design the perfect nursery, call me."

"I will, thanks. And hang in there. You'll figure it all out. Call me if you need anything or if you just need to talk."

"Thank you. I will."

Tyana and Trevor went their separate ways.

Tyana expected Antonio to be finished at the dance studio. They never worked late on Saturdays and typically took Sundays off, but lately Antonio has been working a seven-day workweek. So on a hunch, she drove by the studio first before heading home, and to her chagrin, she spotted his car still parked in the lot, with another car parked next to his. She didn't recognize the car. Her heart sank. She parked her car beside his and went inside to look for him.

When Tyana entered the locked studio, the silence engulfed her initially. No music played in the background. She wandered toward the main ballroom, which was eerily quiet. She figured he might be in the restroom or in his office working. She checked the schedule first to see if he had booked a late student. When she scanned the schedule, she saw that the last student would have been finished hours ago. Good, she thought. She went back toward his office in search of him, but found his door closed. She softly knocked and called out.

"Antonio? Are you in there?" Tyana opened the door, not waiting for an answer.

"Yes! Uh...come on in!" he nervously replied as she walked in. "Hi! What are you doing here?"

"I was going to ask you the same thing," Tyana replied while staring at the older Caucasian woman in his office. She appeared to be in her mid to late fifties. She was in pretty good shape, wearing some casual clothing and dance shoes, and sitting dangerously close to him on the guest side of his desk with his chair slightly facing hers. "Hi, I'm Tyana, I don't believe we've met." Tyana extended her hand to the woman who hadn't so much as flinched from Tyana's unexpected intrusion.

"Tatyana, this is Madeline Kremer. She's going to participate in the competition next month. She's an excellent dancer."

"Hi. Pleased to meet you," replied the woman as she sized up Tyana.

Tyana noticed that she hadn't moved an inch from Antonio. Their knees were practically touching. And the woman wasn't wearing a wedding band.

"Oh, I remember Rita saying something about a student who travels a good distance to come in. Is that you? How long have you been coming here?"

"She's been coming for a few months. Her schedule doesn't always permit her to come during regular business hours, so I teach her late on Saturdays, some Sundays."

"Really. That's nice." Tyana became more curious of this mystery student whom Antonio seemed a little nervous around. "Antonio, can I talk to you for a minute?"

"Sure. Let's go to your office." Antonio touched Madeline's knee and excused himself. Tyana watched curiously. He pulled Tyana by the hand and led her out of his office and into hers.

"So....if you're teaching her why is she hanging out with you in your office? You two looked awful cozy in there."

"Tatyana, we were just finishing up and I'm trying to sell her more lessons and competitions."

"I bet you are. And, you can't do that out there, where you talk to all of the other students?"

"What difference does it make? I came in here to get the information and it was just as easy to have her sit in my office so I can show her the different packages."

"I bet." She stopped herself from bringing up the closed door. "I'll see you at home. When will you be home?"

"Soon. We're almost finished here."

"Good." Tyana walked out of her office and then out of the studio. Antonio nervously returned to his office where Madeline patiently awaited.

When Tyana got back to her car, she started it and proceeded to leave. But before she exited the lot, she changed her mind. She decided to stay and find out more. But this time, she parked on the other end of the lot, which was obscured by shrubbery, but still within sight line of the studio's front door. She turned the car off and waited, and waited.

Thirty minutes later, she watched Antonio and the petite, older woman exiting the dance studio. He walked her to her car door. When she opened the car door, she turned to Antonio and hugged him. He warmly embraced her. To Tyana the hug seemed more of a caressing hug than a casual hug. They held their full-body contact for a long time before he pulled back and kissed her on her cheek. Tyana's blood pressure rose and her eyes bulged; yet remained glued to the couple who seemed quite familiar with one another. She watched them exchange a few more words with their hands touching each other in a fond fashion. Tyana began to shake uncontrollably and tears welled up in her eyes. She could no longer see them through her tears, but she continued to direct all of her attention on her fiancé's behavior toward the woman he referred to as Madeline. Suddenly the woman laughed and then another hug ensued before she entered her car. Tyana quickly started her car and drove off with a stream of burning, salty tears dripping down her cheeks.

Madeline, too, drove off and after one last wave good-bye from Antonio, he returned to his office to lock up. But before grabbing his keys, he sat down at his desk to look over the contract that Madeline signed. He closed his eyes and breathed a heavy, draining, exhaustive sigh. He sat forward with his elbows planted on the desk and his hands placed firmly against his forehead. His nerves knotted his stomach and the stress created a headache. He thought about the competition coming up in a few weeks, he thought about Madeline again, he thought about the wedding that Tyana had placed all of her hopes and dreams on, he thought about his promise to her, he thought about the baby she hoped for, he thought about his own daughter, he thought about his birthday and the birthday presents that his students gave him, he especially pondered the birthday present he received from Madeline right before Tyana interrupted — perhaps the best birthday present of all. With those ambivalent thoughts, he got up, picked up his keys, switched off the lights and left.

When Antonio got into his car, his cell phone rang.

"Hello Babe," he answered.

"Happy Birthday Daddy! I love you!"

"I love you, too, Honey. Thanks for calling. What are you up to?"

"Mom and I were out getting some last minute shopping done for college. Only a few more weeks you know."

"Yep, are you excited?"

"Extremely! You will be going with us on my first day, won't you?"

"Absolutely. I wouldn't miss it. I will however, miss you."

"I'll miss you, too, Daddy. Hey, Daddy, can we go to dinner tonight? You haven't eaten yet have you? I want to see you on your birthday. I have a card for you."

"No, I haven't eaten yet. I'm just leaving the studio; heading home. What did you have in mind?" Antonio was mentally and physically spent and had hoped to go home to quietly relax.

"Pizza?"

"Then pizza it is. Where are you? I'll pick you up."

"Great! I'm at home. Can you come now?"

"Of course. I'll be there in fifteen minutes."

"Thanks Daddy. I love you."

"I love you, Babe. See you soon."

Antonio hung up from Alyssa and called Tyana.

"Hello," Tyana answered, wondering why he was calling and not home yet.

"Hi Babe. Uh…Alyssa called and wants to go out to dinner for my birthday. Do you mind if I spend some time with her? I shouldn't be too long."

"No, go. What am I supposed to say anyway?" Tyana grew petulant and hurt over the numerous dinners and time spent with Alyssa that didn't include her. She didn't blame his daughter for wanting to spend time with her father, she only felt left out because those times rarely included her, and Antonio had never suggested otherwise. In Tyana's mind, that made it impossible for Alyssa to get to know her better and accept her as her father's fiancée. But after witnessing the personal exchange between Madeline and him, she wasn't sure that his dinner plans included his daughter either. She had never doubted his word before so she became confused and unsure of what to think.

"I love you," he expressed sensing some of her tension.

"Antonio, we need to talk."

"Okay." He sounded sad and depressed, matching her tone. "I'll be home as soon as I can." He knew that tone and it wasn't going to be a good ending to a day that started on such a high note.

Chapter

After his futile attempt to concentrate on his work or his plot to leave his wife, Ellis tiptoed into Hailee's and Hannah's elaborately decorated bedroom, which contained every imaginable ballerina figurine, motif, toy, and prop that a child's bedroom could safely hold. He quietly sat down in the vintage Bentwood rocker in the corner of the room and watched the sleeping girls. He closed his eyes and listened to them breathing. He rested his head on the back of the chair and recalled the moment he sat with Tyana in the hospital after she fell down the hotel stairs and lost their baby. He'll never forget how the miscarriage devastated her. He'll also never forget how she ended up in that situation— after she walked in on Charlotte and him in an incriminating and compromising sexual position in his hotel suite, right after he transferred to Charlotte's San Diego territory. He had no earthly idea that Charlotte, too, was already pregnant at that time. He closed his eyes and sighed. Oh, how he wished he could turn back time. He still hated himself for hurting Tyana in the most stupid, unforgivable way. He had never been able to erase the look on her face when she walked into the suite where he busily pleasured Charlotte.

Hailee began to stir. Ellis snapped out of his own nightmare to see what was happening with his daughter. He was hoping that the girls wouldn't pick up on the tension between Charlotte and him. His daughters were sensitive girls and could detect anything unusual or off-kilter. He went to Hailee's side and kneeled next to her bed. She turned over and continued to sleep. He breathed a sigh of relief. He turned toward Hannah and kissed her head.

"I love you Baby Doll," he whispered. He kissed her head once more and then returned to the rocker and continued to watch over his girls until he fell asleep.

♥♥♥

Tyana decided to put her torturous thoughts of Antonio and Madeline on hold until she had a chance to talk to him and find out what was really going on. She had never known him to be untrustworthy or disloyal to her. She grew steadily weary with each passing hour until she finally gave in to her fatigue and went to bed. But when she got there, she couldn't sleep without Antonio next to her.

♥♥♥

Antonio finally dropped Alyssa off at her mother's home at eleven-thirty, kissed her good-bye and drove home. That evening cost him dinner, and five hundred dollars for college and dorm items. It wasn't enough that he paid his ex-lover a generous child support payment each month, but his daughter would intermittently hit him up for entertainment money, a car, a phone, the latest electronics, money for gas, or anything she felt that she needed and knew her daddy would give to her with no questions asked. She had never worked for anything she got, nor did any chores for her allowances. She just asked and received. He substituted his quality time with cash and the items were costing him a lot more now than when she was ten. It's not that he didn't love his daughter, he did, but every so often he dwelled on his past mistakes as an overly-confident and perhaps, slightly arrogant man who knew how to attract the ladies. Many were attracted to him, but no one actually loved him like Tyana did. However, he didn't have the energy to have any more children, not even for her. And since Alyssa was born, he took monumental strides to prevent it from ever happening to him again. He expended all of his energy into the dance studio, trying to keep it thriving and successful. It was costing him.

Antonio walked into the house at eleven forty-five. Just fifteen minutes left of his birthday, and what a birthday it had turned into, he thought, but he was too exhausted to recall each singular moment. He could barely put one foot in front of the other as he made his way toward the master bedroom.

"Hi Babe," he said as he plopped down on the bed beside her. She lay awake with the television on, waiting for him to come home.

"Hi."

"I'm beat. You smell good. I know I don't. It's been a long day. I'm going to rest my eyes here for a second before jumping into the shower. It's so good to be home and off of my feet."

"How was your dinner with Alyssa?"

"I'm stuffed. I ate too much. We had pizza and junk. Stuff I shouldn't have had. But that's what she wanted."

"How much did it cost you?"

"For the pizza?"

"No, for the visit."

"Oh, well, you know how it is with her; she's always in need of something. It's okay though. She's a good kid. She needed some money for some school supplies."

"I'm glad you two had a good time. Are you going into work tomorrow?"

"Have to."

"Why?"

"With comp coming up, I'm booking more hours so everyone will be ready. They freak out all the time at the last minute."

"Who's coming in on a Sunday?"

"Let's see…there's Dottie, Gretta, Shirley, and Birdie."

"That's a lot!"

"I can handle it."

"I know you can handle it, but it's a lot for your day off. Look at you; you're exhausted. Antonio, I really think we should talk—about us."

Antonio sat up to face her. "I know. But can we please not do it now; I really need to get some sleep. I'll be right back. I'm gonna jump in the shower so I can go to bed."

"Sure."

Tyana turned over and thought about the woman he spent his off hours with that evening. Who was she, she wondered? And why was he being so mysterious with these women? More tears stained her pillow. She had been crying for about ten minutes when Antonio joined her in bed again.

"What's the matter?" Antonio asked, reading her body language. She kept her back to him.

"Nothing," Tyana responded.

"Tatyana, look at me." He turned her over. Her face was wet with tears. He kissed them. "Don't be sad. I love you." She started to turn away, but he had a way with his body when it touched her to persuade her to surrender to him, and that she did. With the last bit of energy he had in him, he spent it all with her that night. She was irresistible to him and with her, he ended his birthday the way he began it—romantically. But Tyana still fell asleep with a chasm of emptiness in her soul. The more time that passed without her being married to the man she loved, the more unhappy and troubled she became.

♥♥♥

Sunday ushered in a beautiful, sunny late August day outside, but a gloomy atmosphere inside while Antonio prepared to go to work. He wanted to get in early before the rush of students arrived, so he could pore over the financial statements some more and also make sure all of the competitors in next month's competition were signed up, paid up, and geared up. Attending competitions required extensive amounts of paperwork and preparations. The accommodations had to be made at the Ritz Carlton in downtown Phoenix for the two-day event and he had to make sure all of the music and any props were ready, as well as the Masters of Ceremony and the panel of judges. Everyone needed to be paid. The instructors typically received bonuses for their entries. All of the arrangements fell upon Antonio and Tyana to oversee and/or delegate. But anything delegated had to be confirmed and approved by Antonio. He would never leave anything one hundred percent up to someone else, except Tyana. She was his rock in those situations.

"I'll come in around one to do the paperwork while you're teaching. And then when you're finished, we can sit down and go over everything together so Rita can send it all into headquarters Monday morning," explained Tyana over breakfast.

"That sounds great. I really appreciate all your help with that stuff. You're a life-saver when the comps come around."

"Just doing my job."

"Well, I don't know how I could do mine without you."

"You managed before just fine, I'm sure."

"Well, it wasn't this easy."

"So, when are we going to get to talk? You said you were too tired last night, but then you found enough energy for sex."

"I was mentally tired. And we will, I promise. But I need to get going. My students will be arriving shortly."

"Right. Okay, I'll see you there."

"I love you, Babe. I'll see you." Antonio left.

Tyana sat alone at the breakfast table thinking about what she wanted to say to him if they ever got the opportunity to talk. She played back the night, before making love to him. Tears returned at just the thought of it. She had never felt more connected to someone emotionally and physically, but then more disconnected on issues like his relationship with his students and his lack of attention toward the progression of their relationship. It was as if he preferred doing the same thing day in and day out without deviating from the pattern. He liked the way things were and didn't want to change anything.

♥♥♥

"Antonio, I'm just not getting it. I feel so inadequate."

"You're doing fine, Dottie. Try it one more time. Move your hips more. Here, let me show you." Antonio placed his hands on her hips to help guide her movements.

"Like this?"

"Yes, that's better! Let's try it from the top." Antonio and Dottie championed through their Samba routine as he glanced over to see his next student arriving. Suddenly he began feeling weighted down with the pressure to maintain his positive attitude when, instead, he was sick with worry over Tyana, and the physical pressure to dance with his students all day. He realized that he hadn't allowed enough restorative time for his body. But more than his physical condition, he worried about his mental state. He could feel Tyana's energy drain more and more each day due to her desires to become his wife and a mother. He wanted to give her everything she needed, but he couldn't bring himself to compromise on that one thing — parenthood.

"Great lesson! Thank you and you'll be fine at competition. Just two weeks!" Antonio told Dottie. He waited until she changed her shoes and collected her things to walk her into his office where they chatted for a few minutes about something he wanted to talk to her about.

When they finished and he walked her to the front door to leave, she turned and smothered him in a friendly embrace at precisely the moment Tyana approached the front door. Tyana waited.

Dottie finally released her arms and separated herself from Antonio and walked out past Tyana without so much as a nod. Tyana and Antonio casually acknowledged one another, but Tyana stopped herself from going all the way inside; instead, she backtracked and chased after Dottie. She felt she had to say something to her once and for all. She could no longer ignore the elephant in the room.

"Dottie, wait up!"

Dottie turned around. Tyana caught up with her, but all of a sudden felt nervous when she opened her mouth to speak.

"Hi. Uh…is there a problem? I mean, do you have a problem with me?"

"I don't know what you're talking about," replied Dottie staring at Tyana with her nose in the air.

"I think you do. Do you have a problem with Antonio and me? You seem to have an attitude toward me for some reason and I…"

"You're the one with the attitude. I'm just puzzled why you think you own him and you're always following him around like a lost little puppy. It's so pathetic."

"Excuse me?" Tyana couldn't believe her ears.

"What, are you deaf?"

"What's wrong with you?"

"What's wrong with *you*? He's my man, can't you see. He doesn't even pay you any attention. So, you need to back off and stop trying to get all up on him," Dottie lashed out, scanning Tyana up and down.

"I think you're way out of line. What makes you think he's your man?" Tyana nervously interrogated.

"It's so obvious. I can tell he wants me. We're just trying to be professional about it in public. But I'm not at liberty to say what happens when no one else is around."

"Oh really."

"Yeah, really," Dottie challenged.

"I think you should stick to the lessons and leave it at that." Tyana was becoming increasingly uncomfortable.

"Sorry. Can't do that. As of Monday, I'll be working with him every day—his offer, I might add. I guess he wants to see me on a regular basis and not just during our forty-minute lessons three times a week."

"What? What do you mean you'll be working here?"

"Just because you wormed your way into being an instructor and up under his nose all the time, doesn't mean you own him, girlfriend. Maybe he's just tired of you and wants to replace you with a real woman."

Tyana had had enough and walked away, heading back into the studio with a full head of steam. She was shaking. How dare that self-indulgent woman trash her like that? She barged into the studio to look for Antonio, but found him on the dance floor with another student. She glared at him from across the room and he received her message loud and clear. She paced while he taught.

She bolted into her office and slammed the door. She started dialing.

"Hi!"

"Trevor! I'm done! I can't do this anymore. I'm done I'm just done!"

"What? Whoa, pump your brakes. You're done with what?"

"Everything!" She started crying.

"Tyana, what's the matter? What happened?"

"I just had a confrontation with one of Antonio's students and she told me to my face that Antonio is *her* man..."

"Oh, please. Don't let those skanks mess with you like that. You know they're just jealous bitches."

"It's more than that. I can't handle it anymore. I tried to ignore it for five years and because we're not married, it's made it even harder on me. We agreed to remain professional in the studio and not flaunt our relationship..."

"Whose idea was that?"

"His."

"So, how is he handling the incidents with his students' behavior toward you?"

"He isn't."

"What about today's confrontation?"

"He doesn't know about it yet. He's on the floor with someone. I came directly in here to call you because I'm so pissed. I wanted to tell her off, but I couldn't. I'm bound by professionalism! I'm about to explode! It took everything I had in me to not slug that woman. You should have seen her. She honestly thinks Antonio wants her. Oh! And get *this*; he hired her to work *here*!"

"He *what*?! Is he insane? If having them there as students wasn't bad enough."

"I know! I can't do this anymore. I'm over it and over the drama! It doesn't even make sense."

"What are you going to do? Are you going to break up with him, quit the studio business, what?"

"I don't know. I've been trying to talk to him for days and he's not been available to me. It's always something with him. He doesn't want any babies, so what else do I have?"

"You love him don't you?"

"Yes, too much. I think more than he loves me."

"Look, um, Cleo isn't feeling well and we're waiting to hear back from the doctor. I might have to take her to the hospital..."

"Oh my God! I'm so sorry. I didn't know..."

"Of course, you didn't know. I want to talk to you more about this, but I really need to be with her right now."

"I hope it's nothing serious. Oh, I'm so sorry."

"It's okay. And, we *all* hope it's nothing serious."

"Okay Trevor, I'll let you go. Please let me know what happens with her and tell her I'm thinking positive thoughts and I'm praying for her."

"Thanks. I appreciate that, Tyana. Good luck with your situation and I'll call you when we learn more about our situation. Love ya."

"Love you, too."

Tyana buried herself in her paperwork while she waited for Antonio to finish teaching. At around two o'clock she surfaced from her office in search of her fiancé. She found him in his office and barged in when she thought he would be alone.

"Antonio we need to talk!" she barked as she swung the door open.

"Tatyana…"

She immediately saw Birdie sitting in his guest chair leaning over his desk with her breasts nearly falling out of her spandex top. She had her arms stretched across his desk and her hands on his.

"What is it?" he asked.

"Never mind." She turned and left abruptly.

Five minutes later, Antonio walked Birdie out with his arm around her shoulder. Tyana watched while feeling more and more resentful of the women who get the amazing, attentive Antonio; the actor and superman escort, who can solve all of their problems, including loneliness. And yet, she gets the exhausted, tired, and inattentive reality star, Antonio. The dichotomy of her reality and their fantasies plagued her.

When he finally came back in and with no one left on the books to teach, she approached him.

"We need to talk Antonio, now!"

"Tatyana…"

Before he could interject, they both saw Madeline walk through the front door. Tyana looked directly at Antonio with fire in her eyes.

"Are you kidding me? She wasn't on the schedule!"

"I know. I forgot to put her down. I can't get out of it; she drives like an hour and a half to get here."

Madeline approached without regard for their conversation or simple courtesy. "Antonio, Sweetheart, I'm going to go into your office and wait for you there."

"Okay, Madeline. I'll be right there."

"Sweetheart? In your office?" mocked Tyana.

"It's okay," assured Antonio.

"One question. Did you hire Dottie to work here?"

"Can we talk about it later?"

"Did you or didn't you?"

"Yes…"

"Are you insane? And, am I not your partner in this business and therefore personnel matters go through me, too?"

"She's not on payroll. She couldn't afford the lessons and the comps and wanted a way to work off her comps, so I offered her the media work: the web site, the flyers, the studio calendar to update and upload, as well as answering the phones."

"I'm out!"

"What?"

"I'm out Antonio! I'll see you later."

"Wait!"

"No! I'm tired of waiting. I'm out!"

Chapter

After another long, taxing day at the hotel on a Sunday, not uncommon for Ellis, partly due to his responsibilities when important clients were on site, and partly due to his avoidance of Charlotte, he rushed home to hopefully be able to tuck in his daughters at their bedtime. Saying goodnight to them became a special ritual for him. The nighttime represented peacefulness to him and added certain calmness to his life when he got to spend those hours leading to bedtime with his daughters. For him, they made it all seem worthwhile. His importance in their life depended upon him being the last one they saw before drifting off to sleep. He always made it a pleasant and happy experience for them. They gave him purpose to his demanding job and his impossible marriage to Charlotte.

"Daddy!" Hailee and Hannah greeted him upon entering the house.

"Hey, what are you girls still doing up? At the very least, you should be in the bathtub!"

"We're watching a happy movie and Momma said we can stay up if we're real quiet. She's reading a contract."

Ellis scanned the trail of toys, books, and dolls strewn across the floor and furniture, but saw no sign of Charlotte. He turned the Happy Feet movie off.

"Well, it's time for bed…let's go!"

Ellis squatted down to allow the girls to step up on his thighs so he could lift them up. That became their favorite thing to do. He figured in a few more years, he'd have to come up with something as equally fun for them.

"Where's your mother?"

"In her office. She told us not to bother her," answered Hailee.

"We would get a present if we're quiet, too, but Hailee wasn't as quiet as I was," added Hannah.

"I see," said Ellis in an annoyed tone. "C'mon." He kissed them both.

He changed his clothes, gave the girls a bath, put them to bed, and then read them a bedtime story from one of their favorite storybooks. Hannah fell asleep halfway through the story, but Hailee hung on until the end.

"Daddy?"

"Yes, Baby Girl?"

"Do you love Momma?"

Ellis' eyes widened by such an easy, yet complicated, question coming from four-year old Hailee. Though the twins were physically identical in every conceivable way, Hailee displayed more precocious developmental skills than Hannah did—at times. She studied the adults, especially her parents, more than Hannah did, although they both were equally attached to their parents.

"Hailee, what do you mean, exactly?"

Ellis often felt like he could have an adult conversation with Hailee on some level—like he could easily forget her age. His curiosity intensified.

"I mean like Megan's mommy and daddy next door. They hold hands and kiss and they go to the swing park together. Momma gets mad at you; she gets mad at us, too. Is Momma mad with us now because Hannah dropped the cookies on the floor?"

"Oh, Hailee, no! She loves you and Hannah very much."

"What about you, Daddy? Does she love you? She's mad at you a lot."

Ellis stalled for a while. He didn't know what to say. He knew he didn't want to pretend anymore.

"Baby Girl, Momma has a big job at work that makes her feel stressed a lot. Do you know what that means?"

"Do you have a big job at work?"

"Yes, I do."

"But you don't be mad at us."

"I could never be mad at you. Let's get you tucked in so you can go to sleep."

He didn't know what else to say. He pulled her to him and hugged her tightly. She gave him a big hug in return. He kissed her and then tucked her back into bed. She intuitively understood his gesture and slid back under the sheets.

"'Night, Daddy."

"Sleep tight, Hailee," he whispered. He wiggled her toes, and then left her to go to sleep.

When he returned to his bedroom, he found Charlotte blowing on her freshly polished fingernails and sipping on a martini.

"Are the girls asleep? I heard you in there still talking. I'm glad you got them into bed, they were rambunctious today," complained Charlotte.

"Hannah's asleep. Hailee is just about there. She had some concerns."

"She's too young to have concerns. Did you get Jack's proposal reviewed and signed? We need that before the meeting tomorrow afternoon. When's your flight to Madrid and how long will you be gone?"

"Yes, I signed the contract. And, I leave on Friday for Madrid. I'll be gone for two weeks." Ellis paused for a short moment, not having given any previous thought to what would come out of his mouth next. "Charlotte, I'd like to take the girls with me this time. I know it's a last minute decision, but I think they would really like it and I'd like it. Annamarie can come also to help out when I'm working during the day, but I'll be with them the remainder of the time."

"That's absurd!" She stopped painting her nails to give him a disapproving stare. Her first reaction came across as suspicion. "What are you going to do with them there? They're going to be in the way. You need to remain focused. These are new clients and this is an important contract." She often used a condescending tone with him.

"Charlotte, stop! The girls are not a distraction to me. And I know how to do my damn job! They're coming with me—it's just two weeks. You're having that reception next week at the hotel anyway, so you won't be spending much time at home with them. It'll give *you* a break, so *you* can focus on what you need to do. Annamarie and the girls might even enjoy the trip." He knew they all would enjoy the break away from Charlotte's reign and constant orders.

"What's your motive, Ellis?" Charlotte's tone turned incredulous.

"I don't have a motive. I want to spend time with my daughters. Is that a crime?"

"You tell me."

"Tell you what? Why are you so skeptical? Oh, because you can't accept that I can have no other motive than love for my daughters, unlike you who would stoop to any level to orchestrate such covert setups in order to get what you want."

"Fine. Have fun in Madrid." Charlotte conceded and left the room.

She knew what he meant and didn't want to play along—at least not yet. She didn't want to give Ellis the idea that she could still be capable of doing anything under-handed again, especially if she planned to win any divorce settlement and custody. For Charlotte, success and winning meant everything.

♥♥♥

Three hours after Antonio saw Tyana storm out of the dance studio, he entered the house, practically walking on eggshells. He found Tyana in the kitchen cleaning up her dinner dishes.

"Hi. Something smells good," he said as he slowly approached her.

"It's just spaghetti, toasted baguettes and salad. Help yourself."

"Mmm…my favorite. Thanks."

He reached out to hug her, but she brushed past him.

"I'm here; let's talk," he conceded.

"I don't know where to start first. I'll start with, I left you at the studio three hours ago and you're just getting home. What took you so long?"

"Tatyana, this doesn't sound like you."

"You're right, but this is what you've turned this relationship into, with all your secret students who aren't on the schedule, but show up at all odd hours of the day and days of the week, who make themselves comfortable in only *your* office. Over three thousand square feet of space in there and you confine them to your office. So, I'll ask again, what took you so long tonight, a Sunday night, to come home?"

"I was giving a lesson, and talking."

"Meanwhile, I'm here and have been wanting to talk to you for days. Why don't I matter to you anymore?"

"Of course, you matter to me."

"Really? Then why aren't we married?"

"I told you we will."

"You've been telling me that for five years. You know what? Forget it. I take back my acceptance of your marriage proposal!"

Antonio looked shocked and somewhat teary-eyed at her comment.

"It's done; I'm done. I can't take it anymore!"

"Tatyana, come here."

"No! Don't touch me. You got your way and dragged me along for this circus ride for five years only to tell me that you don't want a baby with me."

"I don't want one with anyone."

"Sure, you say that after you had a child with someone else. It's always someone else you pick over me! I'm almost thirty-five! Why couldn't you have told me this five years ago?"

"It never came up."

"It never came up because I was waiting until we were married! We aren't exactly announcing our engagement, let alone our relationship to too many people you know, so I didn't want to get pregnant until we were married."

"Tatyana, please calm down. I want you to understand why it's important to me to not have any more children."

"Don't tell me to calm down! And, I don't want to hear it—not now. Are you having an affair with one of your students?"

"*What*? Where is this coming from?"

"Have you or have you not been involved with any of your students or anyone since you've been engaged to me?"

"No, of course not."

"Have any of them offered to have sex with you?"

"What are you doing?"

"Answer me! I need to know what's really going on behind my back."

"What do you mean?"

"Dottie told me that you are her man and that I am nothing but a pathetic puppy who follows you around all the time and that you hired her to work in the studio so she can be near you on a daily basis."

"She did not."

"Oh really? Then let's ask her tomorrow when she shows up to work."

"If she did, then she's stupid. Why would she think I'm her man?"

"Have you seen you two on the dance floor, and off? Don't change the subject! Has anyone come onto you and seduced you for personal, intimate reasons?"

Antonio shifted in his stance and then walked to the table to sit down.

"I can't tell you that."

"What do you mean you can't tell me that? So, then it's true. Tell me! It's true, isn't it?"

"Yes."

"Who?"

"Does it matter?"

"You bet your life it does! *Who*?"

"Birdie."

Tyana turned pale and felt weak. She staggered to a chair and sat down and began crying. "When?" she sobbed.

"I'm not trying to hurt you by telling you this. I never wanted you to know."

"When?"

"In Hawaii — two years ago. She slipped me her hotel key on the second night we were there for a dance weekend trip. I told her that it was inappropriate for me to accept it under any circumstance."

"What about because you are engaged to me?"

"That has nothing to do with it; I wanted her to know that I didn't feel the same way about her that she felt about me."

Tyana continued to cry in her hands. Antonio felt burdened by the truth of the situation, especially because it was torturing her. He got up and put his hands on her shoulder to comfort her. "I'm sorry. Please don't see things that way with me. I can handle those kinds of situations. They mean nothing to me."

"But they mean something to *me!*" She looked up at him with tear-drenched eyes. "Antonio, I want you to leave this house. We're over. I can't do this anymore. You're off the hook; there won't be a wedding." She walked out of the room leaving Antonio standing stunned and in disbelief.

An hour later, he sat down on the edge of the bed where Tyana lay, still crying.

"Tatyana...I'm really sorry. I packed enough for a few nights; I'll get the rest later and we can work out the arrangements to move my stuff out. I'll be at my parents until I can figure out my living situation. Will you be coming into work; will you stay on or are you leaving the studio? What about the competition?

"I will continue to teach for as long as it still works for me. I'll do the comp—I wouldn't let my students down. We can remain business partners for as long as it works for us both."

"Good. I know how much you love to dance. What about the routines that you and I have been practicing?"

"Antonio, we can remain dance partners. I don't think we should continue on as romantic partners. We don't seem to be on the same page any longer, or maybe we were never on the same page.

"I'm sorry; I really wish you didn't feel that way."

"I'm sorry too. You've meant the world to me."

"Tatyana, what can I do to make things better for you?"

"It's too late for that. I think you should go now. I'll see you tomorrow."

"Are you sure?"

"Yeah, please go."

Antonio reluctantly picked up his bags and walked out with his head hanging low and a massive lump in his throat. The man who had managed to get things his way and on his terms had lost the one thing he wanted the most.

Tyana spent the night sobbing.

Chapter
Eleven

The next morning, Antonio arrived at the dance studio uncharacteristically late. Functioning on very little sleep, coupled with the hectic schedule he had been keeping, he was close to exhaustion. His mother tried to get him to open up about why he was suddenly crashing in the guest room, but he kept close-mouthed about his troubles. It was too soon to talk about it; he hadn't yet processed the whole situation, nor did he know what he was going to do. Too many things overwhelmed him at the moment, which didn't leave him much time to focus on personal issues. Although he didn't bend on her invitation to open up, she didn't let the opportunity pass to tell him that she thought he was better off on his own because of the nature of his business. She thought having Tyana there at the dance studio and as his fiancée would only create a distraction where his students were concerned. She saw all too often how the women students took to him and wanted to claim him as their own, which only persuaded them to pour more and more money into the business. He listened to his mother's advice and said nothing, but shook his head. It pained him to think that so many family members weren't supportive of his personal choice to marry Tyana. They knew nothing of what she meant to him and how having her in his life enriched it in so many ways. They didn't know her like he did, therefore, they could never understand. It also disturbed him that very few gave her a chance. Instead they only found reasons to criticize her and blame her for the mistakes he made in their relationship and partnership. They never took into consideration what part his long and grueling hours working in the dance studio played, and how his lack of a personal life created a discord in their relationship; nor the fact that the only time they had any quality time to themselves — far away from the business and outside forces — was during the occasional weekend getaways they would take together, albeit very few and far in-between. They may have had only few stolen moments together, but hands down, they were the best times that they spent together as a couple. Other than that, the studio took up ninety-nine percent of his time and he didn't adjust his schedule for Tyana one bit once they were engaged. He figured that working together would make up for their lack of personal time together as a couple. But little did he realize at the time that it didn't work like that; in fact, it didn't work at all. It only made her a target for the enemy.

As he entered the studio, he walked straight to the coffee pot and poured himself a mug-sized portion of the strong brew and then headed to his office. Rita entered right behind him.

"Good Monday morning boss! You're in kinda late by your standards, aren't you?"

"Good morning, Rita. How bad is my schedule?" For the first time in his career, he didn't have the same enthusiastic energy toward teaching or being the pillar of optimism. Usually he would check his schedule en route to his office, but he neglected to do so that morning. His mind remained fixed on other things.

"I'll go check for you, but I'm pretty sure you're booked solid. I do know that your first client just walked in the door. And, what is Dottie Dawson doing here? She said she's working for you now."

"Dottie is not working for me; she's working for the studio — to work off her comp and coaching fees. I asked her to update the web site, the calendar, answer the phones, stuff like that and only stuff like that. I'll write out a list so you'll both have it. She's still a student and will be paying for her regular lessons."

"Oh, for a minute there, I thought you were replacing me."

"Oh no, never. I'm sorry, I should have told you first, but it was last minute. Hey, do me a favor," he requested.

"Sure, what is it?"

"Keep an eye on her and let me know if she says anything out of line or inappropriate about anyone here, particularly, Tatyana."

Rita looked surprised. She had seen them interact in a very friendly manner on and off of the dance floor, so she wondered why he wanted her on close surveillance.

"Okay. Sure. Anything else?"

"No, thanks."

"Are you okay? You seem....actually, you seem depressed about something." She noticed his bloodshot eyes.

"I'm fine. Who's out there waiting on me?"

"Shirley O'Connor." Rita definitely knew something was up. He always knew exactly who was scheduled and when.

"Tell her I'll be out in a few minutes. Offer her some coffee and pastries."

"You got it! Do you need anything?"

"No, just this coffee, thank you. Oh yes, one more thing."

"Sure, what's that?"

"Could you ask Dottie to come in here please?"

"Sure." Rita promptly left Antonio's office to fetch Dottie.

He sat nearly motionless with his eyes closed for several seconds as he waited for Dottie to enter. All that he could think about was Tyana. He felt that he had let her down in so many ways. He missed sleeping in their bed together that night. He thought perhaps he should have put up more of a fight to get her to change her mind about separating, but he knew she had a valid point. He also wondered if she could be attracted to someone else — remembering that phone call he walked in on.

"Good morning, Antonio! Rita said you wanted to see me?" Dottie grinned from ear-to-ear eager to start her day off with some one-on-one time with her fantasy lover.

"Hi. Close the door and have a seat please." Antonio didn't crack a smile. He was more serious at that moment than he has been in a long time. Dottie's actions and animosity toward Tyana put Antonio in an awkward position and he didn't exactly feel comfortable. He hated confrontation. Dottie gladly closed the door, although she secretly wished Tyana could see her.

"What's up?" Dottie asked with a glint in her eyes and a sizeable slit in her skirt.

"Did you tell Tatyana that I'm your man and did you call her pathetic?"

Dottie froze in her chair as she was taken completely off guard. All of her blood rushed to her head and she started sweating.

"I...uh...what?"

"Do I have to repeat myself? Let's just assume you did because Tatyana wouldn't have a reason to lie to me. Listen, I don't like to ever discuss my personal business with staff and especially not with the students. I expect everyone who enters this dance studio to respect each other and show respect at all times. I hate gossip, I hate rumors, and I hate anything that disrupts the positive environment that I work so hard to create in here day after day. Tatyana is not only one of my most talented, friendly and caring instructors who is an asset to this studio, but she's my fiancée and I love her. I won't have anyone speak to her in a derogatory tone or threaten her. She's not pathetic or a puppy or anything like that. She's here in this studio because I want her here — with me. Why would you say those things to her?"

"You...I mean, I thought...I thought you had feelings for *me*."

"What gave you that idea?"

"The way we dance together..."

"That's dancing. My job is to teach you the techniques of Latin and ballroom dancing and those techniques require the partners, in most cases, to have close physical contact, particularly the dances of love; and I dance that way with everyone, but that does not mean I'm in love with you or any other client. Look, I have a student waiting on me, but I need to know that you understand where I'm coming from."

"Yes, I'm sorry."

"I would normally say that you should apologize to Tatyana, but I really don't want you talking to her unless it's business related. Just show her some respect or I won't be able to teach you anymore."

"Okay," Dottie responded with her head hanging low.

"Thank you for understanding; and thank you for wanting to help us out here, but I will not let your working or dancing here upset or make Tatyana uncomfortable, which in turn makes me uncomfortable."

"Absolutely. It won't."

"Good. Thank you. Also, since Tatyana and I are always busy teaching, please see Rita about your responsibilities and directions where the phones are concerned. She can also tell you what needs to be added to the web site."

"Okay. Thank you." Dottie got up and slowly walked back to work with less enthusiasm than when she entered Antonio's office.

Antonio took a few minutes to collect his thoughts. He felt somewhat relieved that he addressed the situation and protected Tyana, but he also worried that it came much too late to save his relationship. He bore the responsibilities of that demise. He took a deep breath and stood up. He took another deep breath and went out to teach that Monday morning and every morning that week with a little less energy and passion for the dance. The staff began to notice something different in him and Tyana separately and between them. They both seemed troubled.

♥ ♥ ♥

With one day to go before the big competition event in Phoenix and having to deal with so many last minute issues, Antonio and Tyana didn't have one second to deal with their own personal problems. They had never worked together without being romantically involved, so their modified professional relationship was foreign to her and a major adjustment on her part. She still loved him and he loved her, which made it almost unbearable for both of them in the close quarters. Antonio spent the initial days, following their separation, pleading his case and asking for a reprieve, but Tyana couldn't and wouldn't give up wanting children and Antonio couldn't give in either.

Tyana also had reservations about having Dottie working in the office. After the unfortunate confrontation with her, she didn't feel comfortable having her around every day. She also resented the fact that Antonio never consulted with her first before offering Dottie the job. Although Dottie attempted to be cordial with Tyana, Tyana kept her distance and did not reciprocate. She ignored her for the most part.

On the day before the competition, Tyana sat mindlessly thumbing through paperwork on her desk before she grabbed the phone and hastily dialed.

"Trevor. It's me. I'm so sorry; I meant to call sooner. How's Cleo?"

"Hi. She's doing okay for the most part. Her doctor is concerned; there's a slight chance she may miscarry, so they've admitted her just until she's a little stronger and out of the woods. She wants her off of her feet for about a month. Between working and practically living at the hospital, I've been too exhausted to call."

"Oh, I'm so sorry to hear about Cleo's situation. I'll get over there as soon as I can."

"She'll like that. I think she's going out of her mind being cooped up."

"How are you doing?"

"I'm worried for her. I feel so helpless right now."

"You're not though, so don't think it. Just you being there and supporting her means a lot to her, I'm sure."

Antonio popped his head in.

"Look, I have to run, but I'll be over to see her as soon as comp is over. It's tomorrow."

"I know you'll knock 'em dead. Good luck and don't worry; take your time. Are you doing okay?"

"I'm managing, thanks." She looked at Antonio. "I'll call you in a couple of days."

"Okay, take care."

"You, too." Tyana hung up and turned her attention to Antonio who stood in the doorway.

"Are you free?" he asked.

"Hi." Tyana glanced at her watch. It had approached nine o'clock in the evening. "Sure, come in."

"I'm finished for the day so if you have time, I'd like to practice our routines — for the comp."

"Uh...sure. Give me a minute; I'll meet you out there. Is everyone else finished up or should we go in one of the smaller rooms?"

"I think Kyle and Jill are still teaching on the main floor. I'll get the music. Meet me in the Tango Room." Antonio left.

Tyana met up with Antonio a few minutes later in the Tango Ballroom where their music of choice for their routine could be heard as she approached the door. Antonio rushed to meet her at the door and took her by the hand, as he would do with any one of his own students. He treated her especially respectful and courteous. In fact, he handled her in the same manner he did when she was his student and when their sexual tension was evident and at its peak. He truly felt love for her and wanted her to know just how much. They walked onto the center of the floor together as they took their position to begin their routine.

Antonio carefully held her close to his body, so close that she could feel his heart beating rapidly against her body. He spun her out away from him, and then back into his body once again with intensity yet precision, where she nestled in so gracefully. Their footwork matched each other's precisely and their eyes never once looked away. Their spot checks were sharp and their hands connected throughout the dance with impeccable timing. The picture perfect couple maintained perfect poise, frame, and hold, and their rhythm and fluidity never wavered as if they had been dancing together for years—six years to be exact. Tyana still experienced the same tingly feeling that day when she danced with Antonio that she savored on the very first day she ever danced with him. He affected her that way, and unfortunately, he affected so many other women that same way as well. His hands, his legs, his feet, his body, his hips, his looks, his accent…all were his gift, or were they his curse?

Tyana and Antonio danced for the entire hour before they realized the time. When they concluded their routine with a gentle and caressing dip, Antonio leaned in and impulsively kissed Tyana's lips. They were both still breathing heavily from their dancing. She missed his lips on hers, the touch of his hands, the closeness of his body, the butterflies in her stomach…

"Excuse me, Antonio, Birdie Pennington is on line one," interrupted Jill. She blushed when she caught the two sharing a romantic kiss, dispelling rumors that they were having domestic troubles.

After Antonio carefully returned Tyana to her feet, she disapprovingly looked at her watch and marched out first. Antonio rushed to catch up with her.

"Tatyana, wait!"

"It's ten-thirty; I'm tired. I need to go. We're finished, right? I'll see you tomorrow."

Tyana never broke stride; she entered her office where she changed her shoes, grabbed her things, and then left. Antonio took the phone call, but wished he had instructed Jill to take a message instead. He watched Tyana pass by his office in a huff on her way out. He dejectedly knew he lost momentum in getting her back.

When he finally finished up with his phone call and left the dance studio around eleven, he phoned Tyana on his way home.

"Tatyana, it's me, did I wake you?"

"Uh…it's late, I'm about to head to bed. Can this wait?"

"I wanted to say I'm sorry about tonight."

"About what?"

"About the abrupt interruption. I didn't have a chance to properly say good night to you."

"Oh, that. You were just doing what comes natural, I suppose. And, Birdie does what comes natural to her—call you at ten-thirty. Now, if you don't mind, I need to get some sleep."

"Wait! Are we ready for the competition this weekend? You danced beautifully tonight—I wanted you to know."

"I'm ready and my students are all ready. I've done this a thousand times. You need not worry."

"I'm not worried, I'm checking, that's all."

"Well, you've checked. Is there anything else? By the way, what did Birdie want that was so important for her to call you so late?"

"Umm…well, she had some questions about the trip to Mexico, next week."

"Oh. She's going on that trip with you? Of course she is. Maybe she'll slip you her key again. Good night, Antonio." Tyana knew that she went too far, but it came out before she had realized she said it.

"Tatyana, that wasn't fair. I don't want to sleep with anyone but you. Can I come over and talk to you—just talk?"

"Now? I'm heading to bed."

"Just for a few minutes. You haven't allowed me even five minutes to talk to you at the studio."

"Oh, like you could tear yourself away from your students long enough to talk to me."

"I'll only stay fifteen minutes. I want to talk about…having a baby."

"Really?"

"Yes. Can I come over?"

"Okay…for fifteen minutes."

"Deal. I'll see you in ten minutes. Thanks."

Chapter
Twelve

When Ellis had arrived in Madrid with his daughters and au pair, Annamarie, in tow, they managed to get the twins settled in the grand hotel double suite upon check-in and put them down to sleep. The long flight wore them out from all of the attention they received from the other first-class passengers, the flight crew, and the continuous first-class amenities, food, and activities. Once they unpacked the children's things and ordered a meal from room service, Ellis took a long, hot shower to help him unwind and relax while Annamarie retreated to her room across the hall to tend to her own unpacking chores.

Annamarie had worked as the Montgomerys' au pair since the girls were born. Charlotte insisted on having the hired help and began interviewing during her last trimester of pregnancy. She found Annamarie as the perfect match to her personality because of Annamarie's submissive personality. She followed instructions to the letter and especially Charlotte's instructions.

Annamarie, a pretty girl originally from Peru, now at age twenty-four, crafted a remarkable style of handling children. She exuded high-energy which allowed her to keep up with twin four-year-old girls. The girls enjoyed being around her and they responded to her positively, which pleased Ellis, especially. He initially thought Charlotte would take some time off from work to stay at home with the girls until they were a little older, but she had no such plans. It took some getting used to having a stranger care for his children, but Annamarie proved her handling skills and childcare knowledge almost immediately and put Ellis' mind at ease. Actually, he felt more at ease having Annamarie care for them, than he did Charlotte. Annamarie had already raised three of her siblings while her parents worked several jobs each back in Lima.

Annamarie returned to her employer's suite to see if she would be needed for the remainder of the evening. She didn't find him in the living room, so she peeked into the opened doorway to the master bedroom. When she didn't see him at first glance, she called out and started to walk in.

"Mr. Montgomery, are you here?"

"Whoa, just a second!" Ellis grabbed a towel to cover his naked body. As she walked in, he, simultaneously, exited the en suite bathroom to get his toiletry bag left on the bed.

"Oh! Dios Mio! Mr. Montgomery, lo siento. I'm so sorry. I...I didn't mean..." Annamarie turned red and ran out and waited in the living room with her hands over her eyes, totally embarrassed at seeing her boss naked. Ellis darted into the bathroom and grabbed his robe.

"It's okay, no harm!" he yelled as he quickly put on his robe. He came out to find her.

"I'm so sorry. I should have knocked or something. I'm so embarrassed. I never meant to..."

"It's okay. I think I'm more embarrassed here. I didn't know you were still here."

"I came back to see if you needed anything else before I turned in. It's all my fault."

"Annamarie, shh...don't worry about it. Let's just forget it, okay?"

"Okay. I'm sorry. I hope I didn't wake up the girls. Should I check on them?"

"No, I'll do it. We're all good here. You can go now. If I need anything I'll call you."

"Sí, sí, buena. I should go now. Gracias."

"Thanks for all your help on the plane. I know the girls were a handful at times. The meals should be coming up soon. I'm kinda beat—from the flight, so I'll probably just eat and turn in. I'll see you in the morning for breakfast. And, feel free to order anything else you want from room service and charge it to my account."

"Sí, gracias. Buenas Noches, Señor Montgomery."

"Good night Annamarie."

Once he shut and locked the door, he breathed a heavy sigh, tightened the belt on his robe and returned to the bathroom, thinking only about the unfortunate incident. He shook it off and picked up his phone to dial home.

"Charlotte, we're here and all settled. The girls did well on the flight—it tired them out though—they're passed out."

He listened to Charlotte drone on and on about work issues and her successful closing of the Tobin deal.

"That's great, congratulations. Uh-huh…right…when is he coming to town?" He could barely get a word in edge-wise. She finally ran out of steam and the conversation wound down. "Okay, I'll tell them. I'm pretty sure they'll sleep straight through until morning, but I ordered them some food, just in case they wake up. I'll call you later."

They hung up without incident.

Ellis heard a light tap on his door. He checked his peephole first before opening the door to room service. The wait staff deposited the meals on the coffee table. He signed the tab, tipped them, and then led them out and locked the door behind them. He carried the food into the bedroom where he could relax and watch a little television before turning in. He suddenly felt more exhausted than hungry. Before he took his first bite, a tiny voice coming from the other bedroom startled him.

"Daddy!" cried Hannah.

Ellis jumped up and ran through the suite to investigate one of his daughter's cries.

"Who's calling?" He whispered as he entered the room.

"Daddy, it's me, Hannah. I woke up and didn't know where I was. Where's Momma?"

"Shh...don't wake up Hailee. Come here."   Ellis picked her up and carried her to his room.

"Are you hungry? Here, I have a sandwich for you; take a bite and then tell me why you woke up. Do you remember where we are now?"

"We came on a plane, right?"

"Right. Momma's at home. She stayed at home, remember? It's just us here in Spain with Annamarie. Remember? She's in her own room across the hall, asleep. Everyone's asleep and you should be as well."

"Can I stay here with you? I feel funny. I can't go to sleep right now."

"Sure, Baby Doll, eat what you can and then get under the covers, and no kicking Daddy, okay?" he said smiling, and then kissed his daughter.

She giggled and hugged her daddy. Hannah took a few more bites before she scrambled into the middle of the large king-sized bed, settled in next to her daddy, and laid her head on his lap.

♥ ♥ ♥

Antonio arrived at the house in exactly ten minutes as he promised Tyana. She grabbed a robe to throw on, at the same time, thinking how awkward that seemed since she never wore a robe in Antonio's presence before. She let him in.

"Hi, Babe."

"Hi. Come on in."

They moved to the family room. He looked around wanting so badly to return to their comfortable contemporary home. He sat down next to her on the sofa.

"So...I'm listening," she said.

"Tatyana, I'm willing to think about what you want—a baby. I'm nervous and still have reservations for reasons that make sense to me, but I love you and I don't want to break your heart. I will think about it, if it means that much to you."

"It means everything to me. It's been a life-long dream of mine. When I was pregnant with my baby, I got a glimpse of what it was like to love someone unconditionally and what it felt like to become a mother. It was wonderful! And when I lost the baby, I lost a part of me. I've had that empty feeling ever since. It's something that I want; I want it Antonio. I really want it!" She unleashed some pent-up emotions and began sobbing. Antonio immediately comforted her.

"I know, I know. Don't cry. I want to understand and feel that with you, but it may take some time. Can I please have some time?"

She slowly nodded her head. Antonio, relieved to have gained even an inch with her, tested the waters and kissed her lips. It had only been a few weeks since their separation, but it felt like decades to him. He reacted to his closeness to her and pulled her completely into his body. She wrapped her arms around him, having missed his embrace. She felt at home with his touch on her. He kissed her with more hunger and intensity and she matched his intensity. Before another minute passed, they were once again connected physically becoming one in love and in spirit.

Antonio made love to Tyana in the couple's family room for twenty minutes before he picked her up, leaving their clothes behind, and carried her to their bedroom where they continued to make love over and over. They let all of their inhibitions go and fiercely released all of the pain and hurt and sadness they've shared, with each long exhilarating moan and cry as they clung tightly to one another. No space divided them for several more hours when they finally fell asleep in each other's arms. They slept in unison and never broke the seal that permanently bonded them together all night.

When morning arrived with a strong sun and searing temperatures, Antonio and Tyana sat cool, yet confused, at the breakfast table while drinking coffee and wondering where to go from there.

"That was beautiful last night. It was amazing and I don't think I've ever felt such passion like that before," Antonio confessed.

"I know what you mean." Tyana experienced the same phenomenal euphoria that didn't compare to any other, but wasn't sure yet that she should get too excited. "I didn't plan to sleep with you. I'm not ready to get back together yet until we're on the same page. I think as long as you need time to think about the idea of having a baby then we should wait—until you're ready. I don't want to get back into the same routine with you, that's all."

"I understand. I couldn't help myself. I missed you so much."

"I missed you, too. I think that was obvious last night." She smiled.

"Same for me."

"But thank you for at least wanting to think about it. I know that's a big step for you and I appreciate it."

"I better go. I need to go home, take a shower, and pack for the comp this afternoon. I'll see you there?"

"I'll be there by ten for hair and makeup. It's seven now, so I better jump in the shower and get moving."

She walked him to the door where he kissed her passionately. She couldn't resist and kissed him with equal passion. They both felt their bodies heating up again, and experienced a floating sensation. He touched her intimately and she touched him intimately.

"Tatyana, I need you."

"I need you, too."

He closed the door and took her right there against the wall in the foyer. She knew that she shouldn't and he knew that he couldn't help it, but they both grew weak to their familiar urges and wafting pheromones.

♥ ♥ ♥

The ballroom dance competition commenced in Phoenix at the Ritz-Carlton hotel on schedule and everything and everyone looked spectacular. The hotel resembled a jeweled wonderland—adorned in brilliant gem tones that sparkled in every room, corner, nook, and cranny. To keep up the appearance of a cohesive relationship, Tyana and Antonio, who arrived separately, met up almost immediately and checked on some of the students together. As studio owners, their responsibilities never ended, which came with the territory. The festivities seemed to unfold without a hitch or glitch, so far.

They shared a room at the hotel. They attempted to change their reservations once they began to live apart, but the hotel was booked solid. They decided to make do. Tyana left first to change into her exquisite custom designer ball gown in preparation for the Smooth dance numbers. Antonio caught a quick glimpse of her in passing as she headed toward the grand ballroom, and couldn't resist a longing stare at the glamorous woman whom he remained very much enamored with and who he, only a few hours ago, made love to as if his future depended on it.

She looked like a princess. Donned in full costume and accentuated make-up, with her hair swept up in a French roll, she looked like a glamorous movie star, as she sparkled from head to toe. And, she couldn't ignore how strikingly handsome he looked when he returned to the ballroom strutting by in the new black designer tuxedo that she gave him for his birthday. Together, they still managed to remain the focus of attention and the envy of most who christened the dance floor. No one could deny it. If they did, they were perhaps jealous.

Antonio watched Tyana warm up with several of her male students and marveled at her talent. In all of his years in the business, he had known no one who had progressed to the level she did in such a short period of time; and who had matured professionally in the business—to know all that there is to know in a partnership role. But most of all, he had never known anyone who loved him with the heart and soul that Tyana did. She displayed so much eloquence on the job, whether in teaching, performing, or simply interacting with the staff and clients. She never made him or the business look bad.

Birdie Pennington hunted Antonio down like game and abruptly dismantled his private thoughts. She, as always, intended to monopolize his time during most of the day. As it turned out, his students struggled and competed all afternoon for his time and sole attention, which left him no free time to catch up with Tyana or spend time with her, except when they performed their pro dance numbers. Only then did he attempt to communicate with her through the dancing, but she didn't have the same mental connection with him as she usually did. Instead, she had the image of Antonio's last performance with Birdie on her mind during a novelty dance number when Birdie made an inappropriate and unrehearsed move on Antonio during their dance— obviously deviating slightly from the routine they had practiced. It shocked everyone who witnessed it, including Tyana; but especially Antonio. He had to maintain complete composure and continue the highly romanticized routine. Dottie stormed out of the ballroom and didn't watch him dance with any other student. She felt trumped by Birdie. His concentration became compromised from sheer shock of the gesture, leaving him in a vulnerable position. He made it through without missing a beat; however, the damage was done. All that he could focus on were Tyana's eyes, wide with astonishment and above all, fury! Madeline looked on with heightened curiosity. She stood ready to dance with him next.

Birdie's plan worked for her. She clearly wanted to send her message to the audience—meaning her fellow students—that she had no boundaries with Antonio. Antonio, to say the least, hid his embarrassment while trying to comprehend Birdie's provocative advance toward him in public of all places. Talk of the incident became quickly fueled by gossip churning among the other students and guests that there might be more going on between the two. Birdie had a reputation of being exceptionally flirtatious and clingy with Antonio, in which he never did anything about to discourage her. Some wondered for years if there might be something more to her relationship with Antonio than just his dance student. And, his demeanor never confirmed nor denied the gossip. He remained unfazed by it, which gave some the impression that he approved of it. Tyana had asked him previously on several occasions to address her imprudent behavior with him, but he didn't see the harm in it because he knew it didn't mean anything to him. He construed Tyana's requests to tame Birdie, Dottie, and several others who publically and inappropriately acted enamored with him, as her being insecure or even jealous of the women and ignored her requests. Birdie, and a few others, had poured hundreds and thousands of dollars into his business, so he figured a little flirtation wouldn't hurt anything. He didn't want to rock the boat in a tough economy. His decision to ignore those situations certainly came back to bite him on that day. And, by Tyana's body language, he could tell that she planned to hold him responsible for what happened between Birdie and him for a long time.

When Antonio and Tyana finished their own routine that evening and gracefully strutted off of the floor arm-in-arm, once out of the sight of spectators, she snatched her arm free from Antonio's grip and walked briskly away from him.

"Tatyana, wait up!"

She kept walking in a hurried fashion without looking back or slowing her pace. She didn't want to draw attention to herself and risk confronting him in public, as all eyes surely would be fixed on her for the rest of the competition. So, she ignored him and kept walking until she reached the elevator—making a beeline to their suite to change. All of the performances for the day had ended and the Latin heats were scheduled for the next morning. Antonio followed her straight into the suite.

"Don't follow me, Antonio! I know what you're doing and we don't have anything to discuss. Not now and especially not here." She closed the bathroom door, shutting him out.

He had no choice but to wait and to talk with her later. He returned downstairs to his eagerly awaiting students. Tyana sat down to catch her breath. She wondered how she managed to dance flawlessly through the routine with her nerves so frayed. It was only because she was a professional that she felt she had to pull it off. For years she observed the flirting, the suggestive gestures, the personal gifts, the body hugs, displays of affections—including kisses—numerous cards, letters, and the endless compliments directed toward her fiancé and the rude comments directed toward her—all things that would make anyone in her position extremely bothered and frustrated. And with Birdie it was all of those things including the late night lessons and phone calls, and then learning about her advances toward him in Hawaii during a paid trip. She didn't know what to think anymore. But before tonight, Tyana trusted Antonio explicitly that none of it would get out of hand. She now no longer felt grounded and in control. She wanted to lash out at *everyone*! She felt suffocated. That was the last straw. She was publicly humiliated and was made a spectacle of, as if she meant absolutely nothing. She stayed in the suite as long as she could to decompress, but eventually she returned for the post dance festivities.

Tyana and Antonio put on their game face throughout the rest of the evening and played the perfect host and hostess to their students during dinner—never revealing their tense situation. Tyana remained professional and disguised her emotions. She didn't want to ruin the event for her well-behaved students, nor did she want to give anyone more to gossip about. The weekend was about giving the students what they paid for, although she thought Antonio gave much more to Birdie.

During the open dancing and open bar hour, the dance floor became the stage for everyone attending the spectacular event to show off their dancing skills. The DJ played many favorite hits from oldies but goodies to Pop, Salsa, Country, and R&B. The joint was definitely jumping. Many of the single women, including most of the students of Antonio's studio were looking for some dance time with him. He and several of the other popular instructors—both men and women—were in high demand. There would be no rest for the weary. Antonio obliged and danced with as many students as he could, but all the while he kept looking for Tyana. When his favorite Whitney Houston song came on, "*I Wanna Dance With Somebody*," he wanted to dance and feel the heat with only one person. He caught her eye from across the room and she caught his, but before he could get to her, someone grabbed him and stole the dance. Tyana smiled and left the party.

Before the evening ended and before all of the teachers, judges, and students returned to their rooms, Tyana left the fun in progress and returned to her room to be alone. She poured out her soul in the privacy of her bathroom while she took a long, hot shower and sobbed as the water cascaded down her face, washing her pain all the way down the drain—a ritual she had done many times. She purged her craving for Antonio's complete attention, her resentment to his lack of devotion to their relationship, her lost hope of getting married to him and having a baby that they both wanted, and all of her frustrations in general for the way things were turning out between them. When she couldn't cry any more tears, she lay in her bed with nothing but silence around her and fell asleep. She would have many dreams that night; and one nightmare.

Antonio joined her some time later, but he didn't disturb her when he slipped into bed next to her. He let her sleep, knowing what she had gone through that night alone because of him. He watched her sleep for only a few minutes before he, himself, succumbed to exhaustion.

Chapter
Thirteen

During his second night in Madrid, Ellis tossed and turned after spending most of the day trying to figure out how to announce that he has filed for custody of the girls. The divorce papers should be delivered to Charlotte at any moment. He struggled with either telling Charlotte before she received the news along with the divorce documents or let the papers speak for themselves and for him. He adamantly didn't want the girls left in her care while he traveled and conducted business in Madrid, in fear of what she would do in retaliation. He thought it best that they should be with him, then and permanently. He couldn't sleep a wink, knowing she would call at any time to start the battle.

♥♥♥

Day two of the competition continued as scheduled and the grand ballroom was filled to capacity with dancers wearing some of the hottest Latin dance costumes in the business to dance International Latin Style dances. A sea of sexiness could be seen as far as the eyes could visually extend in the crowded ballroom. Tyana and Jonathan, one of the studio's long-time coaches who visited often, warmed up earlier that morning to perform steamy Samba and Rumba routines. Scheduled to go on soon, Jonathan set out to look for Tyana so they could quickly run through the routines one last time. He found her sitting alone outside of the ballroom.

"Hey Love, what are you doing out here all by yourself when all the action is going on inside?"

"Oh, hey…Jonathan. I was just catching a quick break before our performance."

"Here, come-come Love; let's run through the number real quick. I know you know what you're doing, so…for my benefit."

"Yeah, right. You choreographed the number."

"That I did! And, it'll be the best damn choreographed Samba out there! Let's do it!"

They casually danced through the routine one time and Jonathan was satisfied with the results.

"Your hip action is fan*tastic*! You've been holding out on me, girl."

Tyana only smiled.

"What's wrong? Whatever it is, Love, park it between the girls until after we've danced. We're going to take this bitch, you got that? We're up against your hunky man and that trick from the Chandler studio. No contest," he laughed.

"Jonathan!"

"Well… I'm just sayin…"

"Let's go," she laughed as they re-entered the ballroom hand-in-hand.

Tyana and Jonathan stood next to Antonio and his partner, along with two other couples waiting to enter the dance floor. Antonio kept his eyes on Tyana the whole time until the music started. She tried very hard not to look at him, but she slipped him a glance right before strutting onto the dance floor with Jonathan leading the way.

The couple burst onto the floor and went right into their rapid footwork of the quarter-beat Samba dance and immediately into their Samba bounce action, followed by a Samba Strut, incorporating some Voltas and Samba Side Steps. The beat was fast, lively, and rhythmical and Tyana beamed with every precise turn led by her partner. Her beautiful and shapely legs were accentuated when they demonstrated the perfect Samba Roll, as they glided around the dance floor. Her movements made her skimpy, hot pink costume, consisting mostly of layers of shimmery fringe, sparkle and dance from her explosive hip action—almost too mesmerizing to watch. The spectators burst into applause, showing their support for the couple dancing a very sexy Samba routine. All Tyana could think about was the routine Antonio and Birdie performed the day before. She came very close to pushing the boundaries with Jonathan. As if Jonathan could read her mind, he raised an eyebrow as if to say he would follow her lead.

The professionals danced a fun, yet difficult dance, and still challenged their skills with complex choreography. The judges would be faced with an arduous task of judging the Samba heat. The criteria would be based on several different points, such as Line, Hold, Poise, Posture, Timing, Presentation, and Togetherness. All of the couples would score high in Presentation because they were each well trained in selling themselves to the audience and judges. They all understood how important it was for their presentation to shine on the dance floor. They would also be judged on their technique and musicality. And, at that moment, Tyana and Jonathan were scoring a close second to Antonio and his partner. When they performed together as partners, they typically blew the other contestants out of the water. But now they were matched against each other, making the heat a little more competitive and interesting. Each couple had to dance consistently strong because each judge would only catch a brief moment of their routine, making the scoring challenging. One incorrect position or breaking a hold at the wrong time would cost points. Jonathan and Tyana appeared very symmetrical and convincingly connected throughout the dance. They demonstrated total chemistry on the dance floor. Jonathan had been a coach and instructor of Latin and Ballroom dancing for twelve years. Tyana carried an advantage being paired with Jonathan as opposed to any other instructor in the competition, other than Antonio, and that edge was beginning to become quite clear to everyone, including the judges.

When the couples exited the floor, Tyana and Antonio exchanged a glance, but Tyana's spark faded once she felt the carpet under her feet. She walked completely out of the room. Jonathan pursued.

"Hey, aren't you gonna watch the next heat so we can pick apart the teams?"

"Uh…I don't think so. I'm kinda tired."

"Tyana, I've never seen you tired during a competition. With all the adrenaline of dancing and the anticipation of waiting for someone to fall…" He noticed her face. "Hey, what's wrong? Talk to me, Love."

When she saw Jonathan staring back at her with genuine concern in his eyes, she began to come unglued.

"C'mon Love, let's go somewhere private." He grabbed her hand and led her to the elevator and up to his room before anyone saw her unravel. She followed while trying to keep the dam from breaking. Once inside the room, he invited her to sit down on the small sofa. "Okay, what's wrong? You can tell me; I'm not going to breathe a word to anyone, scouts honor, although I wasn't a scout, so I swear on your fringe." That made Tyana laugh.

"I don't want you to worry about me. I'm just tired, I guess."

"What's going on between you and Mr. Fabulous?"

"How do you know anything is going on between us?"

"Love, you two are usually beaming when you're in the same room together. You don't give away anything physically during comps, but it's all there in your eyes and anyone would have to be a blind fool not to notice — like those catty bitches who claw all over him. They should know he's not available to them."

"You know about his students?"

"Pa-lease! Who doesn't? They are fools and they look ridiculous! And, it's not just *his* students. There are more just like them from the other studios who only sign up for comp just to get a chance to flirt with him. They all want to be his dirty dance partner and rub all up on him. And what was Birdie Pennington thinking when she molested him out there on the floor? Jeeesus! I thought I've seen it all at comp. Well, we both know what she was thinking. But that was some ballsy move! And, for a minute there, I thought you were going to do something in retaliation. I wasn't sure what was going to happen out there, but I was ready for ya!"

Tyana looked down in shame. "I thought about it. It's just that..." She started to unravel again.

"Hey, I'm sorry. I should have realized how upsetting that must have been." He crinkled his face.

"No. It's not just that, although that was pretty much the straw that... Antonio and I...please don't say anything to anyone, please!"

"I took the oath of fringe, didn't I? I promise." He paused for about three seconds and then guessed the obvious. "You broke up."

"Yep, pretty much."

"But I thought you two were getting married—someday."

"Right. Me, too. It's not that he doesn't want to, he does; but I don't want to wait any longer. Plus, he's not sure he wants children and I do. And, he's not going to change when it comes to his students. He loves me, but he loves his business more because he thinks it's all he has. He's given one hundred percent of himself to his business which doesn't leave anything for me."

"I'm sorry. It's really hard in this business, I know. I've seen relationships and marriages end over business-related matters all the time. Antonio is an idiot for not giving you more if that's what you want. Who wouldn't want to spend eternity with you or have babies with you?"

"You."

"Oh I'd switch teams for you, Love, no doubt," he kidded.

"Thanks, I needed that," she laughed.

"Listen, if you need anything, I mean this, Love, if you need *anything*, just call me. I'll be there for you. And, you can trust me to not say anything, even to Antonio."

"Thank you."

"Now, we better get back down there or we'll be the next queen and queen of the rumor mill." They both laughed and stood up. Tyana gave Jonathan and big, lingering hug. He kissed the top of her head.

"You go on down," Tyana instructed as they walked out of Jonathan's room. "I'll meet you during the awards ceremony. I'm going to clear my things out of my room. I'll see you later."

"Okay. See you in a bit."

When Tyana returned to her suite to collect her things, she noticed a small gift box placed inside of her luggage, resting on top of her clothes. She picked it up and looked at it for a moment. It could only be from Antonio. She carefully opened it up and stared at the remarkable three-diamond studded pendant necklace. The facets from the diamonds, each one larger than the next, caught the sunlight pouring in from the window. She cupped her mouth and sat down on the edge of the bed and cried. She became overwhelmed by the gift and every eventful moment, both good and bad, of their relationship. Her emotions spun out of control. She couldn't take anymore. The pain and joy simply broke her down.

She carefully held the necklace and wondered if she could ever get her relationship with Antonio back on track. But the bigger question remained, could they progress their relationship to the point of marriage, and could he seriously want a baby? She felt that his asking for time to think about the baby issue was only a stall tactic and that he would never warm up to the idea. And in the meantime, he would only get older, which would only build on his case about his age. Then she thought again of Ellis' girls, and of those fifteen minutes locked in that laundry room with him.

She put the gift back in her bag, grabbed her things and ran out of the suite. She rode the elevator down to the lobby and rushed out of the hotel without looking back.

♥♥♥

Ellis expected Charlotte to call at any moment. When the phone rang, as if on cue, he took a deep breath and answered.

"Ellis Montgomery," he said, preparing for the wrath of Charlotte to rain down.

"Ellis?"

He sat up and turned on the light. He didn't quite make out the voice.

"Yes, this is Ellis? Who is this?"

"It's me, Tyana."

♥♥♥

Antonio searched for Tyana in the crowded ballroom before the awards ceremony began. He didn't see her anywhere. Jonathan looked for her, too. He wanted them to collect their first-place prize together when they announced the placements of the Latin heats. Antonio and Jonathan finally ran into each other and Jonathan told him that she commented about going to her suite to get her things. Antonio wanted to run up and check, but the ceremony had begun and he had to escort his students to claim their plaques and trophies. One by one, he escorted each student to the trophy table, while scanning the room for her. When he didn't see her, he asked Jill to escort Tyana's students when their names were called. She never surfaced throughout the entire ceremony. When it was over, Antonio rushed up to the suite to look for her. He looked all around, but she had clearly left and took her things. Everything was gone, except something caught his eye. He bent down and picked up the sparkling shoe sticking out halfway from under the bed. He held it carefully in his hands as his heart sank.

♥♥♥

"Tyana?"

"Is this a bad time?"

"Uh, no. No, it's not. I mean, it's in the middle of the night in Madrid, but I'm up anyway. What's going on?"

"You're in Madrid? Oh, I'm sorry to..."

"It's okay, it's okay! I'm here alone on business at the hotel; you know, the property downtown; we stayed here once."

"Yes, I remember. Did I wake you?"

"No, I'm still up. Are you okay? You sound like you're crying or upset."

"I shouldn't have called. I better let you go."

"No! Don't hang up! Please. What's going on?" Ellis knew something must be wrong for her to initiate a call to him. The last time they spoke, she made it clear that she didn't have a reason to get in touch with him or want him to get in touch with her again.

"I...I, um, it's an impulse call, I guess. I wanted to say..."

"Tyana, what is it?"

"Daddy! Daaaddy...Daddy! Daaaddy..."

"Hold on. Don't hang up!" He put the phone down and ran into the girls' room.

"What is it?"

"I'm cold and can't sleep," cried Hannah.

Ellis turned on the light. When he got to Hannah, he noticed that she appeared flushed. He touched her forehead. She felt warm and her skin looked pale and felt clammy.

"Shoot! You've got a fever. Do you feel okay? What about your throat?" he asked.

"It hurts," she replied.

"Okay, come with me." He picked her up and carried her to his room. Hailee was still asleep, but he knew not for long.

When he got back to his room he put Hannah on the bed and grabbed his phone.

"Tyana?" He didn't hear anyone on the other end. "Tyana?"

"Yes," she replied.

"Oh, good, you're there. I thought you hung up. Listen, I have bit of an emergency here. Hannah's sick."

"I thought you said you were there alone."

"I meant I'm here with just the girls. Please let me call you later. I really want to talk to you."

"I probably shouldn't be bothering you out there. Sounds like you're pretty busy."

"When should I call?"

"You don't have to bother."

"Are you sure you're okay?"

Tyana thought of everything that had happened between her and Antonio in the last two weeks and especially the last twenty-four hours.

"It's nothing really."

"I'll call you when I get a chance, I promise!" Ellis turned his back to Hannah and whispered into the phone, "Tyana, thanks for calling. I love you." He hung up.

Chapter

Fourteen

Ellis and Annamarie had their hands full with two very sick little girls in a foreign country, leaving Ellis fighting to stay awake during his meetings. When he returned to the hotel suite that evening, the girls were cranky and clingy. Ellis spent as much time as he could with them, but he tried to get them to rest while he attempted to get caught up on his work. Annamarie spent most of her time in the suite with Ellis and the girls, giving him very little privacy to call Tyana.

"Hannah, did you eat all your soup and take all your medicine?"

"Yeah, Daddy," whined Hannah.

"What about you, Hailee?"

"Uh-huh..." replied Hailee. Both girls could barely speak. Their throats still hurt and their eyes were watery. They developed a persistent cough as well.

"Mr. Montgomery, the doctor gave them Tylenol for their fever and body aches. They did nap on and off most of the day and have been taking the cough suppressant for their cough. Would you like me give Mrs. Montgomery an update on the girls?"

"No, I'll call her later. Thanks Annamarie. Just make sure they eat before you put them down and that they have taken their final dose of medicine for the evening. I want to make sure they sleep all the way through the night. They've been getting up so much and they're miserable."

"Yes, Sir."

"I love you my little ones. I want you to feel better." Ellis hugged and kissed his daughters as he tucked them in.

"I love you, too, Daddy," said Hailee. She still looked noticeably pale.

"Me, too," answered Hannah in a weakened and raspy voice. Seconds later, they both vomited.

♥♥♥

Antonio called Tyana later that evening to check on her. He assumed she had gotten the gift.

"Tatyana, can we talk?"

"Antonio, I'm sorry I left before the awards ceremony, but..."

"It's fine. Don't worry; your students were in good hands. What happened? Are you all right? By the way, you kicked my ass in the Samba heat. Congratulations! You guys took first with both the Samba and Rumba."

"All the thanks goes to Jonathan; he did an amazing job at choreographing both routines."

"Yes, but he couldn't pull it off without your talent. I had a hard time concentrating for watching you. So, what's wrong? Never mind, I think I know and I'm so, so sorry. I'm sorry about everything."

"I know you are. I saw that beautiful diamond pendant necklace you left in my luggage. It's gorgeous, but I can't keep it."

"You will keep it. It's from Gloria's collection. She said it means past, present, and future. I hope we can fix our present so we'll have a future."

"I don't know what to say. What happened this weekend took all that I had left in me. It may not have been your fault directly, but indirectly, you are responsible for what happened. She and all the others think they own you to a point where they'll continue to commit these indiscretions and invariably cross the line to get what they want, because you allow it, and it hurts me in the process. And, you made it clear to me that I cannot suggest to you how you should handle your students. It's too much, it's gone too far, and I'm too through."

"With me?"

"With us; with me being your fiancée."

"Tatyana, please don't say that. I can fix it."

"It's impossible. It's who you are; it's who they are. If you're not doing what you want to do and how you want to do it, you'll end up resenting me."

"No, I won't! I can't live without you."

"Yes, you can. We didn't have that much of a life together anyway. You'll never even miss that I'm gone from your life."

"Not true. I *will* miss you. I *need* you."

"But so many need you. I may be able to compete and win on the dance floor, but I can't compete for you, and win. And, I shouldn't have to in the first place."

"You *have* me; you don't have to compete for me."

"I don't have you, though. I thought I did, but I really don't. I'll come in tomorrow as planned, but I'm going to take it day-by-day until I can figure out what my next step will be. We can talk to the lawyers about the partnership. I may want to teach somewhere else, or I might go back into interior design. Who knows."

"You can't just leave! And you *can't* give up dancing!"

"I'm through and I'm tired. Good night, Antonio."

"Tatyana!"

She had hung up.

♥ ♥ ♥

The next day, the dance studio was eerily quiet and empty. Most had taken the day off to recover from the hectic weekend. Antonio, as always, was the first in. Tyana showed up around eleven and went straight to her office.

♥♥♥

The twins remained sick all through that night and into the next day. Ellis and Annamarie worked tirelessly tending to the ill toddlers and trying to get them healthy again. When Ellis returned to the suite after a long, exhaustive day, he checked on the girls first and found them quiet and asleep, and then retreated to his room to catch a nap. It wasn't until then that he wondered why he hadn't heard from Charlotte during all of this time. He had gotten confirmation two days ago that she had been served the divorce papers and notified of his intentions to file for custody of the girls. Her silence baffled him, although he'd had virtually no time to think about Charlotte or anything else, between work and his daughters' illnesses. But he knew he had to face the music and face Charlotte sooner or later. He also needed to let her know that the girls were sick. Annamarie would get suspicious if he didn't call her soon.

Annamarie had gone into the girls' room one last time to take their temperatures while Ellis rested. He lay staring up at the ceiling for a long while before picking up his phone. He started dialing and quickly peeked out of the bedroom door to see if Annamarie was still in the suite. The coast was clear.

"Hello," answered Tyana

"It's me. Did I catch you at a bad time?"

"Uh...no."

"I'm sorry it's taken me a while to get back in touch with you." Ellis' voice carried quite a bit of stress and exhaustion. "Can you talk?"

"Uh...I have a few moments right now." Tyana stood up to shut the door to her office.

"It's been a little hectic. I'm working here for a few weeks. I have the twins with me, but unfortunately, they came down with a bad cold or the flu, so I've been up every night with sick ones."

"You're dealing with them by yourself?"

"No, their nanny is here with me. She's with them during the day and now most of the night, too, keeping an eye on them. She's been a big help, but of course, I can't leave everything up to her because the girls need me. I feel so bad for them." He paused for a few seconds. "Tyana, I filed for divorce. I meant it. Charlotte and I were never in love. We stayed together because of the pregnancy and I didn't want to abandon my responsibility — like now. I don't want to abandon those girls. She's not really a good mother to them. I have to see to it that they get the proper and best parental guidance and upbringing possible. They didn't ask to be brought into this world, so it's my responsibility to see that they're well taken care of. I've filed for custody." He took another pause before continuing. Tyana kept quiet and listened. "I have never stopped loving you and I still love you, but I know it's probably too late for me. I wanted you to know that I would have divorced Charlotte with or without still loving you. Again, I was a fool for hurting you the way I did, and all I want at this point is your forgiveness. I totally understand that you have moved on. It's my own fault that I lost you and lost my chance with you. And for that I'm sorry."

"Ellis, I..."

He heard a noise. "Look, I better go. I love you, Tyana. I mean it. Good bye."

"Good bye." Tyana hung up with the most peculiar feeling in her gut.

When Annamarie finished taking the girls' temperature, she started to leave, but stopped when she heard Ellis talking in his bedroom. She assumed he was talking to Mrs. Montgomery and wanted to tell the couple that the girls' temperatures were coming down. She began to enter, but stopped when she heard him address the caller by the name, "Tyana." She remained close to the door and eavesdropped. When Ellis ended the call, Annamarie tiptoed out of the suite.

Ellis thought about his conversation with Tyana for a few moments, and then got up to check in on the girls. They were sound asleep and Annamarie was gone. He felt relieved, so he returned to his room and picked up the phone again.

"Hello."

"Charlotte, it's me."

"Well, I see you finally decided to check in. What, no more surprise lawsuits expected to show up for delivery, or are you going to confiscate my jewelry or property like you did my children? You will not get away with this, by the way!"

"Charlotte..."

"Don't Charlotte me! You will pay, you son-of-a-bitch!"

"The girls are sick by the way, but I want you to know that Annamarie and I are taking good care of them. A doctor has tended to them and it's just a touch of the flu—probably something they picked up from the flight. They're on antibiotics and they're resting."

"Let me talk to them!"

"Charlotte, they're sleeping! I just told you they're sick—not feeling well. They can't be disturbed. I can have them call you in the morning."

"Those are my children and you won't get them, Ellis, nor will you get this divorce without a fight, if at all!"

"Why are you being unreasonable, again?"

"Oh, you think this is unreasonable? I didn't get married to get divorced!"

"But what do we have?"

"When you get my daughters back home, you and I will discuss our future plans regarding our home *and* the office!"

Charlotte abruptly ended the call. She then clicked back over to her other call on hold.

"Okay, where were we? Are you sure Mr. Montgomery was talking to Tyana? And, tell me again what you heard him say to her—exactly!"

"Yes, Mrs. Montgomery, he said, Tyana, and he told her about asking you for a divorce. I'm really sorry..."

"Yeah, yeah, what else?" snapped Charlotte.

"He told her he loved her. I'm really sorry."

"Oh, he doesn't know what he's talking about. You just keep your ears opened and report back to me everything you hear or else you'll find yourself on your way back to Peru! Like I told you, I will make it worth your efforts with a big fat bonus if you come through with what I want. You got that? Why do you think I allowed you to go to Spain with my husband?"

"Sí, I mean, yes, ma'am."

"Good. Now, stop being embarrassed and figure out a way to get more information on Mr. Montgomery and Tyana before you get back here! I'll call you in the morning to talk to my children. And the next time they get sick, I expect to hear about it immediately!"

"Yes, ma'am."

Charlotte abruptly ended her conversation with Annamarie.

♥♥♥

When Tyana and Ellis ended their brief phone conversation, Tyana made another call.

"Hello."

"Hi Kellie, it's me. Is this a bad time?"

"Uh…no. I've been meaning to call you. How've you been? Oh yeah, how was the competition?"

"It was fine, yes, fine. Antonio and I are breaking up."

"What? No! Tyana!"

"I know, I know. I feel it's for the best—for both of us."

"Right. I'm sorry. How are you doing?"

"I'm still numb, scared, confused, hurt, among other things."

"I'm sure you are. What are you going to do?"

"I don't know yet. I'm thinking about maybe teaching somewhere else or going back to interior design — like you said."

"But I didn't..."

"It's fine, Kellie. You were right; Antonio comes with too much baggage and our love for each other cannot offset it. I'm defenseless. All I wanted was to get married and have a baby."

Kellie didn't respond. Tyana wiped away a tear.

"Kellie?"

"Huh?"

"Are you okay?"

"Yeah. Yes. Are you going to be okay? Is there anything I can do for you?"

"What's the matter? What's going on with you? There's something you're not saying, I can sense it."

"It's nothing. Can I call you later?"

"Kellie, please talk to me. Is everything okay? I've shared with you so much and I feel guilty for putting so much on you about me. Please let me be here for you. You've done so much for me. Just tell me."

"I can't think of a worse time to tell you this."

"What?" Tyana got a bad feeling.

"I'm pregnant."

"You're *what*?"

"I'm so sorry. I didn't do it on purpose. It wasn't planned and I thought it was a mistake, but it's not. I'm pregnant."

Tyana paused for a long moment. More tears and emotions engulfed her. She couldn't speak.

"Tyana, say something. Please. I'm sorry."

"Congratulations."

"Tyana..."

"I have to go. There's some place I need to be right now." Tyana hung up and sat completely still for nearly five minutes while organizing her thoughts. Her oppressive thoughts were interrupted when Antonio entered without warning.

"Antonio, I'm on my way out," she stated coldly, barely making eye contact with him. He stepped in and shut the door.

"Just give me a minute!" he snapped.

"I don't want to get into this here."

"You don't leave me much choice, Tatyana. I can't get through to you over the phone. I want to talk to you. I want you to give us another chance."

"Really? Why, so I can be humiliated again by who, let's see...Dottie with her squawking to the whole studio that you're her man and I'm the pathetic puppy who follows you around? Or by Birdie and all the liberties she's allowed to take with you — publicly!"

"Why are we still talking about that?"

"Because it's still an issue!"

"But I explained..."

"Explained what? Explained the new syllabus that you're teaching Birdie and probably others?"

"You know that's not true! That was an isolated incident and I apologized to you for what happened. She was out of line. It won't happen again, I promise."

"But you can't make a promise like that because you have no more control over *them* than I have over when I can start a family with you."

They both stopped talking and just stared at one another.

"If that's all you have to say to me, then excuse me." She brushed passed him and rushed out. He chased after her.

"Tatyana, wait! No, that's not all!" he shouted, but she was gone. He reluctantly gave up and let her go.

Tyana got into her car and slammed the door shut. She suddenly felt dizzy and light-headed. For the first time since being a partner at the dance studio and being engaged to Antonio, she began to have doubts about her decision to do both. It took her back to when she and Ellis were together and she lost him to Charlotte. She thought of her thriving business that she gave up for a new life with the man who rescued her and made it easy to fall in love with him. Did she do the right thing by giving up so much of what was once her? Did she do it for her or for Antonio first? She wondered. And, would Antonio ever make her first in his life? Ellis didn't. His business got in the way. Then Charlotte got in their way. Will she always play second fiddle? Ellis was now willing to make her first. But did he really mean it? Then suddenly all that she could hear in her head were Kellie's words, "I'm pregnant." Both of her closest friends were about to become parents, and Kellie wasn't even trying. The fogginess in her head subsided and she drove away.

Tyana drove straight to the hospital to see Cleo and to provide support to her friends. After visiting with Cleo for an hour, talking mostly about babies and the pregnancy, Trevor walked her down to the lobby.

"Thank you for coming by, it really meant a lot to my wife. She's strong and tough, but I know this situation is worrying her."

"Sure, no problem. I wanted to help her get her mind off of the seriousness for awhile, so she can relax and look forward to the new baby."

"What's going on with you?"

"What do you mean?"

"I know you seemed all happy-go-lucky in there, but I can see that you're sad. It's in your eyes. I take it that you and Antonio haven't made up yet."

"Trev, I'm thinking about quitting the studio and partnership altogether."

"What? Are you sure? Maybe you should let things cool down some before making that kind of decision. It's big!"

"So were our wedding plans and our future, but I don't think that's going to happen. How can I stay around him after all that has taken place? I can't find the reason anymore. By the way, how much longer before Cleo can go home?"

"Probably in about two or three weeks, depending on her progress."

"Take good care of her and that baby she's carrying. Don't let anything happen to either of them."

"I will and I won't."

"Kellie's pregnant."

"What?"

"And she and Paul didn't want children either. It's like everyone is having a baby except me."

"You will. I know you will. You have plenty of time. Everything seems hopeless right now, but you'll see, in no time you'll be having a family of your own. I know you Tyana. It'll happen for you."

"Thanks. I hope you're right." She paused. "Trevor, I'm leaving town for a while."

"When, and where?"

"Soon. I'm going to visit my parents back home in Seattle. I don't know how long I'll be gone. I don't want anyone to really know. I need some time to be alone to figure things out."

"I understand, and thanks for telling me. But keep in touch and let me know if there's anything you need from me. I know you're going through a lot, but don't forget that I'm here for you."

"You're a good friend; you and Kellie both. I will let you know if I need anything. But for a little while, I just need to be alone to think. I'll be fine, so please don't worry if you don't hear from me. I'll get in touch once I get some rest and perspective."

"Okay...but be careful and don't make any rash decisions."

"I'll be fine. Give Cleo my love and I'll keep praying for her and the baby."

"Thanks. I'll see you soon."

"I'll see you soon."

Tyana left the hospital and went straight home to pack.

♥♥♥

Ellis forged ahead with his tough work schedule of round-the-clock meetings, conferences, and teleconferences with his office back in San Diego, managing his staff there, as well as his Madrid staff, coupled with his relentless routine in the mornings and evenings, caring for his daughters. Every time he thought he wanted to call Tyana, something would come up to distract him and the moment would be lost.

Finally, after a long, exhausting day, and after Ellis and Annamarie got the girls fed, bathed, and down to sleep, he retreated to his room for some much-needed peace and quiet. Before he turned out the lights, he placed a call to Tyana. Annamarie listened at the door.

"Hi, Tyana, it's me, Ellis. I just called hoping to reach you. It's still a little crazy here in Madrid. I wish I had more opportunities to call you... But anyway, um, give me a call back, please. I really want to talk to you. In case you can't reach me on my cell, I'm staying at the...oh, you know where I'm staying. Feel free to call my suite—any time, or my cell! Uh...I'll be here for another week. Anyway, call me. Please. I love you. I think about you all the time. Call me." Ellis hung up. He felt ridiculous for rambling, but for some reason he got nervous.

Annamarie quietly left the suite and reported back to Mrs. Montgomery what she had overheard, per her explicit instructions. She knew it was wrong to betray Mr. Montgomery, but she was more afraid of Mrs. Montgomery.

♥♥♥

Shortly after mindlessly packing her luggage, Tyana had gone to bed early that night. But before she turned out the lights, she grabbed her phone to charge it and noticed a missed call from Ellis. She listened to the message, smiled, and drifted off to sleep.

The next morning, Tyana listened to Ellis' message again on her way to the airport. She started to dial, but then had second thoughts due to the time in Madrid and put it back.

♥♥♥

Charlotte paced her bedroom floor, plotting her next move against her husband's plan to divorce her. She sat down at her desk, scrutinizing the divorce papers spread out on top in plain sight where she left them. She particularly stared at the section that requested full custody of their two daughters. Without Ellis, Hailee, and Hannah, she felt she would be left with nothing. That would be the furthest thing from the truth, but Charlotte counted on having it all! She wouldn't let him dictate her lifestyle. She would file a counter lawsuit and fight to keep her children, although deep down she knew she had no maternal instincts to raise the girls without Ellis' help. It didn't matter; she would fight for them anyway, just to win and to keep control of Ellis' money, and of Ellis. She continued to struggle with the whole Tyana issue. If it weren't for her, Ellis wouldn't be acting crazy and asking for a divorce. She didn't want to lose her husband and her children to Tyana, she felt adamant about that.

Charlotte stood up, stormed into the bathroom and almost let her emotions get the best of her, but stopped herself before the first tear threatened to drop. Her pride would never let her cry over a man. Instead, she slowly returned and walked into her closet. She approached the row of mahogany wood drawers in the back and opened the top drawer. Inside of the drawer in the very back, lay a single key nestled in a tiny velvet jewelry box. When she opened it and stared at it, her heart began pounding hard against her chest.

Chapter

The twins were still battling their flu-like symptoms, requiring a lot of personalized attention, leaving Ellis and Annamarie exhausted by the end of each evening. So far, they haven't been able to leave the suite since the first weekend upon arriving in Madrid. Ellis felt sorry for the girls because they looked and felt miserable and he could do very little to make them feel any better except hold and cuddle them. They missed their mother and being in their own beds, too. Annamarie packed most of their favorite toys and stuffed animals, but those things couldn't replace their mother. That evening was no different. The girls were still restless and cranky.

"Daddy, I don't feel very good," whined Hailee, "and my throat still hurts."

"Hmm?" Ellis turned over in the direction of his daughter's voice. "Hailee? Is that you?" He opened his eyes to see his daughter standing before him.

"Yes, Daddy. I can't sleep. I'm still sick and I'm thirsty."

"All right."

Ellis turned on the light before getting up. He slowly rolled out of bed, picked up his daughter and carried her into the kitchen to get her something to drink.

He looked at the clock and noticed it was nearly five in the morning.

"Honey, how are you feeling? Do you think you're getting better or worse?"

"I *said*...everything hurts sometimes. I want to go home."

"I know, Baby Girl. I didn't know you were going to get sick. I thought we were going to have lots of fun doing some fun things. I'm sad because you and Hannah got sick. Here drink this."

"I miss Momma. Can I please talk to her?" She took a drink of the juice while still looking at her father with pathetic eyes. "I can't taste it. It's nasty!"

"If you can't taste it then how do you know it's nasty? Here give it to me." She handed the glass back.

"Can we call Momma?"

Ellis looked at the clock again and did some quick math in his head. "Sure, I guess so. Let's go get my phone." He picked her up and carried her back to the bedroom. "Just for a few minutes, okay? I want you to get back to sleep, so you can feel better soon." Ellis waited for the connection.

♥ ♥ ♥

Ever since Charlotte retrieved the silver key from her closet the day before, her mind has been fixated on only one thought. She examined it carefully for a long time. Her hand began to shake. It was quiet — real quiet. She could only hear herself breathing. In the next instant, her phone began blaring a familiar tone, which jarred her from her trance. It startled her and she dropped the key. She grabbed her phone that was lying next to her and turned it over. Upon seeing Ellis' name on her phone, she took a deep breath and then slowly raised the phone to her ear.

"Hello." Her voice quivered in anticipation of hearing Ellis' voice on the other end.

"Hi, Momma, it's me, Hailee. I miss you Momma."

"Oh... Hi, Baby Girl! How are you feeling? You still sound sick like your nose is all stuffy. What are you doing up?"

"I was thirsty and I couldn't sleep. Daddy said I could talk to you because I missed you."

"Oh, I miss you, too, Hailee. I can't wait to see you. Is Daddy taking good care of you and Hannah?"

"Yeah, but we can't feel better yet—maybe in a few days. Then we can go to the zoo and other places. Momma, I'm getting sleepy."

"Okay, Baby Girl, let me talk to Daddy. I love you. Get well."

"Okay. Bye Momma." Hailee handed the phone over to her daddy.

"Hey," answered Ellis, as Hailee laid her head down on his lap.

"Ellis, you should consider cutting this trip short and bringing the girls home immediately. I don't want them so far from home when they're that sick. You can't possibly give them the care that they need. They need to come home where they belong and so they can sleep in their own beds and not in some hotel so far away from home. I don't trust the doctors there. They need to see their own pediatrician here!"

"I can't leave. Annamarie is doing a great job with them under the circumstances. They've been resting and taking their meds; they're starting to feel better. I have too much going on here to pull out now. I can't postpone these meetings and presentations for the next trip—that's too far away. You, of all people know that! Plus, we've got full participation at this conference—a first! Then there's some reception going on this weekend. I was hoping to get out of it, but my hands may be tied on this one."

"Well, figure it out and get them back here!"

"Charlotte, I just told you I can't!" He lowered his voice so not to disturb Hailee. "It's impossible for me to rearrange my schedule now that I'm here. I'll just have to make do with the situation. Why are you being so unreasonable?"

"I guess this is what you get for trying leave me *and* steal my children away from me!"

"Charlotte…"

"Look, I'm sorry, I just miss the girls and I hate that they're sick. I better go. Please make sure they get everything they need and tell Hannah I love her." Charlotte ended the call.

Ellis stared at the phone with a puzzled look on his face. He had never known Charlotte to surrender without fighting to the end, or at least not without giving him a much harder time. He looked down at Hailee who had fallen asleep on his lap. He scooped her up and carried her back to bed. When he returned, he couldn't go back to sleep, but instead, replayed Charlotte's brief conversation over in his head. Something didn't sound quite right in her voice and, in particular, her tone at the end of the conversation. To him, she didn't seem herself and he didn't know why the change in her disposition, but he quickly put it out of his mind. Then he changed the channel in his mind to Tyana. He hadn't heard back from her yet and wondered if he would. He still felt tired, so he laid back down for a short nap.

♥♥♥

Ellis awoke a few hours later to a chaotic morning as he attempted to soothe Hannah's tearful whines when she begged for her daddy to stay with her instead of going to work. He had a difficult time getting dressed for work, while she tugged on his leg. Her illness made her delirious and definitely out of sorts.

"Hannah, I'm sorry, but I have to go to work. I know you don't feel well and I wish I could stay here with you, but I can't today. Please cooperate with me. Annamarie will take care of you and Hailee until I can get back." He turned the television on for her.

"But Daddy, I don't want you to go. I'm sick and I want to go home. I want Momma! I don't want to stay here anymore. I want to sleep in my bed."

"I know, Hannah. I wish I could take you home, but it's a long ways away and Daddy has a lot of work left to do.

But I promise, if I can, I'll come back very soon and take care of you both. I love you so much; you know that, right? Hannah…you know I love you."

Hannah finally nodded her head as she poked out her lower lip.

"What is it, Baby Doll?"

"Why didn't Momma come with us? Does Momma love us?"

"Of course she does. She had to work, that's all. Why did you ask if she loves you both? You know she does."

"Because…she works all the time and talks to work when she's home and won't play with us. She yells at us and says she's busy."

"But I work, too."

"You took us here with you so you won't be lonely. And you let us sleep in your bed when we want to sometimes. Momma doesn't like us to sleep in her bed. She said she needs quiet and we bother her. We give her headaches."

"I'm sure she doesn't mean it that way." Ellis realized what he just said.

He knew exactly what Charlotte did to the girls every time they wanted to get close to her or wanted to sleep in bed with her—she drove them away. He saw how her disciplinary actions hurt the girls and distanced her from them. Just then Hailee entered the room.

"Hi Daddy…" she said sleepily.

"Good morning, Baby Girl." Ellis kissed his daughter. He glanced at his watch.

"I'm hungry."

"I know. Room service will be here shortly, as will Annamarie. I have to go to work soon. Will you be okay today until I get back?"

"Oooh… when can we go outside?" asked Hailee still rubbing her eyes.

"When you're well. You're not quite over your illness and I don't want to take any chances of going out too soon. I know you're bored, but I want you to get completely well first."

"Daddy, do you love Momma?" asked Hannah, still quizzing her daddy about her mother's strange behavior. Hailee perked up.

Ellis looked at both of his daughters as they stared at him while waiting for an answer. He knew they were smart little girls with keen sensibilities. He thought long and hard, taking in a deep breath before answering.

"Come here you two. Sit up here." He helped them up on the sofa. "I love you so much. Your mother loves you, but I think you should know that your mother and I are not exactly…happy together as mommies and daddies…should be."

His mind began to wander regarding their parental responsibility to the girls. He wasn't sure if they fully understood what he struggled to tell them.

"What do you mean?" asked Hailee. "Momma doesn't love you?"

"Well, we…" He didn't know how to explain their situation, other than truthfully. "Hailee, Momma and I care about each other, but we don't love each other as much as we should. Pretty soon we're not going to live together anymore, but I want you two to live with me. I want to take care of you. Is that okay?"

A knock came at the door at that precise moment and snapped the three from their very intense conversation.

♥ ♥ ♥

Antonio had just finished up his workday without any word from Tyana. He said good night to his last client and immediately locked himself in his office and called Kellie in an attempt to find Tyana. He didn't know what else to do. He had tried her at home and her cell all day. He had a bad feeling. He had gotten a little agitated by the mere fact that she walked out and he hadn't been able to reach her to find out what she planned to do. He was starting to worry. His scheduled trip to Cozumel with Birdie was approaching and he wanted to talk to her before leaving.

"Hello, Kellie? This is Antonio."

"Oh. Hi."

"I'm sorry to bother you so late, but I didn't know what else to do. Do you know where Tatyana is? I haven't been able to reach her. I assume she told you that we sort of separated."

"Yes, she told me. But I don't know where she is."

"When was the last time you talked her?"

"The other day…when I told her that I'm pregnant."

"Oh." His body slumped in his chair. "I see. Congratulations."

"No, it's not congratulations! She didn't give me a chance to tell her that Paul is livid. He's demanding that I abort the baby. He said it's not in his plans." Kellie's voice cracked. It became apparent to Antonio that she had been crying and was quite upset.

"I'm sorry."

"Yeah, I bet you are."

Antonio didn't know what to say.

Kellie began to cry harder. "I didn't think I wanted a baby either until I found out I was pregnant. It changed everything for me knowing that this little person is growing inside of me. Now I want this baby more than anything, but I can't convince my husband to change his mind. I don't know what to do. We've been fighting ever since we found out. It's hopeless."

"I'm sorry."

"No, you listen to me! You're a fool for letting her go and especially for not wanting to have a baby with her. Now I know why it's so important to her. She's probably the best thing that will ever happen to you and you've lost it—

maybe for good. You men are a real piece of work! Good luck to you!" Kellie hung up.

Antonio sat stunned. He actually felt sorry for Kellie because she sounded so distraught and exasperated. He couldn't imagine her husband making her get an abortion, but then he thought that by denying Tyana a baby, he was essentially doing the same thing. His heart became heavy. He had to find her. He called Trevor next.

"Hello."

"Hello, is this Trevor?"

"Speaking."

"Trevor, this is Antonio, Tatyana's fiancé. I'm sorry to bother you so late."

"Oh, hi. What's up?"

"Have you talked to Tatyana? I can't find her. I'm worried."

"Uh…"

"Please! This is important. If you know where she is please tell me. I need to talk to her."

"I have talked to her. I don't think she wants to talk to you right now."

"I'm sure she doesn't and she has her reasons, but I'm very worried. She's never done anything like this before—disappear, I mean. I need to know she's okay. I messed up and I need to talk to her. Please, if you know where she is, tell me."

"She did ask me not to tell anyone…"

"Trevor, please."

"She said she's going to Seattle to spend some time with her folks. She was very upset and said she wants some time to think."

"When did she leave?"

"I don't know. Last night? At least that's the last time I spoke to her. That's all she told me."

"Thanks! Thanks so much for telling me."

"Sure. Good luck."

"Thanks, good-bye."

"Bye."

Antonio tried calling Tyana again on her cell phone, but only got her voicemail. He continued to leave messages. That night, knowing that she was in Seattle, he decided to return to their home and stay there. He missed her so much.

♥ ♥ ♥

Antonio undressed down to his shorts and dejectedly sat on the edge of the bed for a few moments knowing Tyana's side of their bed was empty. He felt bewildered and defeated as he closed his eyes and lowered his weary head. When he opened them, he saw something sticking out from under the bed. After bending down to pick it up, he rubbed his eyes to get a good look at the business card. The name on the card read: Ellis Montgomery.

He stared at the card for a long time and wondered how recently Tyana had contact with Ellis. Then he remembered the private phone conversation in her office a few weeks ago. Exhaustion overtook his body, so he crawled under the sheets and shut his eyes. He didn't know what to think now, especially since Tyana had left without informing him. He eventually fell asleep while still holding the card.

Chapter

Sixteen

Ellis motioned for the girls to wait right where they were while he answered the door to the suite.

"Good morning, Mr. Montgomery, I'm sorry I'm late. Are the girls up?"

"Good morning, Annamarie. Yes, they're right in there. Room service has been called, but hasn't arrived. The girls haven't been cleaned up yet; they just got up. We were just chatting in the living room. Can I have a few minutes with them? Then I need to head on out."

"Sure thing, Mr. Montgomery. I'll go into their room and tidy up."

Ellis returned to his daughters. He checked his watch one more time. He should have been in the conference room of the hotel fifteen minutes ago.

"Girls, I'm sorry, but I really need to go. Can we finish our conversation when I get back? I'll try to sneak back up here around lunchtime to eat lunch with you."

"Okay," said Hannah.

"But Daddy, are we going to live with you or Momma?" asked Hailee. She wasn't going to let him off that easily.

"Baby Girl, I… uh, how do *you* feel about that?"

"I don't know. I like it when I'm with you, I guess, but Momma might miss me."

"How do you feel about it, Hannah?"

"I want to live with Hailee and you, Daddy."

"I'll see that we'll be together and that you'll be happy. I want your happiness more than anything. You can see your mother whenever you want, I promise. She does love you, but I feel you'll be better off living with me. I won't let anything bad happen to you. I love you so much. Now, I have to go to work, but I'll be back as soon as I can. Annamarie will take care of you." He kissed both of them and then reluctantly walked toward the door, looking back once before he reached the door. The girls began stealing his heart on the day they were born and today they just took another chunk of it.

"Annamarie, I'm leaving! Take good care of my little ladies!"

"Sure thing, Mr. Montgomery," responded Annamarie.

"Bye Daddy! Bye Daddy! Hurry back," yelled the girls.

He slowly closed the door behind him.

♥♥♥

Tyana sat quietly on the plane, deep in her thoughts and wide-awake, as the other passengers were asleep. She had a lot to ponder and a lot to figure out about her future. For starters, she didn't quite know what to do once she exited from the plane. She couldn't stop thinking about Kellie's announcement. She thought she probably behaved badly toward her in the wake of her news. She wanted to call her, but needed to give herself some time to get her head straight with her own situation.

She meditated long and hard about her relationship with Antonio and what it really meant to her. It was something she had been perplexed with since their disconnect over the wedding plans. She needed to figure out what attracted her to Antonio and what made her fall in love with him in the first place. She mulled it over in her head for a long time before she finally admitted to herself that it was the dancing that initially revealed her heart and attraction to him. She couldn't imagine any other dance partner who could give her the same confidence, the same on-floor presence, and the same chemistry as they became one on the dance floor, and off. Even their hearts beat in unison when they're dancing. Their physical connection on the dance floor definitely transcended through their hearts and right to their souls. She and Jonathan were capable of dancing perfect routines and winning multiple competitions, but only one key element was missing and that was the body/mind bond that she and Antonio had developed naturally—the connective tissue created and sealed by their physical attraction and emotional love. They were in synch in every way on the dance floor. They had body language that spoke only to each other. Their bodies couldn't fit more perfectly on the dance floor if they were made from molds. She had always loved Antonio, but she wasn't one hundred percent convinced now that the love she possessed didn't have everything to do with her love and passion for dancing. They rarely lived their personal lives for more than a week without the influence and interference of the dance business and their performances as dance partners. She knew God had sent to her the perfect man to introduce her to dancing, who made it possible for her to fall in love with dancing, but did He send her the perfect man to love and to live the rest of her life with? She bristled in her seat from her epiphany. She had never thought of it, or Antonio, that way. She accepted him without hesitation as her fiancé on that night in Miami after she had just spent a magical, glorious moment in the ballroom as his winning partner. And, from that day forward she had been thrust into the world of dance—a passion she had embraced from the first time she christened the dance floor. That was all they had really become to each other—partners in dance. She automatically assumed that their partnership in the dance world was synonymous with being partners in love. She no longer thought that to be true. And worse, she now didn't consider him to be capable of that kind of partnership—with anyone.

Though she felt some sort of relief of possibly uncovering the basis and foundation of her relationship with Antonio, at the same token, she felt immeasurable sadness. She had loved him, or what she had come to believe was true love, for five years. She had hoped to build a life together with him only to learn that he had danced on her dreams of "happily ever after" with him. She realized then what most had realized long before, that if he had the same dreams of happily ever after, then he would have actually married her five years ago.

When she could no longer ponder her broken promises and disappointments, she closed her eyes and let her mind slip away.

♥♥♥

Ellis could barely concentrate on his business after the serious and grown-up conversation with his daughters that morning. He knew it would only be a matter of time before Charlotte would hear about their conversation from the girls, and that would only fuel the fire and exacerbate Charlotte's present state of mind toward him and her pursuit of custody.

His client meetings were unusually intense, long, and demanding. He ended up working straight through lunch. He called up to the room and regrettably cancelled his lunch date with his daughters, which made them cry and throw a small tantrum. They desperately needed their daddy's attention, especially now. The earlier conversation had confused them.

Ellis returned to the suite around six-thirty, a very weary and mentally depleted man. The girls had refused their nap all day, expecting that he would come back at any minute. They didn't want to miss their daddy. But missing their nap left them extremely tired and a bit cranky. Ellis found them at the dining table picking at their dinner.

"Hi girls!"

"Daddy, you said you would come back and see us at lunchtime!" Hailee pouted.

"I know, but I couldn't get away. I tried. I missed you so much. Did you take a nap today?"

"No. We waited for you," said Hannah.

"Oh, I'm so sorry. You should have taken your nap, though." Ellis glanced at Annamarie in disapproval.

"I'm sorry, Mr. Montgomery. They wouldn't go to sleep. They insisted on waiting up for you."

"I see. Well my little ones, you know what that means?"

"What?" they asked in unison.

"That means bedtime comes early tonight. Right after you two finish eating, in fact, which better be soon. Annamarie will give you your baths and then it's nighty-night. I want you to get over this flu and you need rest to do that. So, come on, eat up so Annamarie can get you bathed and into bed. I can see it in your eyes that you're half asleep anyway." The girls were eating chicken soup again. He wondered what he'd eat. He was tired of smelling chicken soup.

"But we want to play with you!"

"Hailee, we're all very tired and you're still sick. If you'd taken your nap, we could play, but you didn't. If you don't get well, we can't do anything fun. So, finish up. I'll read one story to you both. I'm going to bed early, too. I'm exhausted. We'll play tomorrow, that is, if you both take a nap tomorrow. Deal?"

"Deal!"

"Good. Now, how about a hug and a kiss from my favorite little girls." He hugged and kissed them.

"We're your only little girls!" said Hailee.

"And that makes you my favorite!"

They hugged him back nearly strangling him.

Once the girls were cleaned up, in their pajamas, read to, and securely tucked in, Ellis relieved Annamarie of her duties and dragged himself into a hot, eucalyptus shower, and then into bed. It had been a long and stressful day. His back and neck felt like someone had been beating on him all day. He had to get through this week and the weekend, and then they were scheduled to return home the following Monday. But that only meant more stress—Charlotte.

Ellis tried to turn off the jack hammering noise of his clients, his boss, and Charlotte, in his mind, as he stretched out to relax his tightened muscles. He worried for the girls. He found out that they talked to Charlotte earlier today—Annamarie told him. She told him that they were upset during the conversation and more quiet than usual. He hated that Charlotte had a tendency to upset them. He wondered how he would get through the divorce and custody hearing without too much delay and drama, but knowing Charlotte and what she was capable of, a delay would be inevitable. He continued to struggle with his thoughts, but after only ten minutes of sorting out his custody angle, he slipped into twilight sleep. From there, it didn't take him long before he became oblivious to anything that happened that day. After thirty-minutes, a subtle knock, barely a tap, came from the door. At first he thought he was hearing things. But, then he heard it again. He jumped up, figuring Annamarie must have forgotten something. In only his pajama bottoms, he staggered out to the living room to answer the door, trying to shake the cobwebs from his head. In his haste, he didn't bother to turn on the light, but wished he had when he stubbed his toe on the leg of a chair. Swearing and doubled over in pain, he fumbled with the chain on the door and eventually swung it opened, but Ellis' brain could not immediately register what he saw on the other side of his door. He stood paralyzed, but not from his throbbing toe. And, for a second, he thought his eyes were playing tricks on him.

♥♥♥

Antonio awoke the next morning and found Ellis' business card next to him. He picked it up and stared at it with a million thoughts exploding in his head. He looked at the time and sighed. He had forty-five minutes before he needed to be at the dance studio. He overbooked that day in order to keep his students current since he was scheduled to be in Mexico for three days with Birdie. He didn't want to leave without talking to Tyana, so he picked up his phone and tried calling her again—hoping to catch her early in the day rather than later. When her phone went directly to voicemail again, he decided he could no longer sit idle without knowing she was fine and in good hands. He got up and rummaged through the desk until he found the address book with all of her family members' phone numbers, and one in particular, her parents' number. He picked up his phone, dialed, and waited. It was Tyana's father who answered.

"Mr. Dominique, Sir, this is Antonio, Antonio Lorenzo. How are you?"

"Antonio? I'm fine. Why are you calling? Is there something wrong with my Tatyana?"

"What? What do you mean? I'm calling to talk to her. She's not there with you?"

"No, should she be? Is something wrong? Is she on her way here? She would have told me."

"I don't know, Sir. It's my understanding that she went home yesterday, to Seattle, to visit you and your wife."

"No...she's not here. Celeste! Do you know anything about Tatyana coming for a visit? I'm asking my wife. Wait a minute."

"Sure thing."

Antonio became more bewildered and now a little embarrassed that he had no clue where Tyana was.

"Antonio?"

"Yes."

"No, Celeste doesn't know about a scheduled visit from our daughter. You don't know where she is?"

"No, I don't, Sir. She didn't exactly tell me where she was going. I thought she might be there."

"Where is my daughter?"

"I'm sure she's okay." Antonio didn't know that and he was positive Tyana's father wasn't buying his pseudo confidence.

"Please find my daughter. I leave her in your hands so you find her!"

"I will. I promise. But if you hear from her first, would you please tell her I called and that I need to speak with her?"

"Yes, of course. Antonio..."

"Yes, Sir."

"She is my world; she's all I got. She's precious to me."

"I know. She's precious to me, too."

The two hung up with heavy hearts.

♥♥♥

Ellis finally spoke. "Uh...Tyana...I'm sorta speechless and at a loss for words. How? I mean, is this for real?" Ellis stammered over his words. He didn't have a clue on what to say or do next. And, it didn't help that he was mentally exhausted, but his adrenaline from seeing her took over.

"Hi. Can we talk?"

"Uh...sure, sure! Come in! I'm just so surprised to see you standing here. Here! I thought the least you would do is call me back; not show up at my hotel room, in Madrid!"

"Oh, would you rather I'd call?"

"No!"

Ellis invited Tyana in and closed the door.

Annamarie heard the commotion and listened from inside of her room to the conversation that took place in the hallway until Tyana entered Ellis' suite. She wanted to know more about the attractive woman who Mr. Montgomery invited into his suite while only wearing his pajama bottoms. She was determined to man her door until the woman left.

"What are you doing here? Why didn't you tell me you were coming all this distance? When did you decide this? How did you come to decide this? I'm sorry, here, come in; sit down."

"Was this a bad idea? I probably should have called first. What was I thinking? I should go."

"No! No..."

Ellis turned on the lamp next to the sofa.

"I needed to get away and I also wanted to see you. You said you were here — alone and it was important that I see you, now."

"Well, I'm glad, but we could have arranged..."

"Ellis, I'm going to cut to the chase. You said you loved me and I want to talk about that. And, for some reason, I couldn't get what you said out of my head. And since I needed to get away anyway, this was the first place I thought of coming to. Are you sure it wasn't a mistake coming here?"

"No! I'm glad you're here. I'm just shocked." He approached her and sat down next to her.

Ellis carefully hugged Tyana, feeling strange about the whole thing. She opened her arms and received him. He embraced her warmly until they both held each other tighter. She trembled, feeling surreal being in his arms like that.

"Tyana, there is one problem though...my girls. They're here, in this suite with me. It wouldn't be a good idea that they find you here, especially now. Charlotte was served the divorce papers and she's not exactly in agreement. She's being difficult and threatening, which I can handle, but if she finds out you're here, there's no telling what she'll do. I don't want you to get mixed up in this.

She's already blaming this on you. I think she knows how I feel about you –have always felt about you."

"I have a room—in the hotel—on another floor. I probably should have called you first. I'm sorry. I'm not thinking straight; I came straight here from the airport."

"No, that's fine. I'm glad you came here. I'm happy to see you! I'm not trying to be forward, but could we talk in my bedroom. I don't want the twins to hear us talking out here. I don't want to wake them and I can't leave them here alone."

"Okay." She followed him to the master bedroom.

"Please sit." He offered her a seat on the chaise lounge next to the window. He sat next to her. "Tyana, why are you really here? What about your...your relationship with the guy? Have you two split up?"

"I think so; I don't know. I left him."

"But I thought you were happy."

"So, did I. I mean, I was."

"What happened?"

"It's complicated." Before she could say another word, her phone rang. She looked annoyed, but when she saw the caller, she answered it immediately.

"Hello....Hi Papa! No, I'm fine, Papa... Papa, really, I'm fine... He did? When? It's okay." She glanced up at Ellis who looked confused. "Papa, I will call you back. I can't talk right now... No, I promise, I'll call you back. I love you. Tell Mother I love her, too... Okay, okay, I will, I promise. Bye Papa." She slowly hung up.

"No one knows you're here, right?" Ellis guessed.

"Not really." Tyana lowered her head realizing how many lives she just impacted by running away.

"So, you basically left your life in Arizona to come here—to me."

"Basically. Everything is a mess."

"Well, I think we're both in a mess." They smiled at each other. "Tyana, I've been thinking about what happened in Sedona."

"I think about that, too. I hated myself for kissing you like that."

"But yet here you are...thousands of miles away from home."

"Here I am. Goes to show you how messed up I am."

"Or how clearer things are for you now."

"I need to know if you really meant that you're still in love with me."

"No, not the way I was when we were together. That was selfish love. Once you were gone from my life, I realized I hadn't loved you the way I should have, or what I thought was love. I've had plenty of time to think of what real love is and it's not letting the one who fills you up inside get away — for any reason. I know this sounds weird, but I think I fell *in* love with you after we broke up. See, what I have with Charlotte started out as only an intellectual attraction. I was initially attracted to her mind for business and for what partnering up with her could do for me, but when she began to seduce me in exchange for her clout; I became weak to her seductive powers and hungry for the success. I knew it was wrong, but I kept thinking each time that it would be the last time and I could pull away from her. Yeah, looking back I knew I was acting like an immature prize idiot. But also looking back I figured I couldn't have been in love with you to have done that to you. Then once she and I were married and had the girls, I had come to respect her as the mother of my children. I was there when the girls were born and it did something to me — it changed me. If there was any consolation to the guilt and anguish I was feeling and the nightmare I put you through, those two beautiful girls were it. I was grateful and my heart opened up. But I could never find it in my heart to actually fall in love with her. All that love that filled my heart transferred to you; and to my daughters of course. But I knew it was much too late for you and me. So now, I have to settle for only asking for your forgiveness—for hurting you and being a jackass and putting you through that hell."

"Ellis, I'm so scared and confused."

"I know."

Ellis took hold of her hands, leaned in, and kissed her. As he continued to taste her—she tasted like honeysuckle—his body began to positively react to his mouth on hers. He let go of her hands and placed his hands on the sides of her face. When he felt her kiss him back, he tilted his head slightly to the right and kissed her with more passion, nearly swallowing her up. He took her breath away. He grabbed her right hand and placed it on a once familiar place for her on his body until he no longer needed to persuade her. She willingly caressed him, yet timidly at first. In her mind, it felt so wrong, but somewhere from deep within, it felt so right. He stopped her only long enough to pull her toward the bed where he rapidly removed her clothing and positioned her on top of the bed and underneath him. She looked very nervous and unsure as he stared at her for a long time.

"Tyana, I love you; I want you." Then he whispered in her ear. "Do you want me?"

She nodded and then closed her eyes. She left everything up to fate.

♥ ♥ ♥

After two hours, Annamarie unmanned the door to her suite and reluctantly called her boss.

"Are you sure? Are you absolutely sure?" asked Charlotte. She paused. Her world stopped and her stomach flipped upside down. She sat down and started to cry, but covered her mouth so Annamarie wouldn't detect her weaker emotions.

"Mrs. Montgomery? I'm sorry."

"Uh...describe the woman to me again and give me every detail, her height, her hair, her voice, she's bi-racial...half white half uh, uh, Romanian or whatever, is that the woman?"

"He called her Tyana, the same name I heard him say over the phone — to the person he said he loves."

"And, she hasn't left?"

"No ma'am. It's been two hours. I stopped watching because I need to go to sleep. I didn't want to compromise my state of mind with the twins in the morning. They usually get up early and because they're sick..."

"That's fine. Go to bed. Thanks for letting me know. Call me in the morning with the details." Charlotte hung up. She cried herself to sleep that night.

Chapter
Seventeen

Tyana carefully slipped out of Ellis' bed at four in the morning and tiptoed to the bathroom. When she returned, she quietly began picking up her clothes, some on the floor, some on the chaise lounge, and on the nightstand. When she looked for her shoes, Ellis began to stir.

"What are you doing?" he asked while reaching over and grabbing her arm.

"I'm looking for my clothes. I should go."

"Not yet. Please. Come here," he urged as he tugged at her arm.

"Ellis...we need to be careful."

"I agree. Just ten minutes."

She put her clothes down and crawled back into the bed beside him. He inched her closer up against his body. He felt so weary. He spoke first.

"Are you okay?"

"Not sure. I can't believe what we did. Ellis, you're married and I am engaged — was engaged."

"Don't do that to yourself. Let me take that burden." He kissed her hand. "What do you want to do?"

"I honestly don't know. I have a lot to think about. A lot."

"It's up to you. I'll support you no matter what you decide." He leaned in and kissed her.

He kept kissing her until he pulled her even closer and then rose up to level her. She melted on the sheets beneath him. All of the familiar feelings came rushing back — for both of them. Ellis couldn't help himself; this was Tyana, the woman he shared a life with for ten years and whom he had prayed for so long to get another chance with her to show her how much she meant to him. With each grind of his body on top of hers, their fondest memories of romantic times spent together returned. He knew making love to her, while still married to Charlotte, was wrong, but he didn't rationalize it as cheating. He didn't love Charlotte, and he owed Tyana so much after what he did to her. After all, Charlotte had manipulated him away from Tyana, so he convinced himself that whatever he did with Tyana now was only the right thing because she was his *real* love. He just hoped that Charlotte wouldn't find out about Tyana being with him there in Madrid, so she won't create more problems for him — like slapping an adultery suit on him.

Ellis refocused his thoughts back on Tyana. They both continued to revive the flames that were ignited so long ago. They created their own pace and rhythm while their bodies became reminded of each other and reconnected as one, once again. Time ticked away until dawn of the morning.

When Ellis felt himself nearing his second release of his entire being with her, he remembered what her passion and sensuality was once capable of doing to him, physically. She instinctively grabbed hold of his hands and they held tightly to each other as they both closed their eyes and let their minds encapsulate the indescribable euphoria that seized their bodies and held them bonded for what seemed like an eternity.

As the sunrise peeked through the narrow opening of the drawn curtains, they opened their eyes. They wanted to savor the reunion, but reality quickly set in and a new day was upon them, as well as more complications.

♥♥♥

Charlotte had barely been able to concentrate on her work all day since her conversation with Annamarie. Her mind spiraled out of control and she was filled with hurt, anger, and fear. Her focus became compromised and she made mistakes at work, which made her even angrier.

That evening, once she returned home, she quickly changed into a pair of designer jeans, a pair of open-toe wedge sandals and a silk blouse. She pulled her hair back into a taut ponytail, grabbed her purse and left the house to drive out to her beach house where she lived when she and Ellis engaged in their scandalous affair over five years ago. She never sold it, but kept it and visited from time to time when Ellis traveled and the girls were in Annamarie's care. The beach house became a stronghold with memories of when he desired her most and she remained in complete control of him. Since the twins were born, she could no longer dominate him or manipulate him into giving her what she wanted most—love. A dire sense of urgency overwhelmed her and she needed to go there immediately. It was already after eight in the evening and it would take her over an hour to get out there, but she didn't care. She would simply keep going until she reached her destination. With the key from the little box hidden in the back of her closet, she drove fast and furious with only one agenda.

When Charlotte reached the beach house, she parked the Porsche and walked across the gravel to the wraparound porch. She looked around for a second before unlocking the front door and entering. She shut and locked the door behind her, and then turned on the light. She stood in the entry for several seconds breathing heavily.

She shook off her nervousness and walked directly to the master bedroom. She sat down on the edge of the bed and slowly opened the top drawer of the nightstand. Way in the back of the drawer, she spotted a cedar box that she had placed there about six months ago. She pulled it out, unlocked it with the key she brought with her from her closet in the family home, and held her breath as she carefully lifted the small handgun, with the pearl handle, from the box and cradled it firmly in her hands. She studied it and slowly rubbed it with her eyes closed. A single tear dropped, which was followed by a few more. She watched each tear fall onto her lap. Loneliness engulfed her. She had to get her family back one way or another.

♥♥♥

Ellis walked Tyana out and stepped just outside of the door with her. They stood face to face in the hallway.

"What room are you in?" he whispered. I'd like to see you later."

"I'm in..."

"Daddy!"

He stuck his head back inside and answered, "I'm coming!" He turned back to Tyana. "I have to go," he said regretfully. "Call me, or I'll call you! I'll find you!" He quickly kissed her good-bye before stepping back inside of the suite.

Annamarie witnessed the exchange between Ellis and Tyana through the peephole of her room, after hearing the voices in the hall.

Tyana walked away carrying her shoes in her arms, and feeling a little dazed from her secret liaison. She wondered to herself if she had done the right thing by showing up. She knew she definitely had to tell Antonio where she was since he had called her parents and gotten them worried, too, and let him know what she planned to do. But suddenly, she became vividly aware that he was probably in Mexico by now with Birdie.

Ellis turned and went back in the room, where he was confronted by his daughter.

"Daddy, I thought I heard someone talking to you. Is Anna here? I'm hungry."

"No, she's not here yet. Hannah, it's not time to get up. What are you doing up now?"

"I heard you, so I wanted to get up and eat breakfast with you. I thought you left us!"

"You're too much. It's six o'clock in the morning. You need to go back to sleep."

"Can I sleep in your bed?"

"Uh, no... Why don't you snuggle back under your warm covers and see if you can go back to sleep in your own bed first? I need to take a shower and turn on the light to do some work and I don't want to keep you awake. Maybe another time, okay? I promise." He kissed Hannah and walked her back to her bed, being extra quiet not to wake her sister.

♥♥♥

While Charlotte sat mesmerized, staring at her gun, she began to imagine what she would do with it, and then suddenly her cell phone rang, startling her and causing her to drop the gun.

"Shit!" She fumbled for the phone in her purse. She retrieved the phone and answered, "What!"

"Mrs. Montgomery... it's me, Annamarie."

"Yes." Charlotte knew what she was going to tell her and she didn't want to hear anymore.

"I'm calling like you said. The woman left Mr. Montgomery's suite a few minutes ago. He kissed her in his pajamas and then she left."

Charlotte closed her eyes and her body deflated.

"Thanks. That's all."

"But..."

"I said that's all! That's enough. Thank you. I'll take care of it from here. Thank you. Call me when the girls wake up so I can talk to them. I don't care what time it is, just do it."

"Yes, Mrs. Montgomery."

Charlotte hung up.

Instead of driving back to the couple's home in San Diego, Charlotte decided to remain at the beach house and spend the night there. She didn't have the mental capacity to drive that distance and it was late. She never got undressed, but instead she lay on the bed and pulled the covers over her. She fell asleep still holding the gun.

♥♥♥

Once Hannah fell back to sleep, Ellis tiptoed out of the room and returned to his bedroom, where the essence of Tyana's delicate fragrance still lingered. He laid across the bed, hugging his pillow where he could detect her scent the most. He wondered why she had come all that distance. What could be so urgent for her to make such a bold gesture? He could tell from the way she made love to him that her feelings for him never left—deep feelings. He knew her very well in that way, and knew she wouldn't give up her body so completely and uninhibitedly if she didn't possess the love in her heart to complement her physical actions. He soon drifted off atop the still moist and delightfully scented sheets with visions of her floating in his mind.

A couple of hours later, a soft, but firm, knock came at the bedroom door, followed by a voice, calling out, "Mr. Montgomery, Mr. Montgomery...are you awake?" Annamarie opened the master suite door only a smidgeon, but didn't dare look in.

"Huh? Yes. Who is it? What time is it?" Ellis came across mostly confused and disoriented. He quickly sat up and scanned the room to get his bearings. He looked for Tyana, but then remembered that she had gone back to her room.

"It's me, Annamarie. It's eight-thirty, Sir. I tried knocking at the suite door, but nobody answered, so I let myself in. I hope that was okay. I thought maybe you left; I got worried."

"Shit! I'm late! I'm running late! Are the girls up? If they are, order breakfast for them! I have to get moving and get out of here! Thanks for waking me. I'll be out in a few minutes!"

"Okay. I'll go look after the girls."

When Ellis emerged from his bedroom twenty minutes later, freshly shaven and debonair, he grabbed a croissant from the breakfast tray in the dining room, kissed his daughters, and sprinted toward the door, yelling out orders for Annamarie.

"But Daddy!" screamed Hannah, upset and defiant.

"I'm sorry, girls. Daddy's really, really late this morning; I overslept. I'll try and come back up for lunch. I love you so much. I'll make it up to you later!"

"But Daddy..." cried Hailee. She wanted a hug.

"Daddy!" shouted Hannah once more, but daddy was gone in a flash.

"Okay, girls, finish your breakfast and I'll be right back," said Annamarie. The girls protested and began crying. They didn't understand what had just happened.

Annamarie desperately wanted to sneak into her employer's bedroom to do some investigation work before housekeeping arrived. It took a while, but she finally got the girls quieted and settled down with a promise of ice cream after lunch. In the meantime, she occupied them with cartoon videos while she checked out the master bedroom.

In Ellis' haste, he didn't gather up any of the disheveled sheets and comforter that had fallen on the floor. Annamarie noticed the messier than usual bed right away when she entered the room—a very different look from any other time, even when the girls slept with him. The sheets were twisted, mangled, and wrinkled from the moisture of their bodies. Some of the pillows had fallen on the floor, too. She searched high and low for any solid incriminating evidence. Just as her eye spotted something shiny on the floor near the edge of the bed, a noise startled her and she quickly ran out of the room.

"Oh! Mr. Montgomery! You're back!"

"Yes, I forgot something. Were you coming out of my room?"

"No...I mean yes, I was looking for the girls' uh...hairbrush."

"My brush is not in there, Anna!" yelled Hailee.

"It isn't? Then where is it? I couldn't find it."

"Their brush isn't in my room. I haven't seen it. Did you look in their bathroom?"

"I told you! It's in the bathroom," Hailee followed up.

Driven by time, Ellis proceeded to his room to look for his envelope. He almost stepped on a pillow that had fallen on the floor during his romp with Tyana. He bent over to pick it up and noticed the same shiny item on the floor that Annamarie saw moments earlier. He reached down and picked up the diamond pendant necklace. He stared at it and remembered seeing it around Tyana's neck. He stuffed it in his pocket and ran out, thinking he was glad he found it and not Annamarie. His heart pounded fast while thinking he barely dodged a bullet and reminded himself that he had to be more careful. This time he remembered to kiss the girls goodbye, which soothed their hostile moods from earlier.

"Okay, I'm out! I'll see you later!" Ellis dashed out.

♥ ♥ ♥

Tyana took a long, hot shower, which began with visions of her night with Ellis, but ended up with her head filled with worry and contemplation about what to do next. She didn't feel that she should hit Antonio with everything, including her lustful night with Ellis, while he was in Mexico, so in the meantime, she first phoned her parents to put their minds at ease about her well being; not necessarily her whereabouts. She felt that they did not need to know, at this particular time, what she was up to, but only that she was safe and okay. She gave them very little information regarding her relationship with Antonio, but promised more details very soon. She planned to explain everything to them once she returned to the States. At that point she hoped to have a better idea herself what to do. She appeased her parents' inquiries—for now. But she knew her time was limited before they would demand more answers.

Her next phone call went out to Trevor since she lied to him about going to Seattle. She didn't feel comfortable lying to her friends or her family anymore. It was late back home, so she wanted to catch him before he went to bed.

"Hello."

"Trev, it's me. I know it's late…"

"Tyana, I'm glad you called. How are you doing? Feeling better? Antonio called me looking for you. Did he find you at your folks? I'm sorry, but I had to tell him. He was very worried."

"No, no, that's fine. Everything is well…it's complicated. I didn't speak to Antonio. He doesn't know where I am. Papa called me because Antonio called them and worried my parents because I'm not with them. They don't know where I am—no one does."

"Where are you then?"

"I'm in Madrid, Spain."

"What? What the hell are you doing there?"

"I'm trying to sort some things out." She paused. "Ellis is here. I've been with him, sort of."

"I'm speechless."

"I know. Trevor, I had to come. I was out of my mind with confusion and despair."

"Didn't I tell you not to make any rash decisions?"

"But the decision was mine to make. It may be the best decision; it may be the worst. Actually the jury is still out."

"So, what's happened so far or dare I ask?"

"I got here last night and I went to his suite to talk. He had no idea I was coming, by the way. He had nothing to do with this."

"So you just showed up?"

"Basically. But it was okay. He has not pressured me; all he's looking for is for me to forgive him."

"And what are you looking for?"

"Answers."

"Did you find them?"

"I don't know. I'm going to stay for a few more days and then I'll come home. At that point I hope to have all my answers. Trevor, I think I'm ready to move on."

"With Ellis?"

"I didn't say that; I don't even know how I feel about him and me, together. Right now I'm just in search of answers. Currently, nothing in my life makes sense."

"You love him don't you?"

"I think I've always loved him and never stopped. His indiscretions broke us up."

"But you love Antonio."

"That, I'm trying to figure out why. I don't really want to say too much about him until he and I have a chance to talk. He's in Mexico right now with Birdie, so when he returns, he and I will get together and I'll tell him everything."

"Are you okay?"

"I think so. Hey! How's Cleo doing?"

"Good news! She's doing much better and the doctor is pleased with the results of her bed rest. They don't want to release her too soon, though, but it's hopeful that she'll be able to carry the baby full term."

"That's awesome! I'm so happy for her, and you. Give her my best and I'll stop by when I return."

"Be safe and let me know if you need anything. And call me when you get back!"

"Oh, I will. Good night."

"Good night."

Tyana glanced at the time and crossed her fingers for her next call.

"Hello."

"Kellie? It's me, Tyana. Did I wake you?"

"Hi. Sorta. But I've been in bed for a while now. Where are you?"

"That's a long story. Listen, I feel bad about our last conversation. I had a lot on my mind and I don't think I handled it all that well—your news, that is."

"I understand."

"So, how are you doing?"

"Not good."

"Why, what's wrong?"

"Well, I never got a chance to tell you that Paul is quite adamant about terminating the pregnancy."

"What?!"

"I've been upset because I didn't know how much I would want a baby until I became pregnant. I can't express that to him or get him to see it from my perspective. He's not bending on this issue at all and it's putting a strain on our marriage. He's given me an ultimatum."

"That's absurd! He's crazy! You two would make great parents."

"Not according to him. He's forty-five and doesn't want that in his life at this point. He's never wanted it. I haven't been able to work. I've been so upset and scared. I don't want to terminate this pregnancy."

"You can't and shouldn't if you don't want to. I mean it is your body. Maybe he'll come around."

"You really aren't getting it. This is final with him."

"So, what are you going to do?"

"And...now you're up to speed. That's what I'm faced with and I have to make a decision because our marriage is non-existent right now."

"I'm so sorry you're going through all that. And, I wasn't there to support you, as a friend should. I'm really sorry."

"I know you got your own problems and me showing up pregnant and talking about abortion isn't exactly helping you, either."

"Hey, I'll be home in a few days and we can sit down and talk about it."

"What do you mean, you'll be home? Where are you?"

"Uh...Madrid."

"As in Spain?"

"Yeah."

"What the hell are you doing there?"

"Thinking mostly. I have to sort some things out and I needed to figure them out now as opposed to later. I'll explain when I get back. I hope to have everything figured out by then. Listen, you call me if anything changes or if you need me."

"Okay, I'll let your explanation, or lack of an explanation, slide for now, but you better tell me everything when you get back."

"I will. Promise. Take care of yourself. I'll see you soon."

"Bye Tyana."

Chapter

Antonio's mind remained segmented during his trip with Birdie, a few other instructors, and students from other local dance studios. The students purchased the opportunity to be escorted to Mexico by their instructors, accompanying a jam-packed itinerary of sightseeing during the day and dancing at various venues during evening hours. The activities included something for everyone, which meant that the instructors always had to be on and up for everything, leaving little or no time for a private thought or personal agenda. Tyana and Antonio used to plan those events together with their students, but it didn't always work out. More single women were available to Antonio to escort than there were single men, or couples, for Tyana to escort. Antonio never lacked an available damsel, eager to spend her savings on him, to journey to some exotic corner of the world. Tyana rarely traveled with the group when she didn't have students signed up. Instead, she stayed behind and managed the day-to-day operations of the dance studio while Antonio trotted the planet. He not only thought about her while he traveled and even missed her the whole time, but also felt uneasy about not having her home to oversee the business in his absence.

At the end of the first night, he nearly collapsed from exhaustion once he returned to his hotel room, which he shared with Gary, another male instructor close to his age. Antonio and Gary had been in the business for nearly the same length of time and respected one another throughout their careers. That trip was probably their eighth trip taken together, so they were hardly strangers to the drill of escorting students. Antonio, close to falling asleep, suddenly felt wide-awake with worry and uncertainty. He couldn't turn his brain off. He hadn't spoken to Tyana for days and now he didn't know where she had disappeared. He felt guilty for being away in another country after what happened between them and not insisting on talking to her before he left. He called her several times, but she still didn't answer or return his calls. He tossed and turned as thunder rumbled outside for a few hours. He lay awake for hours listening to the rain pound against the window.

It turned out that Antonio had a lot to think about. He had decisions to make that he never thought he would have to make. His business always came first—it was that simple. No one or nothing could persuade him to ever re-evaluate that priority. He didn't get to be the big shot dance instructor by letting anything jeopardize his goals of attaining the best; creating the best; becoming the best; all by providing the best service. In his world, he had to think and know that he was the best in order to succeed. But because the business was just as much Tyana's as it was his, he couldn't dream of going on without her. The dance business had come to mean something very different to him in the last five years because of her. If he took the blame for her disappearance, then he had to do something very drastic and take the responsibility of getting her back, and back with him. She meant more to him than just a graceful and talented dancer, dance partner, and savvy business partner.

He continued to listen to the storm outside his window in his perplexed state of mind and reflected on how no woman, before Tyana, had made him feel more confident about his own sexuality; made him feel more loved; or shared such a deep passion. And more profoundly, he had never felt more chemistry and connection on the dance floor with any other woman and partner. He thought their separation would be temporary, but now, he feared he might lose her forever. That reality terrified him. He desperately missed her. He missed her soft, silky skin next to his; he missed the way she tasted—like milk and almonds, her sweet aroma—like a summer's rain, her infectious laughter that sometimes lingered long after the joke, the way she touched him when they made love—comforting and deliberate; and the way she moved beneath or on top of him at just the precise moment to cause him to tremble inside as if he was eighteen again. They got to where they could communicate with each other without words, but through body language exclusively. He lay quietly with his eyes closed and his hands folded trying to recall the details of those special and personal moments shared with her.

The memories that surfaced first included private and exclusive weekend excursions to escape the daily work routine—usually at the request of Tyana. She insisted on maintaining balance in their lives, but failed to consistently persuade Antonio to make the time for them. She also thought that planning their wedding would help create that balance. He particularly reminisced about their weekend spent at the Ritz-Carlton in Phoenix. Antonio wanted to surprise Tyana with their quiet getaway plans because he had been working so many weekends without a break and leaving her without his presence around the house. Planning a trip out of town would be impossible without her knowledge, so he decided to take her away from their ordinary routines instead.

They occupied a magnificent grand suite, which enticed them, on more than one occasion, to spend more time in their royal, king-size bed, than anywhere else in the luxury hotel. That also left them to indulge in the hotel's efficient room service while lying around casually in only their robes. He grinned to himself, as he looked back on that memorable romantic time. Antonio felt his heart beating a little faster just thinking about how beautiful and sexy she looked to him on that particular weekend. He saw her through fresh, rested eyes instead of the tired, burning eyes he usually had at the end of a long, physical day. He felt ashamed of himself for not creating more memories with her or taking time out of his schedule to pay attention to her needs, even the smallest ones.

After dwelling on the pleasant times, his thoughts went to the night in Miami—her last night as his student and first night as his lover. He remembered kissing her for the first time on the beach, after chasing after her and confessing his hidden love for her. He could almost feel the softness of her lips on him. And, a few moments before that explosive first kiss, they had encountered Ellis and his pregnant wife at the same hotel. Less than an hour's time after that life-changing reunion for her, he and Tyana made love for the first time, followed by his proposal of marriage, which she tearfully accepted.

Antonio opened his teary eyes. He missed her and genuinely didn't want to lose her. He closed his eyes again and drifted off to sleep with tranquil visions of Tyana in his head.

♥ ♥ ♥

Charlotte nervously ran around the house gathering last minute items that she intended on packing for her trip—her trip to Madrid to ambush her husband and to commandeer her children. She scheduled a car to pick her up and she had less than an hour to depart for the airport. This was one flight she had no intentions of missing.

♥ ♥ ♥

Ellis worked late and didn't get a chance to spend as much time as he would have liked with the twins, which left them bewildered and disappointed. Now that they were feeling somewhat better, they demanded more attention from him. They became homesick and pouty. He had only a few more days left of his assignment in Madrid and yet the workload seemed to increase as the weekend got closer—which was not what he had planned nor expected. He originally wanted to take the weekend off to spend it with the girls. He owed it to them. He also wanted to allow time in his schedule to spend with Tyana. He couldn't get their unforgettable night out of his head. He wanted to believe Tyana still loved him. And now he was convinced that she did.

When he returned to the suite, he changed clothes, and had just enough time left in the girls' day to read them a bedtime story. He glanced at this watch when he said good night to Annamarie. He had left Tyana a message earlier that day to tell her he would get in touch with her after the girls were settled and into bed. He checked in on them one more time to make sure they were asleep before calling Tyana. They never even stirred.

"Tyana, it's me. The coast is clear on this end. Can you come up?"

"Are you sure it's okay? I really don't want to cause any trouble."

"I'm sure. Please, come up. I'll be waiting. I need to see you. We only have a few more days left here in Madrid."

"I want to see you, too. I'll be right there." She smiled as she hung up.

Ellis checked in on the girls a third time and found them still sleeping soundly. He kissed them both softly and left them to their dreams. He then stationed himself at the door listening for the slightest sound of Tyana's arrival. Within five minutes, she arrived looking very sexy and fresh. He noticed that her hair smelled tropical when he leaned in and kissed her neck. He could hardly wait until she entered the suite before smothering her with affection. She kissed him back.

"I've missed you," he whispered in her ear. "I've been thinking about the last time we were together."

"I thought about you all day, too," she shyly admitted.

"Come on in."

She entered the suite and he gently closed the door behind her. He took hold of her hand and promptly led her straight to his bedroom. She followed without hesitation. Once inside, they sat down next to each other on the chaise lounge.

"Hold on. I have something for you." He got up and retrieved the diamond necklace from his coat pocket. "Here I found this on the floor this morning."

"Oh my God! My necklace! You found it on the floor?"

"Yeah. If I hadn't returned because I forgot something I'd hate to think that housekeeping would have picked it up."

"I'm so sorry. I should have been more careful. What if your girls or their nanny would have found it? How would you have explained it? Maybe we're pressing our luck here and this is a sign that we shouldn't be doing this." Or she thought it was a sign that she should be with Antonio.

"Hey, don't think that. I want to ask you something," Ellis started. "You know how I feel about you, right? But I'm not sure, exactly, how you feel about me. I mean, I know we had a very hot, and I mean, hot intimate night together, but I guess I want to know if you forgive me and if we are moving toward maybe getting back together — after my divorce, of course."

"Ellis," she began as she shifted in her seat, "that's why I'm here. I've been going over and over in my mind what I should do — about everything. Of course, I love you, I'll admit. I couldn't have made love to you if I didn't, but I didn't know that I still loved you until...last night. You had hurt me so badly and in my mind I hated you so much for doing what you did to me and how you did it..."

"I know, I know, I'm so sorry..."

"And, I fell in love with Antonio... Ellis, I don't know if we're moving forward. I mean you're still married.

You have Charlotte to consider and you have your children. I can't add anymore complications and confusion to my life right now."

"Charlotte and I are getting divorced. I have never loved her—you have to know that. If it weren't for my daughters, I wouldn't be her husband. I want to be clear about that. I don't expect you to throw everything away overnight, or at all, for me. I guess I'm confused since you're here and after last night..."

"I know, me too. I'm sorry I came; I didn't mean to confuse you or give you false hope."

"Nonsense. I understand, and I'm not saying that to get you to stay."

"I needed to find out for myself." Tyana stood up. "Maybe I should go." She realized that she still had her desire for a baby to consider and she wasn't sure that even though she still loved her ex that he would want to add to his family. She witnessed him with his daughters and had heard him talk about them to know how much they meant to him and knew to what lengths he would go to keep them safe and protected.

Ellis stood up. "I wish you wouldn't." He put his hands on her arms. "You're going to go back home in a few days and by then you will have figured things out for you, and I will accept whatever you choose to do, so while you're here, this could be all that we'll have—maybe this is it. And it's all my fault that we're even here like this—unsure."

She felt the sincerity and the emotions emerging from his heart, through his strong hands that still gripped her tightly, transferring that energy to her arms. Her eyes began to water.

"What can I do, Tyana? What do you want from me?"

"Please. Just hold me," she responded.

Ellis pulled her into his body and embraced her. They both held each other standing in the same spot for about ten minutes. They didn't kiss or stroke one another, just held the embrace.

"Come to bed with me..." Ellis phrased it as a question. She began breathing again and allowed him to lead her to the bed.

Before getting in the bed, Ellis removed his clothes down to his shorts. Tyana began to remove her clothes with his help, but he stopped her at her lingerie. "Here, get under the covers and lay here with me," he instructed followed by a light kiss on her forehead. As much as his body prepared itself to take her, he controlled himself to allow her to relax and be still with him. He sensed that she had been through a lot, mentally, and he wanted to be a positive and soothing source of energy for her that night.

As Ellis lay next to Tyana, he wrapped his arms around her and she lay comfortably in the crux of his arm snuggling tightly into his body. He relaxed his head over top of hers and they talked quietly in the night until they both fell asleep.

The next morning came too quickly for Tyana and Ellis. Ellis had awakened first. He opened his eyes and focused on Tyana still cuddled next to him with her arm draped across his chest. From the outside, she looked peaceful and content. But her eyelids moved erratically back and forth giving the impression that her life was anything but peaceful and content. He worried about her. When he looked at the clock, reality set in and as much as he didn't want to, he had to bring their private Utopia to an end. The girls would soon be stirring. He woke her with a kiss on her lips.

"Hi Babe. Good morning," he spoke softly.

"Good morning. What time is it?"

"Unfortunately, it's almost time for the girls to start barging in and demanding breakfast."

"Oh! I'm sorry. I shouldn't have stayed all night; it wasn't my intention."

"I know. It wasn't my intention to do this..."

Ellis rose up over her and began kissing her with unconstrained passion nearly taking her breath away. His body quickly heated up by her closeness and scent.

"Are you sure we have time for this?" she panted.

Ellis had not waited for permission to take her; he had only reacted to her lips on his lips and face. "Trust me, it won't take long," he whispered.

Their early morning liaison was fast yet fierce. They were fueled by the risk and danger that mounted with each ticking second. They quietly moaned and grunted until they lay tired, flushed, and breathless.

Tyana scrambled to collect her clothes and dashed into the bathroom. Ellis followed her and pulled her in the shower with him. It was a familiar ritual when they were living together and neither thought anything of it at the time. She quickly washed up and got out. She dressed as fast as she could.

Ellis popped his head out of the shower. "Wait, I'll be out in a second and I'll walk you out."

"No, that's not necessary. Take your time. I'll see myself out. I'll be quiet."

"Tyana, that was nice—this morning." She smiled. "I'll call you later."

"Hey. I'll be leaving tomorrow morning," she announced.

"Wait! Then please, see me tonight. I'll call you."

"I've got to run. If I don't get out of here before your twins wake up then we won't have a chance to say good bye."

"Say you'll see me tonight. I'll call you."

"Okay. Okay. Bye!" She dashed out of the bathroom and carefully and quietly tiptoed out of the suite. When she reached the hallway, she breathed a sigh of relief and her heart pounded fast. She couldn't believe the chance she took by spending the night with Ellis, but she also couldn't believe how comfortable it felt being with him—like no time had passed for them. She smiled all the way back to her room.

♥ ♥ ♥

Charlotte's plane landed in Madrid around noon. Right on time.

♥ ♥ ♥

Ellis spent his lunch break with his daughters, making them delightfully happy; so happy that they didn't want him to leave.

"Girls, girls! Annamarie is taking you out this afternoon to the aquarium to see some fish and turtles and then to a park so you can play or do whatever you want. I have to go back to work, but when I'm finished we'll have dinner together. So stop whining and take your nap or you won't be able to go out."

"Okay..." said Hailee. "Daddy, when are we going home?"

"In a few days, I promise."

"I wanna go home, Daddy," whined Hannah.

"I read you loud and clear ladies. Just a few more days." He thought about Tyana leaving.

"I love you both. I'll be back as soon as I can. Have fun today!"

"Bye Daddy!" It had become a familiar routine to them now.

Ellis gave Annamarie some money and instructions and left the suite. She thought about him and the other woman in his suite. She hadn't heard from Charlotte so she didn't know what to do about continuing to spy on him. She refocused back on the twins.

When he cleared the suite, Ellis pulled out his phone and dialed.

"Hi, it's me. Where are you?"

"I'm in my room, packing, why?" responded Tyana.

"I think I have a few minutes before I'm expected back. Can I come by?"

"Uh...I guess so. What do you have in mind?"

"I'm just taking advantage of some free time and I wanted to see you. You're leaving in the morning and I don't know how much time we have left and I didn't want to chance not being able to see you tonight. We've been lucky so far, but I just didn't want to wait."

"Okay. I want to talk to you anyway."

"Okay. I'll be right there." Ellis got in the elevator and headed to Tyana's floor.

♥♥♥

Charlotte entered the hotel and headed straight to the front desk with only one goal in mind — to get her hands on a master key so she could let herself in her husband's room. After introducing herself to the reservations staff in typical Charlotte fashion, by flaunting her executive credentials, she wasted no more time with idle chitchat. Once she got what she needed, including Tyana's room number, she bolted to the sales offices first to begin her search.

♥♥♥

A soft knock came on Tyana's door. She checked the peephole and began smiling upon opening the door.

"Hi. Come on in."

"Thanks for letting me stop by. I'm sorry, but I only have about thirty minutes." Ellis hugged her. She warmly hugged him back.

"Come in." She pulled him by the hand and together, they walked farther into the room. "Ellis, I...I shared my feelings with you, and more..."

"Are you regretting it?"

"No...no. I'm not. I enjoyed being with you. I found out how I really felt about you — after all this time and after all that's gone down between us. I enjoyed it — almost too much."

"Tyana..."

"No, let me finish. Ellis, my relationship with Antonio doesn't quite work anymore because he doesn't want children — something I only discovered recently — and I do want children, very much. I've been thinking about how you feel about me and also about your situation. I don't think I should mislead you thinking we can pick up where we left off. Where we left off was with me recovering from losing our baby. I've never wanted anything more. Sometimes I feel that pain is still there — more like an emptiness."

"Babe, I know you're still hurting over that."

"How do you know that?"

"Tyana, I know you and I love you. I feel what you feel; I've felt it since you've been here. It's all over your face and in the trepidatious way you make love to me. You're hurting and unsure."

"I don't think we should be together like that again. I have to make my decision with a clear head — a decision that is best for me and only me this time."

Ellis paced the floor with his fingertips pressed against his forehead. He thought about his girls and what it would take to win the custody hearing. He couldn't afford anything to derail his plans.

"Ellis, I want a baby now, not years from now when you're out from under Charlotte's control." She turned away and spoke with her back to him. She hated even speaking her name to him. "I don't even know if you want any more children."

Ellis walked up to her and put his hands on her shoulders from behind her. She walked away from him. His touch sent a tingle down her spine. She stood looking out the window.

"Tyana, I don't know what to say…"

There was a long pause in the room. Ellis stood still searching for the right thing to say to her. He didn't want to blow his opportunity after coming so far with her. He began feeling desperate and nervous—nervous for his life being one big lie—cheating on a woman he despised with the woman he loved.

Tyana became bombarded with flashbacks starting with the day she discovered Ellis with Charlotte and then ending with her falling down those hard, cold stairs.

"*Why*?!" she shouted sharply turning to face him, unleashing her repressed anger. Ellis was startled.

"Why, what?" he asked confused by her sudden change of demeanor.

"Why did you get *her* pregnant?! I waited ten years with you to have a baby and you get *her* pregnant and killed my baby!"

"But I…"

"Why Ellis, *why*?! Why didn't you marry *me*? *Why*? I *hated* you for screwing everything up! I *hated* you! I'm such a fool!"

"What? Tyana…" Ellis quickly and sternly grabbed her but she started flailing her fists into his chest, repeating that she hated him over and over while crying hysterically. He grabbed her wrists and held them tightly.

"Tyana! *Tyana*! Stop! Stop Baby, please. I'm sorry, I'm *sorry*! Breathe. I was the fool who let you go."

"I hate you…I hate you!" Tears spewed from her face. He had not seen so much fear and anguish in her eyes before. Those grief-stricken watery brown eyes stared him hard into his eyes.

Ellis didn't know what else to do so he pressed his lips firmly against hers until she calmed down. She squirmed to resist him, but with each squirming fit, he held onto her tighter and kissed her harder, bruising her lips. She finally surrendered and relaxed her body into his; wrapping her arms around his waist. He slowly pulled back from her so he could see her face. He lifted her chin upward with his finger.

Barely audible and almost in a whimper, she said, "I love you. I never stopped loving you. I know that now. But..."

He pulled her hard into his body and kissed her with fervent passion, and she reciprocated with insane intensity. Their sexual devotion over the course of several minutes led them to falling onto the freshly made bed. He ravenously peeled her clothes off and she eagerly peeled off his clothes with a sense of urgent desperation and hopelessness.

♥♥♥

When Charlotte couldn't find Ellis in his office, she grabbed her purse, clutched it securely and close to her body and headed to the suite. She hadn't alerted anyone of her arrival, including Annamarie, who had taken the girls out to play. When she barged into the suite and began calling out, no one answered. She scoured the suite visually, but came up empty. Her curiosity and anger intensified. She left, slamming the door behind her. She proceeded to the last place she had hoped she wouldn't find her husband — Tyana's room.

♥♥♥

Ellis and Tyana joust on the bed, making love to one another in fierce, passionate fashion — Tyana's eyes streaming tears during the entire event. She was disappointed in herself for exposing her weakness to Ellis and breaking down in his presence, and most of all for making love to him — again. She wanted to leave the country with a clear head and decision. Before Ellis arrived, she had left Antonio a message that she was returning home and insisted that they speak to each other upon her return about their future. Antonio hadn't received the message yet.

"I love you so much," he whispered. "Yes, you're right; everything was my fault and I swear I'll make it up to you if it's the last thing I do," he uttered, seconds before he released his soul with every fiber of his being. He grunted loudly and buried his head in her neck. Tyana released an emotional surge, rendering her unable to speak or move, or even stop him. He, incoherently, spoke softly in her ear, repeating his sentiments of love for her and promising to always love her.

With the seal between them still unbroken and their hearts still palpitating, he lifted his head to look at her. She opened her eyes and looked into his piercing eyes staring down smiling at her.

"I will marry you when..."

"You *bastard!*" screamed Charlotte from across the room. Her eyes were glazed over and wet with her burning tears as she stood frozen only inches inside the doorway of the bedroom where Ellis' tie and shirt lay at her feet.

"*Oh my God! Ellis!*" screamed Tyana, squirming out from underneath Ellis, breaking their seal in the process.

Ellis quickly turned around. "*Charlotte!* What the hell are you doing here?!"

"You will marry her? You will marry her? You're sleeping with her behind my back?"

Ellis and Tyana both scrambled to grab the sheets, covers, pillows, anything they could get their hands on to cover their naked, sweaty bodies. Charlotte stood shaking and stunned having watched her husband make love to the woman she knew he loved. He backed off of the bed and started to talk. Charlotte pulled her gun from her purse with her trembling hand.

"*Ellis!*" screamed Tyana.

"Oh holy....what are you *doing*, Charlotte?" Ellis backed up and pulled Tyana off of the bed so he could stand between her and the gun. "Put that thing down! I can explain. Don't do anything crazy!"

"*Shut up!* Just *shut up!*" Charlotte screamed as tears blurred her eyes. The cunning, calculating, collected Charlotte had snapped.

Chapter
Nineteen

Tyana, terrified, in shock and clutching tightly to the sheet wrapped around her glistening body, stood frozen behind Ellis. Ellis held on to her while he pleaded with Charlotte.

"Charlotte, please put the gun down. We can talk about this calmly, please!"

"You took my children! And I find you here with *her*! You're not going to get away with this, Ellis!"

"I'm not trying to get away with anything. Charlotte please put the gun down so I can talk to you and explain everything. It looks bad, I know, but let me explain."

"I don't want to hear your explanation! You think you're going to get my children?"

"I'm only thinking of the girls' best interest. I don't want to hurt you."

"Shut up! How could you do this to me?"

"Are you kidding?" Tyana stepped out from behind Ellis. Her pent up anger toward Charlotte had finally gotten the best of her and she reached a boiling point. Fear took a backseat to her animosity. "Do this to *you*? You slept with him when he was with me! You *stole* him from me and got pregnant and you married him—all while he was with *me*! You have some nerve, you..."

"Tyana, don't," urged Ellis.

"Tyana don't? This woman has a lot of nerve coming in here threatening me! I've had it with her, with both of you!"

"You two *shut up*!" screamed Charlotte.

"Charlotte, what do you want? I'll do whatever you want, just put the gun away."

"I want my children! I want you to call off the divorce and I want you to stay away from her!"

"Okay. Okay," Ellis replied surrendering to her straight to her face. Tyana looked up at him thinking that Charlotte still had him by the gonads. "Charlotte, give me a minute to get dressed and we'll go back to the suite to talk. But I don't want you taking that gun anywhere near my children, you hear!"

Charlotte lowered the gun. Ellis and Tyana finally exhaled. Tyana ran into the bathroom and Ellis walked over to Charlotte and snatched the gun from her trembling hand. "Go to the suite and I'll be there in five minutes!" Still tightly grasping the sheet around his waist, he grabbed her arm and forcibly escorted her to the door and put her out. "Give me that keycard. Give it to me!" He snatched it out of her hands before she had a chance to offer it up. "I'll be there in five minutes! You better be there when I get there!"

Ellis closed the door, took a deep breath and slowly exhaled to calm his nerves. He gently placed the gun down on the table, and then immediately went directly to the bathroom door. Before he let himself in, he took another deep breath.

"Tyana, are you all right?" He walked in and approached her.

"One minute you're in bed with me telling me how much you love me and that you'll give me everything and the next minute I have a gun pointed at me and you're telling that crazy woman that you'll give her whatever *she* wants. Sounds to me like you over committed yourself."

"What was I supposed to say? I don't put anything past her. She seduced me, got pregnant, trapped me into a sham of a marriage with her, showed up here unannounced, tracked me down, got in here with a key, and she brought a gun! If anything would have happened to you, I couldn't handle it! *I couldn't handle it!*" he screamed at the top of his lungs and then pounded the countertop startling Tyana. He sat down on the edge of the bathtub with his head bowed in his hands.

"I'm sorry; it's not your fault. I don't blame you," she said. Tyana was suddenly seeing another side of Ellis. She had never seen him fighting angry. She surmised that Charlotte had pushed his buttons for five years and he had reached his own boiling point with his situation.

"Tyana, you're right. I have a lot on my plate and my first priority is making sure my daughters are safe and happy. I have to keep my focus on them, and I have to make sure Charlotte stays away from them. She's unstable right now. She's capable of many things, but she has just gone to another level and I'm seriously worried. Shit, I'm scared!" He continued to get dressed.

"But you said you'll give her what she wants and that's you and the girls. Did you mean it?"

"No. Of course not. What I did say and mean was that I love you and would give you everything you want. Tyana, I was serious, but I need time to make sure my children are safe." He buttoned his shirt, snatched up his tie from the floor.

"Ellis, I'm going to press charges against her. I don't trust her."

"Wait. Don't do anything yet. Let me fix this. I will *fix* it!" He grabbed the gun and stormed out.

Tyana took a long shower and went back to bed where she stayed for the rest of the day after placing the safety chain on the door. She relived her moments with Ellis over and over in her head. She mainly focused on him making love to her in a driven way after she told him she wanted a baby. She placed her hand on her abdomen and fell asleep.

When Ellis returned to his suite, he found Charlotte sitting at the bar with a drink in her hand. He closed the door and entered farther into the room. He looked around to make sure the girls and Annamarie weren't there.

"What the hell is wrong with you? Are you insane?!" he shouted.

"You leave me no choice. I found you in bed with that slut!"

"Do *not* talk that way about her! Charlotte, what possessed you to, to...?" He yanked her up from her seat and stood nose to nose with her. It shook her to see him so angry. She had never seen him go ballistic before. It scared her. She backed away.

"Ellis you leave me no choice. You're taking my children and you're leaving me for her."

"You and I have *nothing!* I have given *everything* I have, including all of my patience and integrity, for as long as I could and now I'm done! Do you hear me? You wear me out, Charlotte! *You wear me out!* You've been calling the shots from the very beginning. You've threatened my *job*, my *career*, my financial stability; you've threatened my relationship with my own children. I'm done; *we're done!* You give me this divorce without any hassles or ridiculous demands or countersuits. And I get primary custody of the girls..."

"Or what?"

"Or I will gladly tell the judge and your superiors about this threatening stunt with this gun and your attempt to, what, kill me and Tyana? You will go to jail and will *never* see your children again! And I will take *everything* you have!" The veins in his neck were bulging and his eyes grew wider and wider as he moved in closer to her. His breathing became shallow the angrier he got. He had never felt such hatred for anyone in his life like he was feeling for her right then. And, she was definitely feeling his wrath and it terrified her.

"Ellis, please don't do that! I wasn't going to use it; I was hurt and scared, and..."

"Save it! Tell me *I get what I want* or it's over for you!"

"Baby, I'm sorry. I'm sorry. Please don't leave me. Please!" She reached out to him and grabbed onto his shirt.

"Stop!" He shoved her off of him causing her to stumble backward onto the sofa. He paused. "I'm not going to leave you just yet. I'm going to see that you get help."

"No! I'll lose my kids."

"You should have thought of that before you pulled that stunt. We're leaving in the morning. Now, get yourself together; the girls will be back. And if you do or say anything to upset them, you'll regret it. Do you understand? I said, do you understand?"

"Ellis..."

"Charlotte, don't push me!"

"Yes. I understand."

"Wait a minute. How did you know that Tyana was here?"

"I...I figured she would be here. After seeing her in Sedona, I thought you were having an affair with her."

"I wasn't. She and I being there at the same time was a coincidence. And we did not plan this trip together. I guess you think everyone is as conniving and devious as you are. Well, we're not!"

"Ellis, I didn't follow her."

"Oh really? You plot to bring a gun, which had to be a premeditated plan because of all of the red tape you would have to go through to even get the gun on the plane! You fly all the way here... I know your work schedule, so to abandon your job and jump on a flight to Spain you had to have had a specific agenda or ulterior motive. If I find out that you had her followed or involved anyone else in this twisted game of yours, you'll be sorry, and so will your accomplice!"

"I didn't. It was a hunch. I don't know what came over me. I was angry and afraid once I received those divorce papers."

"That couldn't have been a shock to you. What kind of marriage did you think we had?"

"Ellis," she cried. "I love you. I love you so much. I'm so sorry for messing things up for us, for you! You gotta believe me!" She paused, taking another sip of her brandy, and then continued. "The truth is, I fell in love with you the first time I saw you, but I handled it all wrong. I didn't want you to know. I've had to work so hard to get where I've gotten and I didn't want to show weakness by letting you know how I actually felt about you. Being strong and having to fight against men to get anywhere in this business and gain the respect along the way, I forgot how to be a woman in love with a brilliant man who... wasn't in love with me. I won at everything else; I couldn't face losing at getting you to love me back." She cried harder and cupped her mouth with her hand. Ellis sat stoic and surprised by this revelation and her confession.

She took another drink and wiped her tears. "I knew I wouldn't stand a chance with you because you were different than the other men who only drooled over me. You were very different which made you more attractive to me. You instantly respected me and you actually wanted my help and appreciated my intelligence. As much as I've learned in the business and proved that I could be an executive and make the tough decisions, I still wasn't getting full credit for deals I've accomplished through relentless effort and innovation, but you recognized my successes and actually praised me for them when no one else did. So instead of telling you how I felt about you, I seduced you like I seduced all the other easy targets. No one has ever turned me down, sexually. I honestly didn't think I had a chance at getting you to surrender because you were so smart and savvy; I knew you would see through everything."

"I wasn't coming on to you because I was in a relationship — with Tyana. I loved her, or thought I did. I was cocky myself, but for different reasons. I wanted to get ahead and knew you had the tools and the know-how to help me achieve success by taking the express lane. I was short-sighted to your agenda because I, too, had an agenda—success, authority, expansive compensation." He lowered his head in shame. "But if you knew I didn't love you, why would you want to be with me for the long-term?"

"I didn't think that far ahead. When I learned you were in love with Tyana, it became all about winning. I had gotten you drunk and into my bed to hook you and it worked, but then sneaking around and sleeping with you whenever and wherever we could wasn't satisfying enough. I had to steal you away to get you all to myself—to keep you at my disposal. I've never been in love before and it confused me. I couldn't live without you, or stand to see you go home to her after we'd been together. I'd see you every time I was in town and I couldn't concentrate, I couldn't rationalize, I couldn't breathe at times. It tore me apart knowing you were with someone else and didn't belong to me. You'd make love to me like you wanted me, but then you would never tell me that you loved me. You became my addiction, which eventually superseded the love."

"What about the pregnancy?" he hesitantly asked.

"I swear I didn't set you up; there was no entrapment," she explained. "I was just as shocked about that as you were, but I didn't share my true feelings. Once I found out, I didn't want anything to do with it." Ellis' eyes began to water thinking about his beautiful daughters. "But the more I thought about it, what better way to get you all to myself, including your assets. I wanted to build an empire off of you. And being pregnant with your child provided the perfect opportunity. And the next logical step, because of the job, would be to convince you to marry me. It was easy at that point because you bore the responsibility of the pregnancy."

"Did you know that Tyana was pregnant at the same time?"

"No."

"So that stunt in my suite...you getting me to engage in oral sex with you knowing she would be arriving..."

"I set that up. I changed the arrival time on the note your secretary left on your desk so you would think she was arriving much later. It would give us enough time to rendezvous in your suite. By then you were easy to seduce."

"That was probably your lowest and most evil trick. I didn't know she was pregnant either. She lost the baby that day when I chased after her and she fell down those stairs." Ellis' tears began to flow steadily. "I couldn't have hated you more...until today."

Charlotte began to cry harder. She knew it was over. Her entire world had collapsed and turned upside down with her in it.

Through sorrowful tears she cried aloud. "Ellis, I'm so sorry. I did unthinkable things, which now I regret. I'm so, so sorry..."

"*Don't*! Don't tell me you're sorry! Don't *ever* tell me you're sorry!" Now his face became drenched with tears.

The door swung opened and the twins came rushing in ahead of Annamarie. They spotted their parents immediately.

"Daddy! *Momma*!" they squealed with excitement.

Ellis and Charlotte turned around sharply, desperately attempting to conceal their wet faces. Annamarie gasped at seeing Charlotte in the suite. Then she looked closer at the two people with tear-drenched faces and wondered what she had walked in on. She became nervous for herself.

"Hi Babies!" Charlotte ran to her girls to hug them.

"Momma, are you crying?" asked Hailee.

"Yes, Baby Girl, because I'm so happy to see you and Hannah! I've missed you!"

"I missed you, Momma!" squealed Hannah as she wrapped her petite arms around Charlotte's neck.

Ellis firmly tapped Charlotte on her shoulder, politely reminding her that he meant what he said about removing her from their lives and that she had better watch what she said to them. He also noticed Annamarie acting very fidgety. He watched her carefully before excusing her back to her own suite.

He canceled all of his meetings for the rest of the day and remained with his girls at all times while Charlotte was there. The girls were quickly winding down from their earlier outing and the excitement of seeing their mother.

After the family ate a big dinner, Ellis put the girls down to bed early that night. There was no doubt in his mind that they would remain asleep until morning. He made flight reservations for all of them to return to San Diego the next morning. He did not call Tyana that night, but instead continued to stay up half of the night talking to his wife. The twins insisted on sleeping with their parents, so as soon as they fell asleep, Ellis and Charlotte left the bed and went out to the living room to talk. They sat on the sofa awkwardly facing each other. The script had been flipped, as was the control. According to Ellis' body language, there was a new sheriff in town and he meant business.

"Charlotte, when we get back, I want you to make an appointment with a therapist immediately and get some help to work through your issues and work on yourself. No one in the office needs to know about it. For starters, call the Employee Assistance Program hotline for a referral. If you don't do it, I will. And that's a promise."

"All right. Are you going to leave me?"

"I said I'll help you. I won't abandon you during this transition, but we will continue with the divorce and custody like I want. If you don't live up to your bargain, I will have no choice, but to reveal what happened here tonight. Tyana is adamant about pressing charges and I don't blame her, but I've asked her not to just yet."

Charlotte paused for a long time. "For the first time in my life, I feel helpless and it's scary."

"You brought all of this on yourself, you know."

"I'd see you with the girls and I wanted so desperately to have you love me like you love them— unconditionally. Do you know that no man has ever said, 'I love you' and meant it to me? And it's all my fault. I wanted more than anything to hear it from you. You were so attentive to me during my pregnancy, I thought you might even have a change of heart, but the morning the twins were born, you gravitated toward them and even more away from me. I almost resented them."

"That's sad."

"Ellis, would you do me a favor?"

"What is it?"

"Don't let the children know how much you hate me."

"Hailee and Hannah will never know about any of this if I can help it." He paused. "I know I said I hated you and I was very close to strangling you tonight, but I can't deny that you're the mother of my children and we have a responsibility to them. I will not teach them hate in any form. Kids are very perceptive and we can't even pretend around them. That's why, I, too, am going to get some professional help so you and I can be good parents to the girls, and even though we won't be living under the same roof, I want us to be civil to one another for their sakes. We have to give them a chance, and if we continue on the path we're on right now, we will destroy them in the process."

"Right. I'm sorry I did this to us."

"I'm sorry you did this to us, too; all of us." Ellis' first thoughts were always those pertaining to his daughters.

Charlotte's tears returned. Between the flight and her weariness, she cried herself to sleep, leaning against the back sofa cushion. Ellis eased her head down on the sofa and placed a pillow under her head. He covered her with a spare blanket. He stood over her for several minutes admiring her undeniable beauty. He felt sorry for her. After another minute or two, he went back into the bedroom and slid into bed where his children lay sound asleep and completely oblivious to the mayhem surrounding their parents. He kissed them both on their cheeks and, from pure mental exhaustion, closed his own eyes, but it was impossible to close his mind.

Chapter

Twenty

Antonio could be found working late at the studio every night since returning from Mexico and since Tyana left. He spent most of his late nights going over the financial books. The plan started out as a diversion—to help him to keep his mind off of her and to keep him from missing her. It almost worked. Obviously, reminders of her were everywhere. Her students constantly inquired about her—eager for her to return—creating a buzz around the studio about trouble in paradise between her and Antonio. Madeline had also become a late night fixture at the studio with Antonio since Tyana's absence. Several of the instructors had noticed the mystery woman spending more and more time with Antonio, especially after all of the other clients had cleared out—enough time spent with him to arouse suspicion. She didn't exactly portray an open book and she didn't entertain small talk with the other students or even with any of the other instructors. She and Antonio would usually commence a private lesson during an unscheduled visit and then head straight to his office and shut the door afterward. With the absence of Tyana around the studio, the staff instinctively drew upon their own conclusions about the situation. Dottie, particularly, paid close attention to Tyana's absence and would keep an eye open to seize an opportunity to get closer to Antonio.

Rita, probably the one most aware of Antonio's activities around the studio, decided to do some digging into both the scheduling and financial books to find out exactly what Madeline's motives were for taking dance lessons. She could tell by the type of dance package the students purchased, or even what kind of classes they signed up for, if they intended to compete or if they were only pursuing dancing as a hobby. What she wasn't prepared to find was there was no record of Madeline paying a single dime for her dance lessons. The missing information now raised a red flag with Rita. Antonio, aware of Tyana's return, kept himself on high alert for her phone call letting him know that she had returned.

Tyana had made only one other phone call right before she left Madrid and it wasn't to Antonio. After Ellis abruptly left her hotel room, she spent the rest of that afternoon in her room and in bed calming her nerves and pondering over all of the events that nearly changed her life forever, not only as a result of what happened that afternoon with the love triangle, but also as a result of her relationship with Ellis and Antonio, and more specifically, loving both men and making love to both men. She stayed up nearly half of the night figuring things out in her head, but by morning, she had a clear, decisive plan, although it proved to be one of the most difficult decisions she had ever made in her life. She didn't make it lightly or without serious meditation and regard for what was in her best interest. She had the framework of her plans in her head, but would continue to work out the details in the upcoming weeks. The weight on her shoulders and the tightness in her chest seemed to lessen once she had made her decision.

♥♥♥

Upon landing in Phoenix, Tyana breathed a sigh of relief, happy to be home once again. She walked through her front door and into the dark house at nearly one o'clock in the morning. Even though she slept some on the plane, she went straight to bed and didn't wake up until nine o'clock. She took her time waking up and starting her day. Her nerves became jittery when she thought of Antonio. She knew he was probably already at the dance studio. She thought about calling first, but decided to go see him in person.

She showered, dressed, ate breakfast, and then headed to the dance studio. On her way, she phoned Kellie.

"Hey, it's me…I'm back. How are you?"

"Hi, and welcome back. When did you get in?"

"Around one this morning. I'm on my way into the studio. What's the latest?"

"I'm keeping the baby."

"That's great news!"

"My marriage, however, is over. Paul moved out and is filing for divorce."

"Oh my God! I'm so sorry. I'm also so mad at him right now and disappointed. Men can be so stupid sometimes. To throw away a perfectly good marriage doesn't make sense."

"Well, he didn't see it that way. The baby would have only created complications, was his argument."

"So, how are you feeling?"

"Other than broken hearted, my health is fine where the baby and I are concerned. I'm just scared."

"You'll be fine, you'll see. I'll be here for you."

"Tyana, thanks for taking this so well, considering…"

"Don't you worry at all about me. In fact, I have some news to share, but I'm on my way to talk to Antonio. I want to tell him first. I hope you understand."

"Certainly. You sound happy, so I take it it's good news. Can't wait to hear about it, so tell me when you're ready."

"I will, Kel. You take care of yourself and that baby, and I'll call you soon."

"Okay. Bye."

The two friends hung up. Tyana wanted to call Trevor, but she had pulled into the parking lot. When she spotted Antonio's car, her nerves unraveled again. She took a deep breath, exhaled, and marched right in.

She was immediately greeted warmly by the music wafting through the air and then by some of the staff who saw her come in. Rita actually gave her a big hug and told her how much she missed her. Tyana scanned the perimeter of the ballroom for Antonio, but didn't see him.

"Thanks so much; it's good to be back. Is Antonio around? I don't see him."

"Check his office; he's been spending a lot of time in there with that Madeline woman. She's here all the time." Rita's tone sent loud and clear signals to Tyana about what had been going on in her absence.

Tyana's heart started beating wildly and a massive lump developed in her throat, strangling her words. "Really?" Her voice cracked.

"Yeah, and do you know what else I found out about her?"

"What's that?"

"There are no receipts in the records of her paying for all those lessons he's been giving her."

"I'm sure there are records somewhere."

"Nope. I checked; unless she's paying him under the table."

"Rita, excuse me." Tyana headed straight to Antonio's office. She tapped softly on the door and then opened it.

"Antonio?"

"Tatyana! Hi! You're back!"

Just as Rita said, Madeline had made herself comfortable in his office. She was actually sitting at his desk and he was standing over her shoulder.

"Uh...can I see you?"

"Sure! You remember Madeline..."

"Yes, of course. Can I see you?"

He touched Madeline's shoulder and excused himself. He grabbed Tyana's hand and they headed to her office. Once inside, he closed the door and gave her a big hug. She timidly hugged him back.

"Antonio, who is that woman and what is going on between you two?"

"What? You know Madeline…"

"Yes, I know her name, but…"

"She's a student…."

"Cut the crap; I understand she's not paying for any lessons here and she's always in your office and now she's sitting at your desk!"

"Tatyana. Sit down. How was your trip? Where did you go? I called around everywhere for you."

"Yeah, I know. I'm sorry I didn't tell you. But right now we're talking about Madeline. Are you involved with her? Are you sleeping with her?"

"I am involved with her, but not like you think."

Tyana's heart stopped; she realized at that moment how much he still meant to her. "Involved how?"

"In a business sense."

"Without my knowledge? What kind of business?"

"Tatyana, I didn't want to have to tell you because I didn't need you to worry and it's not your problem…"

"What's not my problem? We're partners! If it's your problem it's my problem. What are you talking about?"

"The business is in trouble; we're not making the numbers we used to and we've had more expenses than what's coming in."

"What? What are you talking about? That's impossible."

"I didn't want to burden you with it; I was hoping things would turn around and I wouldn't have to worry about it either, but they're not. Madeline has agreed to be an investor and has basically bailed us out. She's invested her own money into the studio because she sees the potential."

"What? You're joking, right? And you didn't tell me or yet, consult with me first? What about a loan from the bank?"

"Tried that. We owe so much already. If it weren't for Madeline, I wouldn't even make payroll."

"But we've sold so many students comp, lessons, and the trips…"

"That helps, but the bigger picture uncovers a different story."

Tyana sat down. Too many questions were ricocheting in her head. She almost felt faint. "And what does the investor get in return besides control of the business and the studio as collateral?"

"What do you mean?"

"What do you think I mean?"

"I give her lessons and maybe she'll do some comps if she wants to."

"And work side by side with you for as long as she wants."

"This is her interest now."

"When exactly did all of this take place? When did you two sign your contract?"

Antonio paused. "On my birthday."

"I guess that birthday present trumped even mine. I can't believe you did that and didn't tell me!"

"Tatyana, you left me a message that you were returning and you wanted to talk to me. I've been sick out of my mind wondering where you were. You left me and now you're back interrogating me?"

"Antonio…sit down."

♥♥♥

When Ellis and Charlotte returned home together they decided not to say anything to the twins about the divorce until after Charlotte received professional help and became more stable. He explained that under no circumstances did he want their problems to create emotional distress in the children. Charlotte requested a leave of absence from her job and, at the order of Ellis, began regular therapy sessions immediately. Ellis joined her for the first session to oversee the process and to approve of her therapist's methods, but she would continue subsequent sessions alone. He still felt responsible for her while he was legally married to her. They also met with their lawyers and, without further delay, modified the details of their divorce to award full custody to Ellis with no spousal support provided to Charlotte, but instead she was ordered to pay child support and had limited and supervised visitation. The lawyers and the family court judge didn't quite understand how they had arrived at their settlement jointly without mediation, and they were especially confused over Charlotte's uncontested settlement agreement given her initial countersuit and dispute to the divorce. Ellis, remaining true to his word, didn't disclose his leverage over Charlotte as long as she complied with his demands.

♥♥♥

"What is it that you have to tell me? And where were you?" asked Antonio as he took a seat.

"I was in Madrid," Tyana nervously responded and cringed in anticipation of his reaction.

"Madrid?! Are you serious? And you couldn't tell me something like that before now? Do your parents know? They were worried! Apparently you told your friends you were going to Seattle! I called there looking for you."

"I know. I didn't want anyone to know where I was going. I needed some time to think."

"And you couldn't do that in the United States?"

"I went there to see Ellis." Her insides were doing flip flops.

"Ellis? Tatyana, why did you go to Madrid with Ellis? Are you having an affair?" Antonio, himself, felt sick.

"I didn't go with him."

"But you were with him."

"Yes, I saw him."

"Are you having an affair? Tatyana I found his business card on the bedroom floor. I found it the day you returned from Sedona. Were you with him there, too?"

"Let me explain. Ellis has been in touch with me claiming that he still has feelings for me…"

"What kind of feelings? He loves you? The guy who broke your heart? And, do you love him?"

"Lately I've been confused about us—you and me. You haven't wanted to marry me after five years and you don't want to have a baby and I do…now. Ellis has been promising the world and you can't take time off to do anything with me or even go to the wedding planner's office without a student interfering and you rushing to their rescue—not mine. And, then there's that incident with Birdie at comp, not to mention Dottie's personal attack on me calling me names and calling you her man. Antonio, these aren't things that only recently happened; they've been going on since day one. None of those things probably would have happened if you weren't so weird about letting everyone know we were together and engaged and loved each other."

"You're not answering my question."

"I've put up with so much crap and mostly from your students and yet you never stood up for me. I had to be the better person and turn the other cheek and believe me they took shots at that one, too! Your lack of support for me as your fiancée in the best interest of your business was all for nothing from what you're telling me today—regarding your new investor. Anyway, after five years of waiting until you're ready, I've realized that I can't wait anymore. I don't want to come second to your students, and now Madeline."

"What do you mean? You don't love me?"

"Yes, I do, but I don't think love alone is enough anymore—for us. I got engaged with you before we even had a chance to date or spend any quality time together to get to know one another. Hell, I didn't even know you had a daughter. And I don't blame your mother for never warming up to the idea of you marrying me. You dropped a bomb on her and she never had a chance to get to really know me. She and your daughter and the rest of your family think I've monopolized you and your time away from them, when in fact, that couldn't be further from the truth. I don't see you either and the little time we do have together, I want to be with you—for every second. I guess I'm selfish that way." She paused and then took hold of his hand as they sat facing each other, knees to knees.

"Overnight, I became your fiancée and business partner and became immersed into your empire. I sold my business and lost all of my identity for you because I loved you. I took on a new identity as your sidekick; not exactly what I had envisioned. But I later realized that my love for you was synonymous with my love for dancing and an offshoot from being your dance partner, which came with a lot of perks, and unfortunately, a few disadvantages. You were also there at the right moment to rescue me from Ellis and Charlotte in Miami, so I loved you for that and for being my hero, so to speak. I didn't really know Antonio the man, nor did I fall in love with Antonio the man. I fell in love with Antonio the superstar dance instructor."

"And, you came to that conclusion in Madrid...with Ellis? He influenced you?"

"No, he did not influence me. I was there to figure out what I wanted and needed—this time for me. He professed to me that he loved me and eventually I needed to find out how I felt about him, which would help me figure out how I feel about you and what I really want for my life."

"Do you love him? Are you with him now?"

"Yes, I do love him, but I'm not with him."

"You love him?"

"I discovered that I never stopped loving him and he has never stopped loving me."

"But what about what he did to you?"

"Not forgotten and we talked about it—at length."

"Tatyana, did you sleep with him?"

"Antonio, I'm not proud of myself. I did."

Antonio sprung to his feet enraged. He paced the floor breathing heavily. He almost thought he was going to hyperventilate. "I was worried sick about you and you were in Spain having an affair? And what about in Sedona?"

"No, not in Sedona. I didn't know he was going to be there. We ran into each other there. He was there with his family. I'm sorry. At the point that I slept with Ellis in Madrid, I was certain that our relationship here was over. Yes, we should have talked about it first, but in my defense I tried to talk to you for days and weeks because I didn't know what to do, but you had no time; you made no time for me. That's why I decided to leave, and to go there. I had my answer then about where I fit in your life. I was frustrated and had had enough. Sleeping with Ellis wasn't planned nor did it sway my decision about us."

"So all of this was my fault?"

"It was my fault. It was my fault I let five years go by without figuring out why I love you and why I wanted to be with you and why I wanted to marry you. I let five years go by without talking seriously about having a baby with you. I let five years go by letting you keep everyone in the dark about our engagement."

"I don't know what to say. I'm stunned. This is a lot to take in." He paused for a moment. "Tatyana, I want you to know that I meant it when I said I loved you; I still do. I'm sorry I messed everything up, for you and for us. What do we do now? What are you going to do?"

"We move on; I move on. I guess your investor can buy me out here because I've decided to leave the studio."

"Are you sure? What are you going to do? Are you going to be with Ellis again? Are you giving up dancing?"

"Actually no. I'm not giving up dancing and no, I'm not going to live with Ellis. I'm going to San Francisco to work for Jonathan Jones."

"With Jonathan? I'm confused; you're not going to be with Ellis? I thought you said you love each other."

"That doesn't mean being with him will be the best thing for me right now. That's just reality."

"So, you've talked to Jonathan already about everything?"

"We talked some during comp a few weeks ago and I called him from Madrid, right before I left, to see if he could recommend a studio looking for an instructor and it was his idea to come to his studio in San Francisco. He has a dance partner right now, as you know, but she's getting married soon and he's not sure she's going to stay on, so he offered the opportunity to me. That's an enormous opportunity for me."

"I'm sorry I didn't work out for you here." Antonio felt slighted and a little bit jealous.

"I mean, next to being your partner, of course, which I cherished for five years, it will be a huge benefit to work with Jonathan. Dancing together was the one thing you and I did well. I'll miss that, and you."

"No, you're right. It is a great opportunity for you to work with Jonathan, like you said. He's the best; you're the best. You two did well at comp and you're accustomed to each other. He would be lucky to have you as his partner. I've known him since he began coaching twelve years ago." He paused for a second while taking in the reality of it all. "Tatyana, I'm going to miss you. I've never had a partner and lover like you before. You're special and you're one of a kind. I'm broken hearted—for many reasons," he said with tear-filled eyes. Tyana stood up to face him. He took her hand in his. "Tatyana, when we made love a couple of weeks ago, it felt to me like we were in love. I wasn't expecting this. I'm going to miss that; I'm going to miss you."

"We have amazing chemistry in bed — the best, I'll admit. I'll miss being with you, intimately, too. I do love you; but your love for me is conditional love and our love for each other is most likely linked to our love of dancing. You introduced me to dancing, which is now one of my greatest passions. The day I fell in love with dancing was the day I fell in love with you. Later I realized that I needed more from our relationship — more than just dancing — and you didn't know how to create a world for just us, and no outsiders, and no business interference."

"I'm sorry, Babe. I'm sorry I couldn't be everything you needed me to be. I can't believe this is it." He paused to collect his emotions. "What about the house?"

"Well, we bought it together. We can either sell it or you can buy out my interest and half of the equity," she suggested.

"I'd rather keep it and buy you out. I love that house — it's you. So, when are you planning to leave?"

"In about two weeks."

"So soon? Do you mind if I move back home while you're still there for the next two weeks? I really miss our home. It'll give us some time together before you leave."

"Sure, I don't mind. I'd like that. It's your house, too. I'll talk to the staff and give my immediate notice so we can start transitioning my students."

"You're finished teaching here as of today?"

"Yes, it's best. I need the time to pack and make arrangements."

Antonio reached out and hugged Tyana. "I'm going to miss you, Babe. I love you so much."

"I love you, too, and will miss you. I better get going. Let's go round up the staff for a quick meeting."

"Tatyana, can we do it tomorrow? I need some time to absorb everything. I don't want them to see me still in shock and processing the fact that we're ending our relationship, romantically and professionally. Just one day, okay?"

"Okay." She paused. "Antonio, we'll always have love. Love is the passionate dance between two hearts."

He smiled and then kissed her passionately while Madeline waited impatiently for him in his office.

Chapter

Twenty-one

After a two-hour emotional conversation with her parents explaining her plans to leave Antonio and move to San Francisco, Tyana, exhausted and weary, made another phone call to share her news.

"Hi Trevor, it's me."

"I'm glad you called. I was going to call you. I haven't heard from you since you left me hanging knowing you were in Madrid with Ellis! So, you're back and what's happened since? You came back and came to your senses, right?"

"Well, I think I came to my senses while I was in Madrid. My eyes were opened to a lot of things, Trev."

"Oh yeah, like what?"

"Well, first of all, Antonio and I are officially over and I'm leaving Arizona in less than two weeks."

"What? You and Ellis? You're leaving to be with him? You're kidding, right?"

"I never said that. I do love Ellis and he loves me, but we're not planning anything at the moment. I'm moving to San Francisco and I'll be working for one of our coaches, Jonathan Jones. He has an awesome studio in San Francisco. We'll also be dance partners. He and I occasionally danced routines during competitions."

"I can't believe you're leaving Arizona. I guess that's exciting, though, for you. But the bigger question is, how did you leave things with Antonio and what happened with him? Does he know? How did he take it?"

"Yes, we talked yesterday. I'm not sure he took it all that well, especially since I told him that Ellis and I were together in Madrid."

"Oh. You told him, huh? What did he say?"

"Yeah, I didn't want to lie to him. He asked me about the details when he found out why I was in Madrid. He didn't take it all that well—understandably. We had a long talk about everything. Well, almost everything."

"What didn't you tell him?"

"Trevor, Charlotte showed up in Madrid while I was there. I haven't told anyone this, especially my parents."

"Are you kidding? By the sound of your tone, I'm guessing things got nasty."

"Things got tense alright. She caught Ellis with me in my room, you know...together-together."

"What?!"

"Wait. She had a gun."

"*What*?! Tyana! Are you serious? You're joking!"

"I wish I was."

"Are you okay? Oh my God! What happened? Is everyone okay?"

"Everyone's fine. Ellis kept his cool better than I did and he was able to diffuse the situation. She frickin' flipped out! I actually feel sorry for her. It was very scary though at the time, and I thought it was all over, I mean we were in bed...naked...and she had gotten the key to my room and let herself in. How scary is that? We didn't hear her come in. I don't know how long she had been there...watching. So creepy and the worst thing I've ever experienced. Forget killing me with that gun! I thought I was going to have a heart attack first."

"Damn! I'm so glad you're okay. I guess she got a taste of her own medicine, so to speak. She catches you in bed gettin' busy with her husband, your ex, so, what happened after that?"

"She was *screaming* at him—at both of us! I don't remember too much off the top of my head. I think I lost all consciousness at one point. I do remember that the last thing Ellis said to me before we knew she was there, and that was he wanted to marry me. That's what she kept screaming at us, 'marry *her*, marry *her*?' It was a horrible nightmare that keeps playing over and over in my head."

"Are you going to marry him?"

"No, I mean we haven't actually talked about it. We haven't talked at all since that incident. He was able to calm her down; he got the gun from her and then he ordered her back to his suite. When he got dressed, he left to deal with her. He was so distraught, hurt, and furious that she lashed out and threatened me. I've never seen him so angry and upset before in all of the time I've known him. And the way he stood up for me, it was so heroic. I think she had pushed him too far and he snapped as well. All this time she had *him* under her control, but I think she pressed her luck and went too far. When he left my room, he was definitely a different person. I haven't heard from him since. I've left him alone as he has bigger troubles right now. I just pray for those girls. She had really snapped. I'm glad we weren't in his suite when she barged in. If those girls had witnessed her with that gun, it would have destroyed them."

"That's an incredible story. I'm still trying to digest the fact that she had a gun in the first place and was probably planning to use it. She definitely sounds troubled and very desperate. So, I take it you guys hooked up on a regular basis while you were there."

"Sort of. I love him; we're still in love and we couldn't deny it."

"Risky business. So, what's next?"

"It's all about me now. I'm moving to San Francisco and I'll start new there—away from all these influences and distractions. Ellis doesn't even know. I never told him that I would wait until his divorce is final; who knows when that'll be. I'm not waiting anymore for anyone. I've been coming in second behind insecure clients, demanding businesses and crazy wives long enough."

"I ain't mad at you."

"One thing that has me confused though..."

"What's that?"

"Well, when, you know, Ellis and I were in bed together, I told him that I was leaving Antonio because I want a baby and Antonio doesn't and I said that I was certain that *he* didn't want to add to his own family, especially with everything else he's dealing with. But then he did something that made me think I might be wrong about what he was willing to do for me."

"And what was that?"

"He looked me in the eyes and said he wanted to make everything up to me and then he followed through...you know..."

"You mean...follow through-follow through? As in, he wasn't gloved up?"

"Exactly."

"Haven't you heard of 'no glove no love'?"

"Yeah, of course, but..."

"What about the other times?"

"Well, let's say he had a quick exit strategy."

"Tyana!"

"Well, it's not like we planned any of it and that last time he caught me off guard; and I think him, too. We were completely in the moment. I thought it would be like any other time. I'll admit, not the smartest thing to do or at the most appropriate time, but I had no expectation that, *that* would ever happen or he was that serious. Listen, you're the only one I've told this to."

"Who am I going to say anything to?"

"Cleo. I don't want *anyone* to know how careless I was and how carefree he and I were."

"Well, he was definitely in control of his actions and maybe he wanted it to happen. Not to get too personal, but what about you and Antonio? Any slips?"

"I usually have my ritual, but can't say that to be the case the last time we were together either, right before I left for Madrid. After he moved out, he came over to talk and we ended up spontaneously doing more than talking—twice."

"You guys threw caution to the wind, too? Well, I'll say this, if something was to happen you'll have quite a situation on your hands."

Tyana paused to ponder what Trevor said and to recall her separate liaisons with both Antonio and Ellis. She suddenly became consumed with worry.

"Hey, you there?" asked Trevor.

"Uh…hey, do me a favor."

"What's that?"

"Keep an eye on Kellie after I'm gone. She's pregnant and Paul left her because of the baby."

"What the hell?"

"Yeah, I know. Real nice guy and husband. Kellie's distraught, of course. I hate the fact that I'm leaving at a time like this, but I need some distance between me and Antonio, otherwise, I'll end up staying with him and staying in that rut of not being married. It's crazy, but I love him and miss him already."

"I'll keep an eye on Kellie. Looks like she and Cleo will be having their babies around the same time."

"That'll be good for both of them." Tyana got quiet again. "Look, I better hang up. I have so much to do. I'll call you to plan dinner or something."

"Take care."

♥♥♥

The next ten days passed quickly as Tyana prepared for her move to San Francisco. She spent time with Kellie and Trevor as much as she could. Living with Antonio throughout the duration of her time in Scottsdale created so much ambivalence for both of them. There were nights when they had heated and pointless discussions about her promiscuity with Ellis in Madrid, and yet there were some nights that they succumbed to their own sexually charged energy, which only confused the situation further. In a weird way, they became closer and more in love. But it wasn't enough to get her to change her mind or her plans. When she wasn't challenged by their physical attraction, she could see the big picture, which revealed the negative external forces.

The day before she left Arizona, Tyana received a call from Ellis.

"Hi." Her voice quivered and her heart started beating faster upon hearing his voice.

"I've missed you. I'm sorry for not calling for the last two weeks."

"It's okay."

"No, it's not okay. Tyana, I've had my hands full; I don't know if I'm coming or going. So many times I've wanted to fill you in on what's going on."

"Ellis, you don't owe me..."

"I owe you more than I could ever repay. Charlotte is getting help. We had a long talk back at the suite after I last saw you. I really wanted to kill her. She has some serious issues, but she's cooperating and she's doing things my way from here on out, for a change. The divorce is in progress; I get full custody of the girls and she'll pay child support."

"Wow. Congratulations on the custody. That's huge for you!"

"Thanks. After what happened that day, I would sooner die than to ever let any court award her custody. The girls are coping. They sense something's wrong, but nothing has affected them too seriously. And speaking of the girls, I haven't yet replaced their au pair, but I am interviewing to find the perfect one. I found out that Annamarie was the one who reported back to Charlotte that you were there with me. Charlotte apparently threatened her to spy on me. As soon as I found that out, I fired her. She was disloyal to me and I don't trust her around the girls. So between caring for the girls and overseeing Charlotte's professional care, I'm at my limit. I've taken some time away from work to handle everything, but with two offices, it's not that easy. I refuse to leave her alone with the girls though."

"Ellis, I'm sorry you're going through all of that."

"No, I'm sorry I got you involved. Tyana, I don't know what your plans are, but until Charlotte and I are legally divorced I want to help her through the initial phases of her treatment. She has a half sister who lives in Las Vegas, who's close to her age, but she's just as professionally driven as Charlotte and I'm not sure she could give her the kind of help that she needs right now while her therapy is still in its early stages. She also has another younger sister who lives in Chicago, but she has a kid, so I'm not sure that would work and Charlotte would never go back to Chicago. After the divorce is final, I think she is going to spend some time with C.J., the sister in Vegas. She's an architect. I've talked to both of them about it separately and I think it's doable and her doctor has agreed. Believe me, this whole situation has been a strain on all of us, including the girls; they're still somewhat confused. But on the bright side, the divorce should be final pretty quickly since she has agreed to all of my terms. Look, I've talked your head off and I do have to run..."

"Ellis, wait. I'm leaving Arizona — tomorrow."

"What? Permanently? Where are you going?"

"San Francisco. Antonio and I have split and I left the studio. I told him about us, and what happened in Madrid, but that's not why I'm leaving him. He and I have...well, let's say that we've agreed to dichotomize our lives. I have signed on to work — teach — at a dance studio in

San Francisco with a good friend and professional dancer. We'll be dance partners and we'll compete together."

"So, what does this mean for us?"

"I don't know; nothing at the moment. Antonio has his responsibilities here; you have your responsibilities there, so I now have a responsibility to myself in San Francisco. Let me get there and get settled and when we both have a better handle on our lives maybe we'll figure out our next steps."

"I understand." Just as they were about to end the call, Ellis interjected. "Hey Tyana, we almost had it all," he chuckled.

"Hey Ellis, we could have had it all," she replied with a smile on her face and a glimmer in her watery eyes.

Chapter
Twenty-two

A year had passed and Tyana eventually became acclimated to her new home, surroundings, and life in San Francisco. She occasionally struggled with the breakup and separation from Antonio. The transition proved more difficult than she had figured, but Jonathan helped her grieve during her low points and kept her spirits uplifted during her better moments. Her emotions throughout the first six months were unpredictable, as she had to deal with so many new changes in her life all at once. Her initial plans were to stay with Jonathan, at his request and insistence, until she could get on her feet and find her own place. But since he traveled a lot and she maintained a steady schedule at the studio in the beginning, one day they realized that their living arrangements actually worked perfectly for them, plus they had become inseparable at work and outside of work since Jonathan, too, was in-between relationships. So, she stayed permanently and, in no time, they became loyal to each other. Jonathan looked after her and took her under his wing in the business and as a dance partner. Without the demands of running a business and tending to Antonio's day-to-day needs, she now had more time to focus on her own dancing, which had improved greatly—one of the perks of being the partner of a dance coach. She limited her teaching schedule to be able to travel with Jonathan when he coached, except when he traveled to Antonio's studio, and they also traveled when competing together after she officially assumed the role as his new professional dance partner. She wasn't yet ready to face Antonio, so she took extra measures to not attend events where she thought he could be. But there were no guarantees and she crossed her fingers a lot.

For the first year, things were falling into place and she was having the time of her life. On the dance floor, she and Jonathan soon became the couple to beat. She couldn't remember being happier and completely fulfilled at the same time during any other time in her life, except maybe throughout her first year being with Antonio — living with him as his fiancée and his dance partner.

Tyana and Jonathan occasionally scheduled personal time away together from the dance studio to enjoy relaxing at home or traveling to remote destinations for leisure and adventure. He even accompanied her to Seattle to visit her parents who were overjoyed to spend some much overdue quality time with their daughter, and they enjoyed meeting Jonathan, as well. Initially her parents were confused about their relationship, but after observing how much they made each other laugh until sometimes they cried, her parents became more comfortable with them as a couple. When talking to her parents about Antonio, Tyana had spared them the details about their breakup, but she did assure them that the separation was in both of their best interests. She omitted telling them about the cascade of female students who flirted with him and tried to seduce him on a regular basis while openly disrespecting her, and she didn't tell them about not being fully and warmly accepted into his family's fold. She did, however, share with them their differences of opinion about starting a family once they were married. They supported their daughter in whatever she wanted to do. They were aware of some of the events that took place between her and Ellis that led up to their breakup years ago, and therefore, trusted that she had her life under control. As long as she was happy, that was all that mattered to them. And, after all, Tyana and Jonathan seemed to complement each other in an unusual way. If Jonathan wasn't gay and known to many as being gay, anyone would suspect that they were a romantic couple upon seeing them together and especially by the way he regarded and protected her.

In that year, Tyana never made it back to Scottsdale. She couldn't bring herself to return just yet, not even to visit Kellie and her new baby girl, as well as Trevor and his new baby boy, both born two weeks apart. She wanted to, but she had a lot going on in her own life, and not to mention, returning too soon could set her back after weeks and months to being on the brink of emotional relapse since her and Antonio's mutual disassociation. Jonathan remained as her support system and pillar of strength during those rocky times. She didn't have too many setbacks, due to her own life's distractions, but she did lean on Jonathan a few times to help her cope with her breakup from Antonio and missing her home and friends. However, she made a promise to her close friends that she would plan a visit when things stabilized in her life. In the interim, they chatted endlessly over the computer via video technology, which was the next best thing to being there. That way, she got to see her Goddaughter and Godson from the day they were born.

She was also able to keep up with Kellie on a regular basis during her divorce from her husband, Paul, which ordinarily would have devastated Kellie, but she began dating her divorce lawyer once the divorce became final, in spite of her pregnancy. Jim helped her through the pain of the divorce and shared in the joy of childbirth with her. She couldn't be happier or more sure of anything, with Jim at her side. Jim immediately took over where Paul left off — relinquishing his parental rights. The day Kellie gave birth to her daughter, Ana, Jim proposed marriage. Kellie and Jim set their wedding date six months from that date, which would give her time to lose her baby weight and allow for Tyana's schedule to open up.

Tyana and Ellis spoke occasionally over the phone and he made several attempts to see her in San Francisco, but she tearfully declined his invitations, using her unpredictable schedule as an excuse. She nearly gave in a couple of times, but concluded that she wasn't ready. She liked things the way they were and seeing him would only complicate matters. His divorce from Charlotte was final about two months after Tyana had relocated to San Francisco, which motivated Ellis to want to see her even more, especially since she and Antonio were no longer together. But he still had to seriously consider his children in every decision he made. He thought it was way too soon, after being separated from their mother, to introduce someone new and personal into their lives—someone who, in their eyes, would vie for their daddy's affections and attention. He thought it best to wait until things were a little more stable around the house and with their routines.

After the divorce, Charlotte moved out of the house and bought a place only a few blocks from their San Diego home to remain close to the girls and help her transition with the legal separation from her children. She kept the beach property, but that became joint property in the settlement. Ellis wanted to be able to take the girls there anytime he desired. Charlotte didn't object. She had made some progress with her psychological issues, which uncovered major dysfunctional anomalies that existed in her life long before she had ever laid eyes on Ellis. And, since Ellis didn't express a personal interest in her life beyond the business, he never inquired about her family history and she never volunteered that information. But what he did learn, through the course of her therapy, shocked him.

He learned that her biological father was a savvy and attractive businessman from France, about thirteen years older than her mother, and who callously rejected the news and severed all ties with her mother when he learned of her pregnancy with Charlotte. Therefore, Charlotte was raised by her self-sufficient mother who, in order to survive and support her growing family, became a high-class prostitute and often left Charlotte and her two sisters with neighbors and family members when she worked all night.

As a developing young girl, Charlotte had seen how some of her mother's "boyfriends" had abused her physically and mentally. Many times, she was physically in the house when her mother entertained her regular "boyfriends." She learned early on how sex could be used to manipulate a man to do many things. She remembered her mother being so beautiful and didn't understand how or why she would let herself be dominated and damaged by those egotistical men. Charlotte shielded her younger half sisters, Cynthia (C.J.) and Jasmine, from a lot of that drama, but Charlotte vowed to herself that she would never let a man, or anyone for that matter, control her or overpower her physically or mentally. At a young age, she became focused and determined to develop a strong business mind like her dad. At eighteen, she even took her father's last name. She had followed his career in the business sector. At one point she wrote to him begging to let her come to France to live with him, but he never responded. Charlotte endured tough challenges in her life growing up outside of Chicago and had to take care of herself and her sisters while her mother was either prostituting herself or recovering from some form of physical, mental, or emotional abuse and breakdown.

Ellis was saddened at the discovery of Charlotte's troubled past when he was invited by her therapist to join her in some of her sessions, which helped him to better understand her personality and what instigated her choice to become the type of person who she wanted to be — a beautiful woman with a mind for business and a body for sin. She still had a long road ahead of her in taming her demons and facing her life permanently without Ellis and her children in the same household, but she was making progress.

The twins had started school and were still adjusting to their new nanny, but clung closely to their daddy during their emotional transition and the absence of their mother in their household. Ellis willingly cut back his hours to care for and nurture his daughters as much as he humanly could. Even though they had a nanny, he was with them almost as much as the nanny was with them.

♥♥♥

Tyana had hovered under the radar in the dance arena outside of San Francisco for a whole year since leaving Scottsdale to avoid any run-ins with Antonio. The dance world would always remain a small world in many ways. For reasons of his own, Antonio made a conscious effort to avoid her as well...until one late October weekend during the United States Dance Open and Pro/Am Championships in Orlando, Florida. Antonio and Madeline attended with intentions of competing, and Tyana and Jonathan were also scheduled to compete.

Toward the end of the afternoon heats, Tyana, painted in full, exotic makeup, her long, dark hair pulled back in a stylish high ponytail, fashioned in a form-fitting asymmetrical beaded turquoise and purple costume for her Latin number, and holding hands with Jonathan in a sheer purple shirt, exposing his washboard abs, prominent pecs and bulging biceps, had just exited the ballroom when she stopped dead in her tracks, breathless and speechless. Jonathan tightened his grip on her hand to let her know he was there for her.

"Hi Tatyana." A long pause followed. "Wow! You look spectacular!" Antonio couldn't take his eyes off of her costume, which accentuated her petite, hourglass figure. He had never seen her look more stunning and sexy. Her body looked so different to him.

"Antonio. Uh, hi." Tyana's eyes stared straight into his haunting eyes, but then panned left of him to see Madeline standing slightly behind him.

"You remember Madeline," he awkwardly gestured to her.

"Yes, of course, how are you?"

Jonathan, eager to end the uncomfortable meeting, quickly spoke up. "Hi Madeline, I'm Jonathan Jones, I don't think we've had the pleasure of meeting. I'm sure you know that I coach at Antonio's studio from time to time, but I'm not sure I've seen you there." He shook her hand. "Are you and Antonio competing together?" Antonio and Tyana continued to stare at one another while Jonathan and Madeline conversed about the competition. Antonio noticed them holding hands but didn't think too much of it as he was accustomed to doing the same with his students. Tyana continued to clutch tightly to Jonathan's hand.

Then Tyana noticed something very peculiar about Antonio. Her eyes scanned him and then Madeline over and over until she gasped. Jonathan could feel her tense up and tremble. Her whole body was covered in goose bumps. He looked at her to read her altered expression. What he saw alerted him, so he tried to excuse them, but it was too late. Tyana eyes filled with tears as she stared at Antonio. She spoke in a raspy whisper.

"You're...married?" Her knees locked and her body stiffened. All of the noise around them had gone silent in her head. And, all that she could see was Antonio nodding his head as his eyes, too, filled up. It was not exactly how he wanted to tell her, but he hadn't made any effort to inform her previously to that moment. Then Jonathan zeroed in on the large, ostentatious diamond ring on Madeline's finger and the modest wedding band encircling Antonio's finger.

"Oh, congratulations!" exclaimed Jonathan, not knowing what else to do. He wanted to get Tyana out of there because she wasn't moving or talking. He could see water filling up her eyes.

"Tatyana, may I speak with you for a moment, in private?" Antonio cautiously asked.

Tyana looked at Jonathan who gave her a subtle nod. Madeline looked at Antonio, but Antonio only focused on Tyana.

"Sure, I guess," she replied while feeling nervous and unsure.

He grabbed her hand from Jonathan's hand and they walked about fifteen feet away from Jonathan and Madeline, who engaged in small talk while they waited.

"Tatyana..."

"I can't believe you married her! I can't believe you're married!"

"Please don't think that by me being married to Madeline now had anything to do with me not wanting to marry you. I did want to marry you!"

"Oh sure you did. It took you less than a year to marry her but you couldn't marry me in five years!"

"There's so much more to it. I don't think this is the time or place to get into everything right here without much privacy, but I'm sorry for hurting you. It was the business..."

"I'm so tired of hearing about the business. It's been to blame for everything that's occurred between us. But this?"

"I know it looks suspicious from your perspective..."

"You didn't love me?"

"Of course, I loved you; I do love you. You left *me*!"

"You left me no choice, Antonio." She took a deep breath. "I thought we had something special."

"We did. We had something that can never be replaced or substituted by anyone—at least that's how I feel about you. I loved you and I loved making love to you. I will always miss and remember that about you. No one can make me feel the way you did. I will never experience with someone else what you and I shared. I promise you that. We'll always have that between us and I'll never forget it."

"Then why her? Why *anybody* over me?"

"It's complicated. We decided that it was the right thing to do."

Tyana began to spill tears listening to him explain why he married someone else. "The right thing for who? Was it because I wanted a baby and you didn't?"

"Like I said, it's complicated. I couldn't afford..."

"I can't believe she hijacked my wedding. When did you get married?"

"Six months ago."

"I gotta go; I have to get back..." she said, while swiping the tears from her cheek as she turned away.

"But wait!" He reached out and grabbed her arm.

"That's all I've ever done with you is wait. I'm done with the waiting." She suddenly stopped and flashed to the good memories, knowing there wasn't much else left between them. "I'm sorry, Antonio—for a lot of things that happened between us and to us. We were good together. We had the dream."

"We were definitely good together. And, I am so sorry for not being there for you when you needed me. I was temporarily blind to the things that were important to you. Tatyana, please let me explain the whole thing, but not here."

She glanced back at Madeline and realized that no explanation would erase the fact that he put a diamond ring on another woman's finger and said, "I do" to all of the promises. That's all that mattered to her.

She stared at him with sad eyes and then whispered, "It is to believe in the dream, and together make it real."

"Tatyana..."

Tyana, feeling mocked, briskly walked back to where Jonathan and Madeline were standing with the intention of grabbing Jonathan and leaving. Antonio followed. She couldn't even look at Madeline, so Jonathan started to say something to break the tension, but before he uttered a word, the unexpected occurred.

"Tyana?"

Everyone turned around to see Ellis standing in his tailored designer business suit, looking ecstatic at seeing Tyana. He hadn't recognized or acknowledged any of the people standing around her because his eyes were glued only to her. To him, she was the only one in the grand space. Jonathan looked confused.

"Ellis!" Tyana gasped, still wiping her tears. He instantly hugged her and kissed her cheek — kissing away a stray tear.

Underneath his bronzer, Jonathan had lost all color in his face.

"It's so good to see you! You look so breathtaking! I was hoping to see you here, and then I saw on the registry this morning that you were, in fact, here. I popped in the ballroom every now and then to see if I could catch your performance. I hardly recognized you! It's really great seeing you!" Ellis' face expressed so much joy wrapped around so, so much sadness, which shouted to the world how he felt about her. He drank in her beauty from head to toe. Jonathan took it all in, as did Antonio, knowing what had happened between Ellis and Tyana in Madrid. He thought she might have gotten back with him after they broke up. He felt a twinge of jealousy while watching the two of them together in a warm, intimate embrace.

"Thank you," Tyana responded shyly, sneaking an awkward glance at Antonio. "I can't believe you're here."

Antonio and Tyana's eyes remained fixed on Ellis. Jonathan's eyes were triangulating among the two men and Tyana. Madeline's eyes were stuck on Tyana. And Tyana's eyes diverted to Kiera, who was walking toward them. Her face lit up as she waved Kiera over.

"Hi, I'm sorry to interrupt, but your little guy here was getting restless. I think it's feeding time again," said Kiera addressing Tyana.

All eyes cut to the tiny baby in Kiera's arms. Tyana carefully lifted the hungry baby from his nanny's arms. He eagerly took to his mother's scent and voice.

Antonio spoke first. "Tatyana? You had a baby? This is *your* baby?"

Madeline turned to read Antonio's face. Tyana looked nervously at Antonio and then at Ellis. Jonathan put his arm around Tyana's waist as she quickly diverted her attention to Kiera. "Thanks Kiera, we were just heading your way."

Kiera, sensing an awkward moment among the group, decided to excuse herself expeditiously. "I'll be checking things out down here while you feed the baby. Call me when you're finished and I'll come get him."

"Okay," Tyana answered Kiera. "Everyone, meet my little miracle, Oliver. Yes, I had a baby."

"Tyana...," uttered Ellis, confused and curious as he and Antonio both scrutinized the baby and the situation. "He's...absolutely beautiful. How old is he?"

"He's um...four months old next week," She revealed.

Ellis performed some quick math in his head, which would put them in Madrid around the time the baby was conceived.

"He's perfect, Tatyana, just like his mother who is a true champion. I'm happy for you," added Antonio, who wanted to say more, much more, but refrained in the presence of his wife and the others. He continued to stare at Tyana while he also did some quick math in his head, which would put them together intimately right around when they split up, and after she returned from Madrid. As he stared at

Oliver, he felt an ache in his heart for the amazing woman whom he loved and who loved him in return and wanted an exciting career with him, as well as a family. He suddenly felt selfish seeing her radiant face.

"Thank you. He's *my* little champion whom I love very much. I've waited my whole life for him." She began to tear up while thinking of all the years she had dreamt of having a baby and it had finally happened. She kissed her baby's little hand and then his cheek. "Mommy loves you," she whispered.

"When did you find out you were pregnant?" asked Antonio. Ellis glanced at Antonio wondering if there was a possibility that Antonio could be Oliver's father.

"After I moved to San Francisco." She glanced at Jonathan, remembering back on the emotional day she discovered her pregnancy, with him by her side.

Ellis spoke up, still curious for answers. "May I please hold him?"

Tyana looked at Jonathan first. "Uh, sure."

Ellis carefully scooped up the baby from Tyana's outstretched arms, while searching her face for any secret sign or message. After having twins, he appeared to be a natural at handling the baby. He cradled him securely and stared at him while occasionally glancing at Tyana. She never took her eyes off of Oliver. Oliver, wide-awake and still searching for mommy's milk, curiously stared back at the strange man who held him securely. To Tyana, time seemed to have stopped when no one said anything as Ellis smiled and coddled the baby while being pleasantly reminded of a new baby's smell. The tender moment caused Tyana's heart to flutter continuously. Oliver began to grow impatient for his lunch. Ellis looked at the small baby for a long time before letting him go. "You named him after your father."

"Yes, he's Papa's namesake. I better take him; it's past his feeding time." Ellis gingerly passed the baby back to

Tyana. "I apologize for the short introduction, but we must go."

Jonathan took Oliver from Tyana's arms and held him so she could say good-bye. "Come here, son. Daddy missed you so *much*!"

Both Antonio and Ellis directed their confusion toward Jonathan and then to Tyana who focused only on her baby. She kissed her baby boy again before Antonio hugged her and then Ellis took his turn. He hugged her tightly while whispering something in her ear. When they released their embrace, she took hold of Jonathan's awaiting hand, being slow to let go of Ellis.

"It was good seeing you both," she addressed Ellis and Antonio. "We'll catch up later, I promise, but right now Oliver needs me."

She smiled at Ellis first, with sincere eyes, and then at Antonio, with sorrowful eyes. She waved good-bye as she walked away with Jonathan's arm around her and her head tilted against him. Antonio and Madeline returned to the ballroom, but Ellis stood watching Tyana walk away until she disappeared among the crowd.

♥ ♥ ♥

"So, that's Ellis, eh?" whispered Jonathan as he and Tyana walked back toward their room to feed Oliver.

"Yep. What was your first clue?"

"I see what you mean. Besides that, he's hot and strapping! You had *two* hot guys vying for you, Your Sexiness. I think I'm jealous," he laughed. "I had heard, the last time I was at Antonio's studio coaching, that he had gotten married—Rita told me. She misses you, by the way. I was so busy I don't remember seeing Madeline there though. According to Rita, their marriage news definitely caused an uproar with everyone. I really didn't talk to him that much anyway—he stayed busy as well. But when I came back I just couldn't bring myself to tell you. I almost wished I had. By the look on your face, I thought you were going to plotz."

"I almost did. Thanks for being there to catch me. I can't believe he's married, and to her! To anyone! She came out of nowhere and baited him, or maybe he baited her. I wonder how all the others are reacting to her snatching him up like she did?" she smirked. "I guess she gave him what I couldn't." She turned sad once again.

"Well, according to Rita, some of his fans quit and some of course, will never leave him. He's a god to them. She did say that most of the staff who knew you well, she included, felt bad for you and thinks he made an enormous mistake for letting you go...I definitely think he was a fool to let you go, but on a selfish note, Oliver and I are glad he did. Do you still miss him?"

"Sometimes; but you helped me through the worst of it."

"Don't take his marriage to her personally. I also heard from my 'sources' that she's loaded and he married her for her flush bank account; she proposed to him sort of, as a business proposition you could say. She dangled her money in his face like a carrot as bait to save his business. He gets what *he* wants and she gets what *she* wants. Is that what he told you over there?"

"Not exactly. I don't think I gave him a chance to explain. Though I'm not sure he would have told me the entire truth—he didn't before now. I didn't know the business was in that much trouble for him to do something so desperate. He did a good job at hiding that stuff from me. Maybe because I was so focused on getting married and planning our wedding he didn't want me to know about the finances. I dunno. It's kinda sad and tragic in a way. So, maybe he doesn't love her then. If he did then he would have come to me wanting to end our relationship because he fell in love with someone else. He certainly wouldn't admit wanting her for her money. And, why her if it wasn't for the money? Do you think she's his type?"

"He was crazy about you. If you ask me, I don't think he would choose someone like her over you unless he had an ulterior motive, like her money. He loves what her money can do for him and his studio. We both know how important his business is to him. If he did marry her for her money, then you know what that means, don't you?"

"What?"

"She's calling the shots because she bailed him out from under the studio debt. That makes him her bitch!"

"You're funny. And, I can't believe you *kept* this from me! Thank you. I love you."

"Me, too, Love. Did you think I was going to let anything or anyone upset you while you were pregnant with this little munchkin? Not on your life."

"You're so good to me."

"I'd like to think that I have a vested interest," he said and then kissed the top of her head. "So...are you going to tell them? I think they were dying to ask, especially Ellis. He nearly shed his skin when he saw you with the baby."

"I'm not sure I need to. It wouldn't change anything."

"It might. Did you see the way Madeline was staring you down?"

"Yeah. I had a strong feeling when I used to see her with him at the studio that there was something else fishy going on between them. He told me once that dancing was her interest now, but I think he was trying to tell me that the studio was her interest now, which included him. I still don't understand why he just didn't come to me and be honest with me from the beginning. But instead he put me through so much frustration and I ended up going to Madrid and ended up in bed with Ellis, and Antonio then ended up prostituting himself for the money that he needed. And, now he has it. I'm still shaking."

"Well, he made his bed now. The studio may be saved, but now he has a new wife and a new boss."

"Wife. Wow. Who knows...maybe he does love her. And maybe his mother is happier now, too."

"Do you miss Ellis? He's been wanting to see you for a year and now I'm sure he's guessed why you've been putting him off." They both reflected back on her pregnancy and how she deliberately hid it from both Ellis and Antonio.

"Don't think badly of me, but I didn't know how much until today. But I'm happy for him. He got his divorce from Charlotte and has custody of his daughters—that means a lot to him. Antonio got what he wanted—to save his dance studio. I know how much that means to him. And, I finally got what I wanted most—my Oliver."

"And, you're still dancing. I think they're both still very much in love with you."

Tyana went silent for a period of several minutes as she processed the whole Antonio/Ellis encounter in her head once again. Her emotions crept to the surface. It seemed all too surreal to her—seeing both of them there at the same time as her and Oliver. Reading her mind, Jonathan left her to her thoughts until they reached their hotel suite.

Once they entered the room, she made herself comfortable on the sofa in preparation to feed Oliver. As Oliver eagerly took to his mother while securely gripping his tiny fingers around her pinky finger, Tyana stared blankly off into space, almost forgetting where she was.

"What are you thinking, Love?" Jonathan asked when he returned to where she sat.

Comfortable in her own tranquility, she took her time answering. "I was thinking about love."

"What about it?"

"Well, I was thinking that with Antonio, I regrettably learned that passionate love can bite; with Ellis, I am a witness that magical love can overcome even the most afflictive obstacle; with you, Jonathan, I'm lucky that loyal love can grow; and with my precious son, Oliver here, I'm blessed with happily ever after love that is pure, genuine, and unconditional...and a dream come true. I am eternally grateful for being Oliver's mommy. He has enhanced my life more than I could have ever imagined. And where others may have failed me, he never will."

About the Journey

YOU DANCED ON MY DREAMS: BEYOND THE BALLROOM is actually a compilation of two of my earlier works, LIFE IS BUT A DREAM and DANCE ME TO THE END OF LOVE. However, this book not only merges the two books into one dynamic story, it cements the journey that began at the turn of the millennium; ending five years later with this installment.

YOU DANCED ON MY DREAMS: BEYOND THE BALLROOM is a work of fiction.

♥ ♥ ♥

Dedication
To Love, the passionate dance between two hearts.

♥ ♥ ♥

Acknowledgments
Book cover: RAW Designz. Columbus, Ohio
My hard working team of proofers and editors

Passion's Dance
A poem by Theresa E. Liggins

When you come to me and gently take my hand,
You take me to a place, a place I've never been.
It doesn't really matter how long we dare to stay,
As long as we, together, are magically swept away.

Our souls helplessly collide as we passionately embrace the
love of dance,
You lead me; I eagerly follow, watching you command a
king's performance.
We speak not a word, allowing only our bodies to
communicate,
For only the moment we're given, feels like eternity we take.

Our hearts responding in sync, beat to the rhythm of our
forces,
Nature takes the lead, and dances us down the paths to
harmonious courses.
As the crescendo transcends us to the grasp of passion's
fires,
We take to each other's moves with determined desires.

The energy is strong, the passion, deliberate;
Our bodies, precise, responding to a perfect fit.
Our hips grind hard with fluid motion; our hands clutched
tight,
Our eyes meet briefly, our lips without a doubt, want to take
flight.

The beat of the music begins to slow down,
The beats of our hearts continue to pound.
We hold tightly to one another as we reluctantly return to
reality,
We begin to realize the power of our intense chemistry.

The passionate dance, embellished with desires, eventually comes to an end,
Is it really the end or maybe where we begin?
We walk away slowly, left with the question, what does this all mean?
Until we seek the answer, we'll dance together in our dreams.

Other Books by Theresa E. Liggins

The Escort, Et Cetera

The Escort II – Princess and the Surrogate

The Escort III – Son of an Escort

Under the Purple Moon

Under the Cover of Darkness

To Love and To Cheat

About the Author

Theresa E. Liggins began her prolific writing career in 2001 when her ballroom dance training became the inspiration of her first novel, LIFE IS BUT A DREAM, and then its sequel, DANCE ME TO THE END OF LOVE. She turned her newfound creative outlet into a dream come true with the creation and publication of her novels.

In addition to her writing and ballroom dancing, Liggins is an avid photographer, specializing in photojournalism and nature-inspired photography, as well as an interior designer/re-designer, incorporating the ancient Chinese principles of Feng Shui. And, for over thirty-five years, Liggins has employed her analytical and technical skills with major corporations.

Theresa E. Liggins currently lives in Columbus, Ohio where she was born and raised. However, for many years she has called Northern California home and backdrop for UNDER THE PURPLE MOON and its sequel, UNDER THE COVER OF DARKNESS. Chicago, Illionis, where she frequently traveled and also lived for a number of years, inspired her provocative series and trilogy: THE ESCORT ET CETERA, THE ESCORT II – PRINCESS AND THE SURROGATE, and THE ESCORT III – SON OF AN ESCORT. She has two pretty awesome sons and two amazing granddaughters.

To learn more about Theresa E. Liggins and her books, visit: www.romanticreations.com.